BRUTAL & STRANGE

JIM FUSILLI, EDITOR

BRUTAL & STRANGE
STORIES INSPIRED BY THE SONGS OF ELVIS COSTELLO

Collection Copyright © 2023 by Jim Fusilli
Individual Story Copyrights © 2023 by Respective Authors

All rights reserved. No part of the book may be reproduced in any form or by any electronic or mechanical means, including information storage and retrieval systems, without permission in writing from the publisher, except by a reviewer who may quote brief passages in a review.

Down & Out Books
3959 Van Dyke Road, Suite 265
Lutz, FL 33558
DownAndOutBooks.com

The characters and events in this book are fictitious. Any similarity to real persons, living or dead, is coincidental and not intended by the author.

Cover design by Margo Nauert

ISBN: 1-64396-345-7
ISBN-13: 978-1-64396-345-7

TABLE OF CONTENTS

Complicated Shadows Meg Gardiner	1
Motel Matches George Pelecanos	9
Tramp the Dirt Down Catriona McPherson	23
Almost Blue Jim Fusilli	35
Everyday I Write the Book Gar Anthony Haywood	51
Waiting for the End of the World Peter Blauner	63
Living in Paradise Raquel V. Reyes	71
Busy Bodies Ed Lin	83
(The Angels Wanna Wear My) Red Shoes Rob Osler	99

Favourite Hour Martyn Waites	113
I Want You Alex Segura	123
Watching the Detectives Mary Anna Evans	135
Opportunity Reece Hirsch	157
My Aim Is True Gary Phillips	171
Accidents Will Happen Naomi Rand	187
Permanent Lent Peter Spiegelman	201
The Beat Raymond Benson	219
Our Little Angel Mark Billingham	233
About the Contributors	259

COMPLICATED SHADOWS
by Meg Gardiner

Ceci calls him at work, the garage out on the highway. "I found something."

"For real?" Danny's deep into an engine rebuild on a scorching desert afternoon. And he's heard it before.

"I'll show you." She quiets, sounding bruised. "Please."

That voice, dark satin, slides across his skin. "I'm closing today. Six thirty."

When he locks up, Ceci's little Toyota is idling out front in the sunset. Her brown eyes shine with fervor, and maybe beneath that, a promise. After. If he plays it right, maybe afterward they'll have tonight.

He jingles the keys to his F-150. "We going off-road? My ride's better."

She eyes the Ford like a new truck doesn't impress her, or maybe he stole it. She pushes open the Corolla's passenger door. "Got my gear in the trunk. Let's roll while it's daylight."

Danny could laugh. She's been tough to impress since grade school. As if China Lake is Beverly Hills, and she doesn't clerk at the Rite Aid or live in a paper-walled apartment near the Navy base. But she's leaning across the front seat toward him, her skin glowing in the golden evening light. A thin silver chain clings to her chest from the heat, dipping under her tank top. He slides in. She puts it in gear. Her perfume is cinnamon. The Sierras cut the western horizon like a shadowed blade.

He lowers the sun visor. "Where we going?"

"The Yellow Aster."

Wind whistles through the open windows. His throat tightens. "Turn around."

"That mine is the only place where she—"

"You might as well drive off a cliff. Since you want to do something pointless."

She grips the wheel and accelerates along the blacktop. Telephone poles strobe past, tar black against the sandy ground. "It's not pointless. Something's out there."

Danny should have known it. Suspected it, at least, when she called. Something's out there? She means someone.

Her. Tania.

A snapshot is rubber-banded to the sun visor, faded and creased. Ceci and Tania, the summer after high school. Eyes blazing with life. White teeth. Tanned shoulders. Frayed cutoffs. Tania with those red curls and a bubblegum pout, Ceci laughing.

Tania, Danny's prom date, sparring partner, fuck buddy, lender of last resort, first call for bail money. Who would hold hot merch for him and slide him oxy from the pharmacy where she worked. Who danced with fury, and fought the same way. Who always came back to him.

Tania, who has gone dark.

Why Ceci thinks Tania fell down an abandoned mine shaft, Danny doesn't ask. But the last thing he wants is to scrabble through miles of derelict tunnels as the sun goes down.

"I need your help," Ceci says. "I checked out the mine online. A historical website, and county records. All those tailings were just left in place when it shut down, and the tunnels were never blocked off. There's still tons of ore out there." She turns to him, punctuating it. "Tons."

Gold.

People moved to the high Mojave for gold, and silver, and borax, and to hide from the law and ex-wives, back before the Navy came. Been digging holes in the earth here 150 years. Mostly played out now. That mine, the Yellow Aster, it's built on bones out beyond a ghost town. It'll be dusk by the time they get there.

He lets his shades mask his gaze. "So what is it you want to show me?"

She pulls the silver chain from beneath her tank top. It's clipped to a two-by-two-inch zip-top baggie.

She clenches the baggie in her raised fist. Sun and cloud shift over it. Inside it, flakes glitter.

"For real." The bruise is gone from her voice, replaced by iron.

Danny can't look away. "How'd you…"

"The main tunnel leads back to where the mine train wrecked and the ceiling came down."

Gold, Jesus, right there, gleaming. He can't even blink.

But it's a bad omen. "Why'd you go poking around that place?"

Ceci sighs. The wind ribbons her hair and the sun kicks against the windows. Distantly, a thunderhead boils in the heated sky, dark and brilliant-edged. Her smile flickers, melancholy.

"Tania told me once."

His shoulders drop half an inch. Melancholy is a better omen. Sadness leads to surrender, and it's best if she gives up on this quest.

"Tania talked about exploring the mine, talked about digging up her golden ticket." She exhales, almost a laugh. "God. That girl eats nails for breakfast, but she lives on hope."

"Maybe she got her fill," he says. "If she went to the mine, she kept it to herself, and didn't ask you along." He lets that land. "She up and left, Ceci."

"Without telling anyone? Been two weeks, Danny, and not one word."

"Because you don't go flashing gold around this town. You

shove it in your pocket, and you drive to L.A. to sell it, and maybe you keep on driving."

Ceci shakes her head. "Tania's clothes are still in the closet. The fridge is full of moldy food."

"You broke into her place?" Ceci is more thorough than he imagined. The thought alarms him.

"I know where she stashes a spare key."

"You talk to the cops about this?"

She crimps her lips shut. So, she hasn't. Huh.

"Something happened to her," Ceci says.

The snapshot batters in the wind. The car labors up a hill, its four-cylinder engine struggling. Even with the two of them it's heavy, like it barely has the strength to get this far from the city limits.

"Oh, sugar." Danny cups the back of her neck. "You are too softhearted. Tania left."

The rest of the thought remains unspoken. *And she left you here.*

Ceci blinks, and swallows hard, and keeps her foot down.

"So," Danny says, "you think we're going to poke around the Yellow Aster and find, what, clues?"

She roughs away tears with the back of her hand. Shakes her head. "We're not going to look for Tania. I already did that." Blowing out a breath, she straightens. "We're going to find more gold."

The flakes in the baggie sparkle and flash. She side-eyes him, and in the cascading dusk her look is all at once something new. Not desperate or rampant with fear. It's covetous.

"Keep driving," he says.

Past the dead town she turns onto a dirt track. Sunset pins a peak and the thunderclouds dapple the desert floor with shadows. She pulls up to the mine in a scrim of blowing dust. Under the shoulder of a towering hill, abandoned buildings slump, graying. She kills the engine and they get out into the sudden quiet and stare at the Yellow Aster's remains. Bent railroad tracks and rotted ties lead to the mine entrance.

"You sure?" he asks.

She glares at the black mouth of the mine tunnel, and he waits. Does she know something about Tania going away? Something he doesn't?

"Why me?" Danny asks.

Slowly, she turns. "Don't you know? Really?"

She looks fierce, like she wants to laugh, maybe eat the whole world, bite it in half. That brown hair swirling in the twilight, eyes shining like pennies.

"I can't do this by myself," she says. "It's a two-person job."

He hesitates. Makes sense, but not enough. "Why me?"

He needs to know. So he'll know what to do in the next few minutes.

She gives him a look that is so full of want that it's almost heartbreaking.

"We could get out," she says. "You and me. Vegas, maybe. San Diego."

So, he thinks. It's that simple. Except she isn't going anywhere. She's twenty-six. You get out of China Lake at eighteen. Twenty-one tops. At twenty-six, the road out is too long. Too steep. It's too late even to enlist in the Navy. The town has you.

Go? Your time has come and gone.

But that glare—he's never seen such complicated shadows in her eyes. He's seen her sing, and laugh with Tania and spit fire at her, seen her in tears and on a glittering high, but not this. Not like something rare and dangerous is on the line. Something she wants beyond all reckoning. If he gets it for her, he can have her, too. And maybe then he can have the gold all to himself.

Did it once.

Do it again.

Ceci is so vulnerable, so naïve. So slight, a shove at the small of her back would send her over the edge.

And he can put any blame on her. All at once, everything seems diamond clear.

"Let's do it," he says.

She holds his gaze for a lightning moment. Nods. "Got shovels and a rock-pick hammer in the trunk. Plus my flashlight, it's dark as hell's ass crack in there. Give me a hand."

He watches her rear end sway in those jeans as he follows her around the back of the car. Sizing up her center of gravity. She pops the trunk. The night is falling full on, getting late, but this chance won't come again. The trunk yawns open.

"Hey, baby."

Almighty fuck.

Inside the trunk are two fiery eyes. Bared teeth. Bandage on her forehead. Tania. Holding a shotgun.

He lurches back but Ceci racks the slide on a silver pistol. "Nope."

He stumbles another step. "You…"

She centers her aim on his heart. It's a Colt .45. He stops.

How did she know? He had dumped his gun. Had stood at the edge of the black mineshaft, echoes fading, and let it drop. Went home and washed off the stink of gunpowder and put on a sinless smile. But some reek had lingered, stuck to him, Christ in hell.

He raises his hands. "I didn't mean it. I was shooting at rats. It was target practice."

A hiss emanates from the trunk, where he sees the play of a darker darkness, and he wants to bolt. Tania. Who should be gone for good. Who Danny thought he'd made disappear. He smells cinnamon again. It's not perfume—it's gum. The gum Tania always chews.

Ceci tosses a pack at him. He fumbles it.

"I found that inside the mine entrance," she says. "Tania dropped it while you were pushing her into the tunnel."

It's like a stone that's got his name carved on it. Tania's not dead, she's here. With her finger on the trigger of a Remington twelve-gauge.

Gold once littered this hillside but it's the map Tania drew, the one showing the path to the seam she found in the mine, the map Danny tried to kill her for, that now shines under the flashlight. The map he grabbed from her before he shoved her toward the drop, before he opened fire and kept shooting into the shadows. He couldn't see clearly, an all-swallowing emptiness in front of him. He fired into the devious non-light until ricochets spooked him to a stop. Then he peered, gasping, at the black bottom of the shaft and thought he saw her body. He threw the pistol, his beautiful silver Colt .45, into the pit after her. And walked away with the map. The one that showed him where to find the gold that paid for his new F-150, parked back at the garage.

And Danny knows: Tania made a copy of the map, stashed it at her house, and Ceci found it. There's a tunnel at the bottom of the shaft, and a back exit to the mine he should have looked for instead of roaring back to town. Ceci found the tunnel, and Tania, and got her out. And she found his gun.

"My truck's parked at work. I'll be missed."

Ceci gives her head the barest twist. "You won't. You brought the keys. We'll take care of it."

Tania rises, a cold phantom, graveyard white. "Shooting at rats? You're just in time."

The shotgun barrel catches the light as she raises it and takes aim.

MOTEL MATCHES
by George Pelecanos

The motel was out on Route 301, one of those low-slung outfits with a restaurant and bar as part of the package. A half century ago it had featured gambling machines. Back then, in the bar, B-girls pushed watered-down drinks on men who, if they had the itch, could finish off the night with those same young women in the motel's designated rooms, which smelled of Lysol and nicotine and were available to be rented by the hour. The owner got a cut of the women's earnings and a taste of that ended up in the hands of the local law. The establishment was called The Plantation, and few Whites were offended by the name. This wasn't the Deep South, but it was Southern Maryland. South of the Mason-Dixon Line when it still meant something.

That was in the 1960s, decades before Tom Lecky was born. Back then, gambling had been legal, surpassing tobacco as the top source of revenue in Charles County. Nightclubs like the Stardust, the Wigwam Casino, and the Desert Inn flourished on Route 301, which some called Slot Machine Alley. The Stardust hosted acts like Johnny Cash, Dolly Parton, and Conway Twitty. Slots were in lounges, gas stations and beauty parlors. For a time, the cash they generated outdid the machines in Vegas.

That all ended in 1968, when gambling was deemed illegal in the county. The Wigwam became a bakery and, along with its trademark giant teepee, was eventually torn down. Now 301 was one big suburb of Washington, D.C., pretty much all the way down through Waldorf and La Plata to the Potomac River Bridge.

The Plantation had changed hands many times. Its latest iteration was The Shindig Inn, transformed by a youngish entrepreneur who had ridden the pool hall revival in D.C. It was a kitschy recreation of a 60s motel and lounge, with craft beers and designer cocktails. The jukebox was stocked with the music of country stars who had once performed on the strip, along with R&B singles from the same era. The motel rooms were furnished space-age style and could be had for three hundred dollars a night. They were rented by young lovers, married people out for something different, and adulterous couples who had a foolish aversion to risk.

Lecky was seated at the bar, nursing a Bulleit bourbon neat, having asked for something up the shelf, but not *too* far up the shelf. He was waiting for a woman to arrive. Next to Lecky was an older guy, dark skinned, late 60s, fairly fit and relatively unlined, cleanly dressed, with closely cropped gray hair siding a bald dome. He had taken the stool beside Lecky a short while ago.

"You like this one?" said the guy to Lecky, nodding toward the juke. Someone had punched in "Another Saturday Night," and its Caribbean lilt was filling the bar.

"Yeah, I've heard it before," said Lecky, who recognized the tune from a shampoo commercial he'd seen many times. "It's pretty good."

"I go by T.J.," said the man, extending his hand.

"Tom Lecky."

They shook. Lecky wasn't averse to talking with strangers in bars, but he didn't encourage it. You never knew what you were going to get.

"That's Sam Cooke on the juke," said T.J. "The boy could sing."

"Yep," said Lecky, lamely. He remembered something, vaguely…"'Back on the Chain Gang,' right?"

T.J. chuckled. "You're thinking of that female singer. Sam's song was just called 'Chain Gang.'"

"He the one who had hot oatmeal poured on him by some girl?"

"That was Al Green, and it was grits. No, Sam got shot to death in a motel a lot like this one, what they used to call a motor court. In Los Angeles, out by the airport."

"Jealous woman?"

"It was a woman who killed him, but it wasn't a crime of passion. Sam was a player, for sure. Married, but, you know. He had took this young woman he'd met to the motel room, and they were getting ready to do that thing. She told him that she couldn't get with a man unless he was clean, so he went into the bathroom to wash up. When Sam came out the bathroom, the woman was gone, and so was his money and his slacks. She was a professional and she had rolled him. He put on a jacket and his under-drawers, and went to the motel's office, where he confronted the tough woman behind the desk. Sam thought she was hiding the treacherous ho in the back of the office. He got physical with the motel lady, roughed her some, and she shot him dead."

"Damn."

"Yeah, boy. She killed Sam good. But here's the rest of the story that some don't know. Sam had been mentoring a young singer named Bobby Womack. I'm saying, Sam and him were friends. You heard of Bobby Womack?"

"Can't say I have."

"Real good singer, later got famous in his own time. Anyway, Sam wasn't even cold yet when Bobby Womack started a physical relationship with Sam's wife, Barbara. Bobby commenced to wearing Sam's nice suits and driving Sam's Ferrari around town. Wasn't long before Bobby and Barbara were married."

"Some friend."

"There's a lesson in this," said T.J.

At about this time a woman with long chestnut hair, carrying a briefcase, entered the bar. When she came in, in a tight skirt and heels, heads turned. She was toned and pampered.

Lecky had been glancing toward the front door, waiting for the woman to arrive. They caught each other's eyes and both of them smiled. Lecky pointed to an empty two-top and made a "give me a minute" hand gesture. She nodded and took a seat.

"I gotta go," said Lecky. "Nice to meet you."

"And you as well," said T.J.

Lecky paid for his bar tab with cash, grabbed a book of the motel's matches and stuffed them into the side pocket of his sport jacket. He'd use the matches to put fire to a cigar, his guilty pleasure, on the ride home, and then ditch the matchbook before he got to his house.

T.J. watched Lecky approach the fine woman at the table, who stood to hug him. Lecky had been wearing a wedding band, but T.J. was certain that this fellow and the woman were not man and wife. You could just tell.

T.J. knew something about being married. He'd been with the same woman for over forty years, until her death from ovarian cancer. Now he was living with guilt, for a lot of things. He should have treated Rudine better, mainly. And he wished he could hear her voice again. That was the tough thing about losing a loved one. You could never talk to them again.

Looking at Lecky and the woman, now seated and conversing, T.J. thought, *You should have waited to hear the lesson from the story.* You could get caught. Or worse.

Lecky smiled at the woman, whose name was Joan Levine.

"Good to see you," said Lecky. "Thanks for coming."

"My pleasure."

Lecky gave her his sincere look. Pretty Korean American woman with breast enhancements, married to a Jewish man. She looked like a TV anchorwoman. He imagined her nude, stretched out on a bed…if only women knew what men were thinking. Maybe they *did* know.

"Want a drink?" said Lecky.

"Do we have time?"

"There's no rush. I'm drinking bourbon. How about you?"

"They have good mojitos here, I'm told."

Lecky looked around. "Let me find someone..."

"Aren't you worried that someone will see us?" said Joan. "I mean, how would you explain it?"

"Caution to the wind," said Lecky, rakishly.

Joan shook her hair away from her face. "You're not timid. I like that."

Lecky grinned. *God, you're hot.*

Lecky was driving home with his window down, smoking a cigar. Listening to a System Of a Down song at high volume. He was forty-two, but right now he felt twenty years younger. Four bourbons and he was pretty lit. He'd have to keep an eye on the speedometer, and mind his manner when he walked into the house.

He lived in a community of middle-class homes that were spaced just enough, and cosmetically contrived, to give the appearance of wealth. Brick fronts, vinyl siding. Imports in the driveways, BMW and previously owned Mercedes SUVs, bought primarily for their badges and not for their quality. Lecky's home and his vehicles were like the others.

He owned a couple of packing and shipping businesses, franchises for one of the big national names, one in Waldorf, one in LaPlata, both on 301. To get in originally he needed a one-hundred-thousand-dollar investment and fifty thousand dollars in proven liquidity. Lecky at the time had little cash, so he went to his father-in-law for the seed money. Wendy's father had done well in real estate, and he could afford to help his daughter and her husband, but he didn't know if Lecky had the experience to run a business on his own, as he had only previously worked for others. Wendy convinced her father to give Lecky the startup money, and Lecky had prospered. Now he was in a medium-grade country club, golfed regularly, drove a Range Rover that he never took off road, and wore a secondhand Rolex on his wrist. In Lecky's mind he'd made it, and sometimes he liked to boast about it. He never mentioned to anyone that he'd had help.

Entering the house, he hung his jacket on a peg by the door and went to find Wendy, who was back in the family room watching one of her streaming shows. The kids, two boys, twelve and fourteen, would at this hour be sleeping in their rooms. Lecky had been chewing on a breath mint since he'd parked.

"Hey," said Lecky, standing far enough away from Wendy so she could not pick up on the remaining alcohol fumes. As for the cigar smell, he couldn't do much about that.

"Tom," said Wendy, turning her head only briefly in his direction. "Did you get your work done?"

"Yeah." He'd told Wendy that he had to go in to the store where he kept his office to do some paperwork, as tax season was on the horizon. Covering himself he said, "I stayed and had a drink out of the office bottle. Just to unwind some." He wondered if his voice was too loud.

"Okay. There's some pasta in the fridge if you want to heat it up."

"Thanks."

Lecky looked her over, in her sweatpants and oversized hoodie, slipper-socks on her feet, having a glass of white wine. Some wives had an embroidered pillow, said, "Maybe" on one side and "Not Tonight" on the other. They'd flip it and leave it on the bed, depending on their mood. They thought it was clever. Wendy's outfit was her version of the "Not Tonight" message. The sartorial version of No.

Lecky stayed up for a while after Wendy had gone to bed. He watched a repeat of a college basketball game and in the second half fell asleep in his recliner. When he woke up it was two in the morning. He went upstairs to their bedroom. Wendy was breathing heavily, turned away from his side of the bed.

As he got undressed, he stumbled getting off his socks. Wendy woke, but kept her eyes shut. Hoping he wouldn't try to touch her. He had reeked of alcohol and mints when he'd come home. Her husband wasn't much of a lover, or any kind of lover at all. He never kissed her anymore. He'd get on top of her, prep himself with some lubricant (he had no interest in foreplay), and pump away until he came. Blessedly, he didn't last long.

The next morning, while Lecky was at work, Wendy made a phone call. These calls cost her money, as did the services of the man she spoke to. But Lecky would never know about that. She kept a separate money market account in her name, from which she could draw without her husband's scrutiny. Married couples had secrets.

After the call, after she had digested what she'd heard, she sat for a while at the table off their kitchen, contemplating. She then went to the foyer of the house and took Lecky's sport jacket off the peg with the intention of walking it upstairs to hang it in their joint closet. She was always picking up after him. A sport jacket didn't drape correctly if you left it on a peg too long, but Tom never thought of such things.

Before she folded the jacket over her forearm, she reached inside one of the side pockets and found a book of matches from The Shindig Inn.

Her husband had just worn this jacket the other day, and he had hung it on the foyer peg, and as always she had taken it off the peg and transferred it to a proper hanger. There were no matches or anything else loose in the jacket that day. She knew because she had checked.

What had been relayed to her was true. Her husband was at The Shindig Inn the previous night, when he came home talking too loud and smelling like a distillery and cigars. But he said he'd been at the office and merely hit "the office bottle" to unwind.

Liar.

Sure, he lied to her, many men lied to their wives. It was an avoidance thing. Stay clear of an argument. It's easier to say you're at the office than at a bar, if only to avoid conflict. But

Wendy wasn't the type of woman who would harsh her husband out for wanting to relax occasionally, alone. Was she? It's just that he'd done it so many times. And this time he wasn't alone.

He'd never taken *her* to The Shindig Inn. That place was for people looking to have some fun. Lecky didn't take Wendy to fun places anymore. If Wendy asked to go somewhere like that, he had a negative response. *I'm tired. Why do you want to go to that place? It's only for young people. The drinks are expensive there...*

He could go to a spot like The Shindig, but not with her? Was he embarrassed to be with her? Sure, she'd put on some weight. It was natural for a woman her age, and she'd never lost the pregnancy pounds from the carriage of her two boys (and by the way, *fuck* a husband who couldn't forgive that).

Okay, maybe she didn't dress as "hot" as their friend Joan Levine, who Lecky loved to look at, with her Louboutins and her fake tits. Joan hadn't delivered two kids. Joan didn't have to *raise* two kids. Joan didn't have to get them off to school in the morning, drive them to practice and games...*Joan* had the time and energy to go to the gym, where she used a personal trainer. And Joan barely worked (she said she "bought and sold" jewelry, whatever that meant), because her husband, who was a partner in a D.C. firm, made real money. The four of them had dinner sometimes. Lecky couldn't keep her eyes off of her.

Now Wendy knew that Lecky had met Joan at The Shindig Inn for cocktails and a room. Or, on another night for all she knew, some other whore. Probably wasn't the first and only woman for him.

Wendy would confront him tonight when he came home.

Lecky had been feeling shitty much of the day from the drinking he'd done the night before. It had been a "never-again" morning but now he thought he might have a taste later in the evening, just to make himself feel normal again.

After he got home, Wendy prepared dinner as Lecky bantered with his sons, who were playing Madden on the family's sixty-five-inch smart TV, set in the family room off the kitchen. One of the boys, the eldest, looked like Lecky. The younger one more strongly resembled Wendy. Lecky, if he were to be honest, favored the older boy. Didn't all men want sons who looked like them? Was that shallow of him? Wrong or no, that's how Lecky felt.

After dinner, after the boys had gone up, Wendy told Lecky that she wanted to talk with him.

"Sounds ominous," said Lecky, but Wendy didn't smile.

"Let's sit in the dining room," said Wendy.

So it *was* serious. They rarely sat in the dining room, one of several rooms they didn't use much in their oversized house. The room had pocket sliding doors with glass panes that could be closed for private conversations.

Wendy poured her second glass of Barefoot chardonnay, met him in the dining room, and closed the doors. She was wearing jeans with an elasticized waistband and a large sweater with side pockets that she had bought on sale at Macy's. Lecky was seated in the chair at the head of the table, the only one that had arms, the alpha-of-the-house chair. He had poured himself two fingers of Wild Turkey 101.

Wendy pulled out a chair. Before she sat she reached into a pocket of her sweater and produced the deck of matches from The Shindig Inn. She dropped the matches in front of him and had a seat.

Lecky made an effort to hide his expression of surprise and self-disgust. Okay, he fucked up. He'd meant to get rid of those matches but he was torched and he forgot. Now, there could only be one strategy: deny.

"Explain that," said Wendy.

"Explain *what*? I used those matches to light the cigar I was smoking when I drove home last night. I know you don't like when I smoke, but...do I have to tell you everything?"

"You said you were at the office last night."

"I was. I wasn't at The Shindig, if that's what you mean. Those matches were in my glove box. From...I got them some other time, when I stopped there for a drink after work. *One drink.* Like I said, do I have to tell you my every move? *God.*"

"Why are you lying?" said Wendy.

"I'm not."

"I know you were there last night." She couldn't tell him how she knew, but her tone said she was serious.

"Oh, you *know*," said Lecky. "That's bullshit."

Wendy stared at her husband with determination, disappointment, and, at that moment, hate in her eyes. And, despite her anger, something close to pity. Her husband was on the cusp of losing his looks. His hairline had receded and his middle had begun to spread. He looked like a doughy kid who was refusing to admit he'd done something wrong.

Her anger was tempered by affection. Yes, he annoyed her, with his sloppiness and bad habits, and the old jokes he told over and over again. But there was a reason they were together after fifteen years, and it wasn't just for the sake of the kids. Not that long ago, they had been crazy about each other. The passion part of it was gone, but there was still a connection.

"Why can't you just talk to me and tell me the truth?" said Wendy.

"I'm not lying," said Lecky. "And I'm going to tell you something. When you know what this is, for real, you're going to be sorry."

"Fuck you, Tom."

Wendy got up and left the room. The remainder of their night was spent in silence. She went up to bed at eleven and didn't say good night.

Lecky sat at the desk in the back office of his Waldorf store, eating a Subway BMT sandwich with chips and a Diet Coke. He knew he should be watching his weight, but he hadn't lost control of it yet, and there was always the gym at his country club. Maybe he'd swing by today on his way home from work. Maybe.

His cell rang. He saw that it was Joan Levine, returning his call.

"Hi, Joan," said Lecky. "Thanks for calling me back."

"Long time no see," said Joan, and Lecky smiled.

"Listen…"

"I hope you're not having buyer's remorse."

"Nope. Just hoping to confirm the delivery date."

"As far as I know, you're still on track for delivery in two weeks. It's coming from California, not from a store…custom-made takes time, Tom."

"I know. Just hoping to put out a little fire at home."

Joan chuckled. "Well, we all have those little fires in our marriages. But this is going to put a big smile on her face. Trust me."

"I do."

"I'll keep you posted," said Joan, and cut her end of the call.

Lecky sat back. He and Wendy had their fifteen-year anniversary coming up. Joan had sold him a "recommitment ring," a band set with diamonds, to be worn on the same finger as Wendy's wedding ring. Lecky knew that Joan sold custom-made jewelry, and he'd seen such rings on other women in their circle of friends, and liked them, so he'd called Joan up and asked her to meet him somewhere to talk about it. Thought he'd make it fun, so he chose The Shindig Inn as their meet spot. Joan had brought a book of photos in her briefcase, and he'd chosen one.

He couldn't tell Wendy, even after she'd made her accusations. He'd spent fifteen hundred dollars on the ring, he wasn't going to spoil the surprise, so he'd just have to wait for two weeks to be vindicated. In the meantime, he'd endure the silence and drama in his house. She was going to be embarrassed for a minute, but she would love that ring.

Maybe it would strike a flame in their relationship, if only for a night. Sure, it would never be like it was when they met. As far as marriage went, he knew what time it was. A guy at the bar of his country club had once told him, "If you put a penny in a jar every time you fuck your girlfriend, you'll soon fill up the jar. And if you marry that same girl, and you take a penny out of the jar every time you fuck your wife, for the rest of your life, you'll never empty the jar." Okay, the guy was a drunk and a barroom philosopher, but he had a point. Lecky didn't expect much. The passion part of their marriage was gone, but he had deep feelings for Wendy. He'd like it if she moved away from her matronly, sale-rack wardrobe and paid more attention to her looks. He'd like it if she grew her hair long again. He'd like it if she lost some weight. But he often woke up in the middle of the night simply to look across the bed and assure himself that she was still there. It wasn't just that he cared for her. He loved her. It was just a different kind of love than the one they had shared when they met.

As for Joan Levine, Wendy was off base. The truth was, Lecky wouldn't lay a hand on Joan Levine, even if he had the opportunity. Not that he'd mind. Joan with that cascading hair, those tight pencil skirts she liked to wear, and the high-heeled shoes with the red soles. But it was just too risky. Too close to home.

A man, sixties and fit, sat behind the wheel of his Lexus sedan, waiting and watching. He was in the rear parking lot of three-star chain hotel in a southern suburb of Washington, D.C. He was retired from the Metropolitan Police Department, where he had put in his twenty-five as a patrolman, plainclothes man, and, eventually, Homicide detective. He now carried a private ticket. He lived in Prince George's County, Maryland. His name was Thaddeus John Simms. When on the job, if he was inclined to give his name, it was simply T.J.

His wife had never called him by that abbreviated moniker. Rudine addressed him as Thaddeus, or, if she was being stern, Thaddeus James. She was even-tempered, though, and rarely lost her composure. When he was MPD, Thaddeus often brought his stress home with him, and it couldn't have been easy on his wife.

But she handled him with patience. Made sure the home atmosphere was peaceful. Good music playing soft in the house, Frankie Beverly and Maze, Michael Henderson, Gil Scott-Heron, Chaka Khan…and flowers, fresh cut out of the yard. She made things nice.

He was an interior guy, didn't like to talk too much about his feelings, despite Rudine's efforts to bring him out. And there was her love of Jesus and the church, which he couldn't get with, not really. He'd seen too much on the street. Kids murdered and abused, where was God's "purpose" in that? Thaddeus would often shut Rudine down when she tried to talk to him. They did talk plenty after she got sick but, all those years before her diagnosis, there had been too much silence and wasted time. It was his biggest regret, among many. He wished he could talk to her now.

If she were here, she'd chuckle in that husky way of hers, talking about this fool Tom Lecky. "Some men will walk right past a good woman just to get to a tramp."

Thaddeus had put a tracker on Lecky's Range Rover and used a GPS monitor to follow Lecky to this hotel, an adulterer's favorite off the main highway. The place had a rear entrance with an elevator that went straight up to the rooms. Thaddeus had taken photos of Lecky walking across the lot to the entrance, a backpack slung over his shoulder. And soon, bet it, a sunglass-wearing woman would pull into the lot and make her way up to Lecky's room.

Maybe it would be that fine Asian woman who Lecky had met at The Shindig Inn. Maybe it would be someone else. Man like Lecky had made up his mind that it was cool to do that thing, and he was going to do it. He sure wasn't thinking about what it might cost. Like Sam, when he'd decided to take that woman to the motor court out by the airport in L.A.

Thaddeus had tried to warn Tom Lecky when he spoke to him at the bar. Thaddeus was working for the wife, but he was giving Lecky a chance to think about consequences.

Rudine would say, "A man forgets what he has at home. Hopefully, he wakes up and learns." And then she would look at Thaddeus with her knowing eyes and say, "You should know."

If only Thaddeus could hear her voice one more time.

He picked up his phone and deleted the photographs he had taken. He then ignitioned the Lexus, put it in gear, and drove out of the lot.

It brought Thaddeus Simms no pleasure to take a man down. Especially when he himself had made the same kind of mistakes as Tom Lecky. The spiritual side of Rudine had taught her forgiveness. Eventually, Thaddeus had put an end to his ways and come to a comfortable place with his wife. Maybe this Lecky fellow and his wife could come to that same place, too. In time.

TRAMP THE DIRT DOWN
by Catriona McPherson

'So when will we get together again, the three of us?'
'Depends on the weather.'
'Christ, could we sound any more like witches if we tried?'
They don't sound like witches. They sound like themselves. So much like themselves it's as if someone's written their lines: Christine obviously thinking everything can be sorted in ten minutes if they schedule a meeting; Laura fretting about getting home up the track to her house in the rain that's been hammering down all day; Anne-Marie, who never misses the chance to remind them she works in the theatre world.

'Don't swear,' Laura says. 'It's sacrilege. Or something.'
'This isn't a church,' says Christine. '"Chapel of rest" is just an expression.'
'Chapel that taste forgot,' says Anne-Marie. She has already had her say about the satin-striped wallpaper and mushroom-coloured carpet, the not-real-velvet curtains that hang halfway down the wall, neither sill-length nor floor-length, as if they were bought without a measuring tape ever being unrolled. Worst of all is the two-seater sofa and little matching armchair, foam-stuffed and covered in pastel poly-cotton that's pilled all over, more offensive in its blandness than actual ugliness could ever be.

Laura has inspected the furnishings mostly because she doesn't want to look at what's in the middle of the room. None of them do.

The lamps are the only items of décor that don't seem as if they belong in a therapist's office, or the relatives' room of a cancer centre, maybe the bit of a modern police station where fragile witnesses are coaxed into speaking. But best not to think about police right now.

They give out a very specific, unsettling kind of light, those lamps. It's bright enough to let mourners move around without tripping, but dim enough to leave kindly shadows in the centre of the room. Where the coffin sits. On trestles that look so…

'Annie-Mee,' says Laura, 'what's the word for those trestle thingies? There's a coffin in this room every day, right? So shouldn't there be a more…like something designed…?'

'Ad hoc,' says Anne-Marie. 'That's the word. And yes, there should.'

'Except that would be overhead,' says Christine. 'Hard to pass on to the customer.'

Laura sighs. She learned to sigh silently when they all shared a bedroom.

'It must be exhausting,' Anne-Marie says, 'to always be on the lookout for someone trying to swindle you.' She's never been one for silent sighing.

'Don't have to look very hard right now,' Christine says. She's ended up holding the sheaf of brochures and she fans them back and forth, the heavy paper flopping and smacking, so glossy it sounds wet. Laura feels her throat soften.

'Stop!' she says. 'Don't waft, for God's sake. Don't move the air. What *is* that smell?'

Anne-Marie cackles. 'Seriously? What do you think-?'

'The other smell,' says Laura. 'Whatever they're trying to mask it with.'

'Because the smell that needs the masking is-'

'Don't be so-'

'Plug-ins,' says Christine. 'Industrial strength. They probably get them at trade expos.'

'Specifically to mask the smell of...' says Anne-Marie.

'Our dear mother, yes,' says Laura. 'But there's no need to be so bloody crude.'

'Since you've broached the subject though,' Christine says, 'we need to make some decisions. *We*. As in, I am not going to let you both pull the old "you know about these things, Teen. Why don't you just take care of it all and let us know what we owe you" number.'

'We need to wait for the death certificate,' says Laura. Christine frowns. A dart of expression, a second long at most, but Anne-Marie smirks and waggles her eyebrows. So Laura smirks too. Of course Christine hated being reminded of an essential fact, even after she's just pointed out that she's not in charge. When the frown clears, she laughs at herself. She always could and usually does. The three sisters settle again.

It's the last unshaded moment they ever share.

Second last. When the knock comes at the door, Anne-Marie says, in a tremulous voice, 'Oh my God. Who's tapping? Mum? Is that you?'

'Shut up,' Laura says.

'Come in,' says Christine, crisply, all set to be displeased at the interruption.

But the funeral woman doesn't come in. She only pokes her head round. And the look on her face has changed since the smarmy head-tilt that made Laura want to scream when they got here. Now, her mouth is pursed and her eyes are narrow. She looks...shrewd.

'So sorry to disturb you,' she says. 'Only...it's about the cert.' They must all look as blank as Laura feels, because the woman hurries on. 'The death certificate. You know we can't do anything without the death certificate? And there seems to be some kind of hold-up.'

'The hospital told us the register office was running slow,' says Christine. Did they? Laura can't remember much about that night, but didn't the woman at the hospital say it was the undertakers who were running slow—"working two weeks out" she'd said. Laura remembers pausing a minute to decipher the meaning. She's almost sure it was the undertakers.

'Or maybe "difficulty" would be a better word for it,' the funeral woman says next. 'Did you know there was a postmortem?'

'Of course we knew,' Christine says. 'Routine procedure since she died alone.' Anne-Marie is staring at the floor and, even in this half-swallowed light, Laura can see her chest rise and fall quicker than it should. Individual strands of mohair on her jumper are waving in the air like the tentacles of a sea creature.

'But they've released the…her,' Laura says, nodding to the middle of the room without moving her eyes in that direction. 'So doesn't that mean they're…?'

'Well, it depends,' the woman says. She sounds flooded with regret but she looks perfectly comfortable to be saying this. More than comfortable. Pleased. 'You had mentioned cremation. And that would be a problem. More of a problem than burial. Since, you know, after a burial you can always…'

Dig her up again.

No one says it but all four of them might as well have bellowed it at the top of their lungs. It ricochets around the room anyway, as if there are hard surfaces for it to bounce off and bounce off and bounce off again. Not at all as if the close carpet and vinyl wallpaper, the upholstery and drapery and cloths and covers and lining and pillow, have soaked it in.

'Thank you for the information,' Christine says. 'There's no rush, is there? I'm assuming you have enough storage capacity to let us wait until the register office catches up with itself.'

She's still pushing the idea that people are busy, that there's a back-log. She's resisting the hint that there's any kind of a problem. Well, Laura thinks, why wouldn't she?

Only, Anne-Marie has been scrabbling through her bag for something and she looks up while Christine is speaking. The glance she throws is panicky and she gives her head a tiny shake too, sending a message.

'Just so's you know,' the woman says. 'For planning.' She bows her way out backwards and closes the door without a sound.

'What?' Christine says, turning on Anne-Marie.

'You hit the wrong note, Teen. Too brisk. You made her suspicious.'

'Of what?' says Christine. 'God's sake, the amount we're coughing up to them I shouldn't need to crawl too. I hope there's a feedback questionnaire at the end of all this, I can tell you that much. I'll put "If your staff are required to wear black they should also be required to use Head and Shoulders". How can someone go out in the world looking like that every day?'

'So anyway,' Laura says, 'it sounds like we can bury her now or cremate her later.'

'Or bury her later,' says Anne-Marie.

'No way,' says Christine. 'Pick the cheapest available coffin. No funeral. Ashes returned in a Ziploc and straight in the nearest bin. Clear the house. Sell the house. Split the swag. Live our lives. At last.'

Laura feels an ache in her throat as if she's going to cry. If only the funeral woman came back in now, she would see what looked like mourning. She would see one of them being normal.

'I know,' says Anne-Marie, reaching out and taking hold of her hand. 'The relief, Lolly. We beat her.'

'Don't say that!' Christine barks. Then, 'Oh. You mean "beat her" as in won? Sorry.'

'Of course,' says Anne-Marie. 'Not "beat her" like she beat us. Well, beat you.'

'You know why I reckon she never beat you, Annie-Mee?' says Christine.

'Not a clue,' Anne-Marie says.

'Witnesses. We were too big to see it and not know it was happening. By the time you came along. I can only vaguely remember Lolly-' She draws a sharp breath in over her teeth as if she's just got a paper cut. She takes hold of Laura's other hand. 'You were tiny,' she says.

'I can't remember,' says Laura. 'Thankfully.'

'The body remembers,' says Anne-Marie, in the voice that gets all the audio-narration work.

'The stuff we do remember is worse,' says Christine. 'The stuff she thought she could deny is so much worse.'

'Have you—have either of you—ever talked about it?' says Anne-Marie. Laura feels Annie's hand grow slick inside hers, a sudden sweat.

'Not my style,' says Christine. 'Droning on to a therapist and then writing a hefty cheque. You?' She looks at Laura, who shakes her head. 'And we'll all have thrown out the letters, haven't we?'

'No one in their right mind would have kept the letters!' says Anne-Marie. 'I wonder if anyone ever saw them at her end. Before she sent them.'

'You're kidding,' says Christine. 'She had the whole world fooled except you two and me.'

'Good,' says Anne-Marie. 'That's good then. No motive as far as anyone knows. That's a start.'

'*What?*' says Christine. She snatches her hand away from Laura's grasp and rubs it on her trousers, as if she's started sweating too.

'And I can get rid of the evidence,' Anne-Marie says next. She holds up a handful of crumpled paper.

She must have been tidying her handbag out, Laura thinks. 'What's that?' she asks.

'Receipt for petrol and a sandwich,' says Anne-Marie. 'I paid cash. Or maybe I should hang on to them. Say I was going somewhere else. In case of CCTV. The only thing I really need to ditch ASAP is the parking ticket. It's probably still knocking about the floor of my car.'

'Do you know what she's on about?' Christine asks Laura.

Laura has opened her mouth to say no when a memory

swoops in and engulfs her. The memory of feeding coins into a slot, picking at a corner and unpeeling the back, rubbing it hard with a fingernail to make sure it stuck to the damp inside of her windscreen. She made a proper job of it; it's hanging there still. 'Shit,' she says.

'The thing is,' says Anne-Marie, 'that last letter was different from the others, wasn't it? Assuming yours were the same.'

They used to compare them. Crying and drinking, laughing and raging, they used to read bits out to each other over the phone. They were always identical: three handwritten letters full of the kind of hints and jabs that worked on them when they were girls, that made them the women they'd become, that couldn't hurt them anymore, as long as they laughed and raged as well as cried.

'I didn't read it,' Laura says. Then immediately she adds, 'Sorry. That's not true. Of course I read it. Different how?'

'Threatening,' says Anne-Marie. 'Didn't you think so? Nothing you could bank, obviously. But a whiff of threat?'

Christine is nodding. 'Changed days. A lot to lose,' she says. Those were the words in that last letter, right enough.

'A lie goes round the world while the truth's...What was it?' Laura says.

'Pulling its socks on,' Anne-Marie finishes for her. 'The higher you climb, the harder you fall.'

'You're right, Annie,' says Christine. 'She *was* threatening us. I assumed she meant to embarrass me professionally.'

Laura smiles. What else would Christine think? 'We're only halfway through our home-study,' she says. 'If she was going to derail anything for Rob and me it would be the adoption.'

'Even *she* wouldn-' says Anne-Marie. But she stops herself. 'Sorry. Of course she would.'

'When I heard she was dead, the first thing I thought was I can't offer a grandma as part of the wider family now. I wondered if that would be a mark against us.'

'Not with aunts like this,' says Christine. 'What did you think she could still do to hurt you, Annie-Mee?'

'Seriously?' Anne-Marie says. 'What could she do to the face of #MeToo in community theatre? One well-placed story about a vulnerable teen...And when I say well-placed I mean the *Daily Express*, obviously.'

'How could anyone that age still-?' Laura says, but Christine makes a noise. It's the kind of noise you'd use to train a cat not to scratch or stop a puppy from jumping up on guests. They agreed a long time ago not to waste any more of their lives wondering how she could be that way, what she got from it, why she had them at all when she loathed them so much.

'So,' says Anne-Marie, 'the thing is, I went to see her.'

They sit in silence while all the tendrils of new meaning unfurl themselves from the core of that simple sentence and attach to the world. They hook into the petrol and sandwich receipt. They pin down the words "motive" and "evidence" that have been swirling around in the air. They reach out of the door to where the funeral woman sits with her shrewd look.

'When?' says Christine.

'Wednesday.'

'Wednesday!' says Laura.

She was discovered on Thursday morning when the postman couldn't jam any more junk mail into the basket behind the letterbox and he lifted the flap to peer in. 'Old lady fell down the stairs,' he said on the 999 call. 'I can't tell. I don't think so.'

'She was just lying there,' says Anne-Marie. 'Did not look good, I can tell you. Not pretty. But not done. So...I made a decision.'

Laura is aware that she isn't breathing.

'One the one hand, call an ambulance, get her to hospital, onto a drip, maybe a feeding tube, splint her broken bones, sit by her bedside, find her a nursing home, and let her stew there for another year or two until she *is* done. Or do what any animal lover would do for a stray dog.'

'Stray bitch,' says Christine. 'That came out worse than I

thought it would. Sorry.'

She doesn't sound sorry. She doesn't sound shocked either.

'I had a bit of a rummage,' says Anne-Marie. 'Did I say she was face-down?' Laura snaps her head up and stares at her sister. 'Anyway, I managed to get one hand over her mouth and the other hand over her nose. You'd think that thick-pile carpet would have done the job on its own, wouldn't you? Well it didn't, so I stayed like that till I was sure and then I left.'

'Fingerprints,' says Christine, of all the things someone would say after they'd heard what she and Laura have just heard.

'I used my palms. She'd have liked that, don't you think? Flat of the hand.'

'Jesus,' Laura says. But it's true. She can still hear the voice telling them all it's not hitting if you use the "flat of the hand".

'And yet somehow none of us ever punched her,' Christine says. 'I'm proud of us for that.'

'So when you called me, Lolly,' says Anne-Marie, 'and told me "a fall, dehydration, a gradual end" I thought I was home free. Only I realise now I didn't look for cameras on the road. And I bought that bloody parking ticket. I bought a sandwich! Those barcodes are laser-precision, you know.'

'There aren't any cameras on that road,' says Christine. 'Not between your place and the house.'

The house, Laura says to herself. They've never called it "home". Or "Mum's". Rob used to laugh at her and ask her where she thought *they* lived.

'Not between my place and the house either,' Christine is saying when Laura starts paying attention again. 'And I wasn't dim enough to buy a parking ticket. Have you ever even seen a traffic warden patrolling there?' She rolls her eyes.

'You mean, generally?' Laura says. 'Teen? You mean you weren't dim enough to waste your money on parking tickets generally?'

'No, I mean on Tuesday. When I decided I had had enough of her crap and I went to the house to straighten her out once and for all. And found out the job was half done without me.'

'What do you mean?' says Anne-Marie.

'She had already fallen down the stairs,' says Christine. 'She was lying at the bottom, obviously injured. So I did what I thought was best.' She actually manages to flick a glance towards the middle of the room. Christine's always been the strong one. 'She was lying flat on her back so I put her in the recovery position, like we learned in First Aid at Brownies.'

She blinks her eyes, bats them really, a parody of an innocent child.

'Because,' she goes on, 'of the nice thick carpet, Annie-Mee. I thought the same as you.' She turns and smiles at Laura. 'Which means decisions, Loll. You've got a big decision to make. About Annie and me. You can tell right now. You can wait and see what happens with the postmortem. You can tell once you see the report. It's up to you.'

'I-' Laura says, but she's saved by another one of those soft knocks on the viewing-room door. It's the dandruff woman again. Laura looks away from the pale drifts that have settled into the folds of her black neckline. They didn't bother her till Christine pointed them out. But then she's always followed along behind the other two, hasn't she?

'Just to say it's come through,' the woman tells them. 'Quicker than I thought, after all.'

'The death certificate?' Christine isn't quite her usual self for all her bravado, because she hasn't managed to hide her surprise.

'No, no, no,' the woman says. 'Sorry. I mean the PM report. The go-ahead. One of you needs to register the death and *collect* the cert, then bring it back to me.'

'Ah,' says Christine, in command of herself again and lucky as ever. She got away with it. 'Thank you,' she says. 'We hadn't quite decided which way to go and this helps, obviously.'

With another bow, the woman withdraws.

'So, Lolly,' says Anne-Marie. 'If you keep quiet, it'll all blow over. You'll be able to blackmail us for the rest of our lives.'

'No, I won't,' Laura says.

'We're not saying you'd do it,' says Christine. 'Just that you could.'

'No, I couldn't.' Laura takes one second to be sure and then she smiles at her sisters. 'She tried so hard to work us off against each other, didn't she? To stop us from being friends, being allies. She'd love it if you two were divided from me by guilt. If I was divided from you by...'

'Sanctimony,' says Anne-Marie. 'She would. The only thing better than that would be if we were all estranged from each other. She wouldn't like Teen and me being brought together by our dastardly act.'

'Trouble is,' Laura says, 'I pushed her.'

She thinks Christine gasps. She thinks it's Christine. It's one of them. It's Anne-Marie who finds her voice.

'Teamwork,' she says. 'Sisterhood is powerful.'

'I started it,' says Laura. 'You two came after me.'

'Right then,' says Christine, after the briefest pause. 'Who's going to the registrar's? Do we need to traipse back here and tell Ms. Snowstorm what we want done? Or can we tell her now? What *do* we want done?'

'Like you suggested,' says Anne-Marie. 'Cardboard coffin, Ziploc bag. Dump the ashes in the nearest bin.'

'I'm not paying for an urn, I'll tell you that much.'

'We can't dump them,' says Laura. 'We need to bury them.'

'Do we?' Christine's ready to move on.

But Anne-Marie says, 'I agree. We need to bury something.'

'Why?' says Christine. 'So we can dance on her grave?'

Laura reaches out to take her sisters' hands. 'Something like that, yeah.'

ALMOST BLUE
by Jim Fusilli

Boyer mostly kept to himself: a drink at Belma's before a sandwich in his room; movies, especially when the temperature soared; on the weekends, maybe a show at one of the downtown clubs. Most nights, he hung up his jacket and slacks, put on some music, then worked a crossword puzzle before tossing himself into bed, hoping the terror dreams did not return.

In the morning, Boyer reported to Chesney's, where he ran the new Hi-Fi department, pushing phonographs to novices and audiophiles alike. With a vague sort of charm, a shock of black hair, and a body that filled out a suit just right, he had won over management and kept up with the rapidly changing industry. He got along well enough with Sasser, the little guy who sold records at the counter next door. If someone asked about LPs, Sasser sent him to Boyer. If the customer was sticking with old-fashioned 78s, Boyer walked over to tout the finest and the latest gear. The job went down like a Harold Arlen melody.

When the lights dimmed, he put on his hat, punched the clock, and walked to the employee parking lot. Twenty minutes later, Belma's, bourbon on the rocks, *Audio* magazine, blue halos of cigarette smoke, Chet Baker on the jukebox.

No one could tell that he was barely holding on.

And then came Marion.

***

"Mind if I join you?"

At a table for two in the company cafeteria, Boyer looked up from his magazine and saw before him a tall, flawless woman, wavy black hair, high cheekbones, enticing lips. Narrow waist and impossibly long legs. Carrying a cup of black coffee and a slice of peach pie, she wore a white bathrobe with the Chesney's logo across a breast.

"Sure," said Boyer. "Why not?"

"Crowded today."

Not too, thought Boyer as he pushed aside his chicken chow mein.

"You're Boyer. Right?"

He nodded.

She sipped her coffee, first blowing across the cup.

"I'm Marion," she said. "I model in Women's."

"Do you?"

"I hear things, Boyer. You're on the go."

"Says who?"

Marion cut a sliver of pie, savored it slowly.

"Sylvia."

"Sylvia. Well then…"

"She models too. And then she models for Morgan Chesney. If you catch my meaning."

The founder's grandson had some sort of position in the front office. He had lost a leg below the knee at Kakazu Ridge, but didn't let it keep him down.

"You're going to be regional manager. They want Hi-Fi departments in every store in the state."

"And then what?"

"There's no limit, Boyer." She reached over, nudged his cuff, and looked at his watch. "I'm due. They ought to give Hazel a whip and a chair."

Boyer watched as she unfolded upward. He peeked when she

leaned over for one last sip of coffee.

"Want the pie?" she asked. "I recommend it."

He watched as she shimmied toward the elevators.

Marion liked to be seen. Modeling for the well-heeled in Chesney's plush showroom wasn't enough. She paraded into nightclubs, coasted into restaurants; at Santa Anita, in high-waisted slacks, short sleeves, jacket over her shoulders, sunglasses, she took a position at the rail and men suddenly lost interest in their tout sheets and the horses skittering into the starting gate. Boyer didn't much mind, though he was stretching his paycheck about as far as it would go. Whenever he was in town, they ended up in his bed. As moonlight eased through the blinds, he would watch her from the other side of the room as she slept, her body on display only for him.

"You know, Boyer," she once said, "I didn't always look like this."

She wore his bathrobe. Three fingers of his bourbon in a glass.

"No, I wouldn't think so."

"I didn't know how to dress it up. To use it." She sat at the foot of the bed. Boyer gave her room by inching toward the headboard. "Got myself in a lot of trouble."

"Capital T trouble?"

She nodded.

"Where was this again?"

"Outside of Dayton. Nothing more than a bus stop and a Rexall's. You wouldn't think anything could happen there. And yet..."

He waited for her to go on, but she took a long pull on the bourbon and left the bed. Walking away, she let the robe drop to the floor. Ten minutes later, she was gone without so much as a wave goodbye.

* * *

Boyer thought he saw behind the façade. She was a kid, twenty-two years old, and she was damned determined to make something of herself, to never look back. He knew she would trade up at the first chance—why settle for the regional Hi-Fi manager when Sylvia had Morgan Chesney?—but one evening, as he watched her run the stopper from her perfume bottle between her breasts, Boyer realized he liked having her around, that she had revived the spark in his life that had been missing. No longer was he going through the motions.

Then, as they were dancing slow and close in his room to a dreamy Chet Baker ballad, he said it, whispering.

"Do you?" she asked. "Why?"

"You look good in blue."

"Just blue?"

She nipped at his ear.

Stepping back, she reached for his belt.

Boyer was on the road two, three days a week now, staying in hotels, coffee-shop eggs and toast, supervising installation at the stores, training personnel. Half the time, she didn't answer the phone, which left him yearning. So this is what it's like, missing somebody, he thought as he stared past sheer curtains at the stuttering neon across the street. He counted the hours until he returned home, ran traffic lights when the city was in sight.

"Hi Boyer," she said when he entered. She was sitting in his chair, slacks, high-collar blouse, barefoot. Bourbon and bonbons, listening to Mel Tormé.

They kissed for a good long while.

"In the mood for a night out?" she asked. A sapphire-blue dress was on a hanger on his closet door. She didn't steal it, not really. She would return it to wardrobe before Hazel knew it was gone.

"Your call, babe."

"It's a little stuffy in here."

"You could open a window."

"Or you could buy me a T-bone."

He dipped into his jacket pocket and withdrew a long, narrow jewelry box. "Turn around."

He linked the clasp on the nape of her neck.

Without a word, she walked to the mirror.

"You're sweet," she said as she touched the blue topaz teardrop.

Boyer loosened his tie knot. "Let's order in," he said. "I head to La Jolla in the morning."

"No, no, Boyer," she said. "You want me to show me off, don't you? In that dress, on your arm. Wearing this bauble. The light catches it just so. Heads turn. They're looking at us, Boyer. See?"

Sasser intercepted Boyer in the parking lot.

"Hazel is looking for you." He was in shirt sleeves, carrying his jacket by the hanging loop. "She called a couple of times last night."

"Called you?" Boyer looked at his watch. He no longer needed to punch in, but he liked to be on time. "She say why?"

Sasser shook his head.

"All right..." Boyer said, peeling off and entering Chesney's. He took the escalator up to Women's.

Passing a petite Mexican woman arranging flowers in stout painted vases, he found Hazel in her posh white office beyond the showroom floor. When he knocked on her doorframe, she peered over her bifocals, gathered the invoices she had been reviewing, and directed him toward a Louis XVI armchair facing her hand-carved desk.

"Mr. Boyer."

"Miss Heinemann." She was a large, hulking woman who revealed a trace of a German accent when she spoke. Under upswept silver hair, she had severe features, a bulb-like nose, and surprisingly soft green eyes. The Chesneys thought the world of her, even if most of her girls did not—fashion punched well above its weight, lifting the entire operation above the ranks of other department stores. Customers valued her impeccable taste and tolerated her abrupt manner.

She clasped her hands together. "I have been meaning to speak to you."

Boyer said nothing.

"This Marion, she was not for you."

"'Was not'?"

Heinemann frowned. "You don't know?"

"Know what?"

"She is gone, Mr. Boyer. As are several dresses, shoes, pieces of jewelry—our best and most costly. Cosmetics too. Cash here and there. I ask again: Have not the police contacted you?"

"I got in late last night. A three-hour drive."

"We will keep this quiet, of course. There will be rumors, but…You would be wise to avoid complications. Already you are fortunate that you are not likely to be implicated."

Boyer said, "Why not?"

"Because Mr. Morgan Chesney is gone too. This is not a coincidence."

Boyer nodded slowly, letting it all sink in. After a long moment's silence, he said, "You were going to warn me?"

"We have had many opportunists here among the girls. They model, they are friendly, proper, and the women of means tell their sons, their brothers. Introductions are made. Of course, on occasion, the wife brings the husband and his wallet and…But it is always subtle. Discreet. And no one steals, Mr. Boyer. The man is enough. Not for Marion, apparently." She shook her head. "Our reputation…Does she care?"

Boyer stood.

"I myself have told the police that Morgan Chesney is no party to her crimes," Heinemann said. "Also, I can guarantee you she will drop him as she has dropped you: As soon as the next step on the ladder is in view."

"Okay," said Boyer. "I...Yeah, that's—Thanks."

As he crossed the showroom, Sylvia entered, harried in flats and slacks, her red hair bobby-pinned, coat over her arm. She veered until she was in Boyer's path.

"God damn it, Boyer."

He looked at her with empty eyes.

"Damn, I knew she'd do it. A guy with the company car can't match the guy who hands out the company cars. And you had no idea?"

Some, he thought. "None."

"Me? I'm a dope. But I gotta say, Boyer, I never took you for a sap."

What Boyer saw, heard, and smelled in the Ardennes Forest took the fight out of him. Lucky to be alive, to be whole, to turn an interest into a career, to have a few dollars to throw around: What right did he have to ask for more? Put your head down, move forward, ignore it all, keep it as simple as can be. Don't feel. Survive.

Now he was worse off than before Chesney's hired him, before he left the psych ward at Walter Reed. Wallowing in misery, he could not escape her. There was no refuge, not even in hotel rooms and highway dives where she'd never been. In the distance, a shadow under a lamppost: Marion. A swaying tree: Marion. More than once, he woke when he heard a footstep creak in the hall. "Marion?"

He rearranged his furniture, but he could not erase her memory. The things she left behind went in a box in the back of his closet. He took out the box, opened it, ran her nylons through his fingers, studied the blue topaz stone in lamplight, put the box away. On the road, he wandered the streets, head down, hands buried in his pockets. No crossword puzzles, no Chet Baker or Mel Tormé, no joy. No Marion.

Said Sasser, "Far be it for me to advise, John, but why not look it like this? You had a quality piece of ass for a few months and now she's someone else's misery."

Said Sylvia, "Mr. Boyer, I'm sorry I said what I said. Both of us, we deserved better. If you're looking for a shoulder to cry on…"

At work, he pressed on. He surpassed his quota, setting up departments and monitoring performance. He ached, but was no longer miserable. When in town, he took to eating in the cafeteria again. He wasn't quite ready to paint the town, but he went to the movies. He ordered the blue-plate special. The page he tore out of phone book that listed private investigators? He put a match to it and let it flutter down to the sidewalk below.

Sasser pulled him aside.

"John, I think we have a problem."

"You do?"

Boyer waited while Sasser punched the clock and then they stepped into twilight together.

"Bunning. He's not cutting it."

"Is that so?"

Boyer already knew the numbers were down in Hi-Fi at the flagship store.

"A dullard. No zip. The slow play worked for you, John." Sasser paused. "Don't get mad at me, okay? I think when, you know…You weren't around. Bad habits set in with him."

Boyer had interviewed him twice. "Knows the products."

"Jeez, by now I know the products and I'm eavesdropping. Isn't selling them the job?" As they strolled the parking lot toward Boyer's company car, Sasser laughed. "You, John, the way you used to hook them in. Earnest, mature, patient…Then, once they signed, they'd come over and I'd replaced their 78s with new LPs. Bonanza! Now? They nod, linger, disappear."

"I'll talk to him," Boyer said.

Sasser held up a hand. "Before you do, there's someone I want you to meet. A real dynamo. I guarantee she can sell sand to an Arab."

"'She'?"

"Meet her, John. Quiz her. Then imagine her working the customers…"

Boyer said, "What's she to you?"

"John, huh? Sally's just out of high school. She shops with us. Buys a ton of LPs. Knows her music."

Boyer hesitated. Maybe he could offload Bunning. Men's shoes, maybe.

"I'll be back next Tuesday. Have Personnel set it up."

A happy Sasser slapped Boyer on the arm.

Sally was the full dose all right, with enough energy to power Paris and a smile as bright as a full moon. Tall, hefty around the hips and bust. auburn hair in a bob, she did not walk so much as bounce, exuding appealing self-regard. Sasser had it wrong: She had graduated high school two years ago and was taking classes in electrical engineering at the community college. Sally not only knew what was happening now in audio, she knew what was going to happen tomorrow. She turned up at the interview with a folder full of correspondence from Bell Labs about stereophonic sound, the next big thing. It would take a couple of weeks to move out Bunning, but as far as Chesney's was concerned, she was on board.

"I've an idea, Mr. Boyer," she said as he treated her to lunch in the cafeteria. "Why not take me on the road until I can start here?"

"No budget, Sally."

"I don't care if you pay me. It'll be a treat."

He was due upstate on Wednesday. "We'll need a chaperone."

She laughed. "Heck, I'll sleep in the car, Mr. Boyer. Or drop me at an all-night diner."

Sally rolled off Boyer and said, "Oh yes…Yum, yum." She turned on her side to face him. "Well?"

Spent, Boyer stared at the ceiling.

"Moves with malice, doesn't it? My body." She tapped her stomach. "I don't know why women clamor to be skinny. How can they make the earth quake?"

He was thinking of Marion, who had her tricks but after a while was all but stationary under him. She had made it seem like she was doing him a favor.

Never once did he complain. He had considered himself a lucky man.

"Want to go again?" Sally asked.

Sales of amplifiers, turntables, needles, and speakers were up at the flagship store. Customers who weren't sold right away returned if just to enjoy the salesgirl who brightened the entire Music department. When she visited Boyer in his little office upstairs, she was nothing but professional as they went over the numbers. Teasing with a straight face, she asked, "Any complaints, Mr. Boyer?"

"Sasser says you're taking advantage of the employee-discount on LPs."

"Guilty."

Along with her toothbrush, perfume, a few undergarments, and casual clothes, she brought records from her collection to Boyer's apartment. He'd find her waiting for him, Mexican food from the takeout joint around the corner, the room sweetened by Joe Williams backed by the Basie orchestra or Sarah Vaughan with Clifford Brown.

One evening, she came out of the shower to find him listening to *Chet Baker Sings and Plays*.

"I don't know how you can put up with that," she said, as she dried her hair with vigor. "Cat can play, but his singing is a snooze. It's got as much zing as a boiled potato."

She was wearing his robe, as Marion had.

She changed the LP, tossed aside the towel, and held out her hands as the creamy Basie horns ushered in Williams on the ballad "Nevertheless."

"Come on, Boyer. Dance me."

A few minutes later, she said, "It's too soon to tell."

"What?"

Mimicking the lyric, she said, "Maybe I'll live a life of regret / And maybe I'll give much more than I'll get."

When the song ended, she kissed his cheek, then lifted the needle before the next track kicked off.

"I know about her, John," she said. "At the store, people talk. And even if they didn't, I can tell. Your torch burns blue, doesn't it?"

"Sally..."

"But you've got nothing to worry about with me. I am having the time of my life. Not counting Toohey in the second grade, you're my first love."

He stepped back and looked at her. That smile, the twinkle in her eyes...

She wasn't Marion. Not one part of her was Marion.

"I don't deserve you, kid," he said.

"My call," she replied.

Sally answered the door, thinking Boyer, home early, had lost his key.

Two detectives. Haggard in baggy suits, tired fedoras.

"Marion Gunderson?"

"Not me," Sally replied. She was still in the green swing dress and low heels she wore to work.

The other cop said, "Is John Boyer around?"

"He's on the road. Barstow, I think. Why?"

"You are?"

"A friend." She gave her name.

"Have him call us," said one as he produced a business card.

"Are you going to tell me what this is about?"

The two cops looked at each other. "Morgan Chesney is dead."

"Wow. Morgan Chesney. What happened?"

"Maybe Boyer will tell you after we talk to him."

When the cops departed, Sally went to the radio in the Hi-Fi cabinet.

Chesney fell off a cliff not far from his hotel in Sonora, Mexico. The announcer confirmed the police in Mexico were looking for Marion, described as his companion.

Boyer came in an hour later, carrying his suitcase, sandwiches, and bottles of beer. She could tell he hadn't turned on the car radio.

Taking the deli bag to the kitchen, she told him to sit. He tossed his jacket on the bed. She explained.

"They say if she had something to do with it?" he asked.

Sally shook her head. "The radio gave me more than they did. John, a man with one leg on a cliff. Wouldn't you say that is…unexpected?"

He stood and retrieved his jacket.

"I'll go with you," she said.

"No sense in dragging you into this."

He walked to the mirror, tightened his tie, tugged on his lapels. He saw that she was looking over his shoulder, her smile replaced by a purposeful frown.

"What?" he said, turning.

"They're going to ask you if you've been to Mexico lately."

"Will they?"

She said, "They came here, John. The cops."

He shrugged.

"John, you've got it all going for you now…"

He went toward the door.

ALMOST BLUE

* * *

Oh John, Sally thought as she watched him get into his car down below.

She thought telling him that she loved him had driven a wedge between them. But no. It was something else.

Two weeks ago, she called the Chesney's down state. Marantz was going to roll out a new amplifier with superior frequency response. If they ordered now, they'd give Chesney's a sizable discount plus a price cut on last year's model. Sally could order a couple for the flagship store, but she needed Boyer to make the deal for the chain.

Not only wasn't Boyer at the La Jolla store, he hadn't been there in more than a month.

She thought to tell him: John, it's a company car. They're going to check your expense reports against the odometer. They're going to show your photo around Sonora.

Marion knew the names of the hotels he preferred. She knew his routine. Tracking him down had been easy. So was getting him to bypass La Jolla and cross the border.

She told him to wait at a dusty cantina thirty miles inland. Sweat soaking through his shirt, jacket over the rails behind him, the beer did him no good. It was a goddamned steam bath in here.

She was late, but so what? It was Marion. Real, not an apparition.

Sheer scarf tied under her chin, sunglasses, a baby-blue blouse with its sleeves rolled to her elbows, beige slacks covering her impossibly long legs. He stood, but she waved him back down.

"I've got to get gone," she said. "He's...He's a sick son of a bitch. You have no idea."

She removed her sunglasses. Boyer saw she had been crying.

"I had it good with you, Boyer. Christ, I know that now.

You…You really loved me."

"Did I?"

She touched his hand. "Would you take me back?"

"Marion…"

"Sylvia said you've got a girl. Is that it?"

Boyer saw how it would play out. A disaster. It was only a matter of when she would leave him on the side of the road. The Chesneys wouldn't stop coming after him.

Maybe he was dying in the snow in the Ardennes Forest, a German machine gun slicing him in half like it did his entire platoon. Maybe this was all a dream that would end the moment his life gave out.

He looked deep into her eyes.

"Your girl. Is she me, John? Almost me?"

Or not a dream. Her lips, the slope of her breasts, the birthmark on her stomach.

How much misery would he take on in a trade for a few more weeks in her arms?

"What do you need me to do, Marion?"

The cops interviewed him at the flagship store and told him not to leave town but knew he would. A lieutenant whose wife thought Hazel Heineman and Chesney's hung the moon said he'd drive the tail car himself.

Before taking off, Boyer went home. There wasn't a trace of Sally anywhere in the apartment. No toothbrush, no *DownBeat* magazines, no Joe Williams, no Sarah Vaughan. No comet streaking across the night sky. No Sally.

Somewhere there's a man worthy of that kid, thought Boyer as he stuffed a suitcase. He put under his arm the cardboard box that held what Marion left behind.

Boyer was unaware she had come back to town. She waited until the girl left, used her key and stuffed Morris Chesney's wallet inside the box.

Now Boyer set out for a hotel she said she'd check into. It was only a few miles from Chesney's Bakersfield store.

She was halfway to Nevada when he arrived.

EVERYDAY I WRITE THE BOOK
by Gar Anthony Haywood

There is no such thing as the Book of Love. It doesn't exist. It is a literary unicorn. People have their favorites on the subject, sure, but no one book says everything there is to say about it. Poetry, prose, fiction or non-fiction—it doesn't matter. There's just too much ground to cover.

And what is love, anyway? A feeling, a sensation. Ask fifteen people and you'll get fifteen different answers. For some, love is the very intake of breath that keeps us all alive; for others, it's a dagger warmed over burning coals that's then driven through the heart. Again and again and again. Love is pain, not ecstasy. It is the fire you are drawn to, only to have it burn you down to your very bones.

That's the way Joanne looked at it. Love to Joanne was a drug she feared like the devil himself but couldn't kick. She needed love, to be in love and have someone love her back, but she'd been hurt too many times not to always expect the worst. I'd had my share of being hurt myself, but it hadn't jaded me like it had Joanne. I was convinced happiness was inevitable, the just reward for those who kept the faith and waited until the right partner came along.

I was the right partner for Joanne and she was the right partner for me.

This wasn't because I had never betrayed a woman's trust,

because I had. Monogamy had not come naturally to me. But by the time Joanne and I met, on the other side of my foolish and degenerate youth, I'd developed the power to control my baser instincts, to recognize the value of denial over temporary gratification, so being faithful to one woman was not a feat beyond my reach. I'd done it once or twice and could do it again.

I was sure that, in time, Joanne would see this. In the face of my steadfast refusal to cheat on her, her lack of trust and optimism would melt away. I had to believe that or let her go, and I couldn't let her go. Joanne had become my drug.

I fell for her the minute I laid eyes on her, sitting with a group of friends two years ago at a sushi bar in Little Tokyo. Glowing ebony skin, braided and beaded brown hair, a smile that lit up the room like a flare—she was a revelation, and I had no choice but to leave my seat at the bar and approach her. I left the bar with her phone number that night, high on the idea that I had just set my life on a new and exhilarating course.

And I had. The next twenty-three months would prove that. If I'd ever been happier, being in love with a woman, the experience escapes my memory. And I was sure Joanne felt the same way about me. We grew in each other's company, stronger and more content to be alive, neither of us looking ahead to the next better thing because nothing could be better than what we already had, and what we were going to have for many years to come, as long as we paid it the proper attention and respect. All I had to do to keep Joanne was want Joanne.

Joanne, and nobody else.

A man sees a woman he wants many times every day. Someone who catches his eye and turns his mind toward wet kisses and a bedroom strewn with discarded clothes and condom wrappers. It's an impulse that means almost nothing because it's gone in an instant and almost never leads to anything. The women who elicit this reaction are generally imperfect, endowed with one or two qualities the man finds attractive and little else. They come and go and are quickly forgotten.

But then there are women who strike a far deeper chord in a man. As rare as the last of a creature bordering on extinction, they draw his attention and refuse to release it. The power they hold over him is absolute, as impervious to his resistance as gravity itself. They render him stupid and reckless. They force him to speak nonsense and act the fool. They are the epitome of his greatest desires, the ideal he imagined he would never actually live to encounter.

This was Reina Davis to me.

If Reina had never entered my life as a new hire at Temple Synchronics, the South Bay tech company I worked for at the time as a senior project manager, my relationship with Joanne would likely still be intact. But from the moment she was introduced to my team at a staff meeting, I knew that Reina would disrupt my world as profoundly as the moon affects the tides. She was beautiful and lean, raven-haired and green-eyed, and she projected raw, prideful sexuality without an ounce of effort. I shook her hand that first day feeling helpless and clumsy and not giving a damn if she noticed. I was ruined.

Over the next several weeks, we became good friends and nothing else. I had a steady girlfriend and she had the attention of every other man—and some women—at the company. But the more time we spent together, at the office and at after-hours events, the more obvious it became that friendship wasn't where either of us wanted to leave things. It seemed that, as much as I wanted Reina, she wanted me. We were a chemical combination entirely in balance. The chances that we would never take our mutual attraction to its most logical conclusion defied all odds.

This isn't to say, however, that I had any illusions about Reina as a long-term partner. She wasn't built for that kind of relationship and I wasn't in the market for one. What I wanted from Reina was the experience of having her, once, twice, maybe three times, and that was all. She was a box to be checked off my bucket list, a crowning sexual achievement I could for years afterward look back upon fondly, and with no small measure of pride. Opportunities to realize a dream like Reina only came a man's way once or twice in his lifetime and I didn't want to miss this one.

But what to do about Joanne?

Joanne was my future and my true love. All the plans I had made that were dependent on being with her would all go to waste if I had my fling with Reina and Joanne somehow found out about it. There would be nothing I could say or do to erase the pain my adultery would inflict upon her; she would leave me and never come back.

Unless…

Unless I gave her a reason to forgive me. Fixed things so that, if she learned I'd been with Reina, as much as that would hurt her, she'd feel obligated to look the other way and give me a pass.

Because she had betrayed me first.

One night. I just needed her to lay down with another man for one night.

I wasn't going to like it. My idea or no, knowing she'd been with someone else was going to linger in the mind and gnaw at my pride. But every time I thought I couldn't go through with it, I'd catch a glimpse of Reina in the office and become convinced all over again that she was worth any temporary jealousies I might suffer. Joanne would have her night of weakness, I would have mine, and we'd move on as before, perhaps having grown even closer to each other than ever.

All I had to do was find the perfect man to seduce her. Somebody I could trust to bed her down once and then go away. He needed to be desirable but flawed, within what I knew were the boundaries of her tastes but far short of her ideal so as to eliminate any risk of her developing any real feelings for him. It had to be a man who would take money to do almost anything, including have sex with a woman not of his own choosing.

It took me three weeks to find him, but find him I did.

"This is some kind of joke, right? Or part of a weird sex game?"

"No. It's not a joke and it's not a game. At least, not exactly," I said.

His name was Trenton Giles but all his friends called him "Trent." I'd approached him at the bar in Manhattan Beach where I'd discovered him three nights before. He was a regular there. He was handsome enough to get a girl's attention but only with considerable effort, and effort was no problem for him. His confidence was inexhaustible and he dressed like somebody with a five-figure clothing budget. I watched him get lucky with beautiful women a lot more often than I saw him strike out.

"But he's a total asshole," Sid, the bartender, had told me when I asked about him my second night in attendance. "He's everything I hate about this place."

Sid was off tonight, and that was just as well. He would have had to wonder what the fuck was I thinking offering Trent a drink and chatting him up like we were old friends after Sid had been kind enough to specifically warn me about him.

"So what is it, then?"

I had to tell him something at least close to the truth. "It's a test. I need to know if I can trust her. She wants to get married and I'm not going to marry her until I'm sure she'll be faithful to me. This is the only way I can be sure."

"Faithful? What does that even mean?" He laughed and finished off the last of his Jameson.

"Yeah. It's an old-fashioned notion, I get it," I said. "But the lady's a looker. Guys come at her all the time, and if she's not going to be up to saying no once we're married, I'd rather know that now. Divorce might be fine for others, but not for me."

"And if she bites? How far do you want me to go?"

"As far as she'll let you."

He thought about that for a minute. "A looker, you said. What kind of looker?"

I showed him a few photos on my phone. He didn't whistle, but his face went slack and his eyes filled with white. "Jesus," he said under his breath.

It cost me a couple more shots of Jameson to get him to buy in. Mine was a wild proposition and even a shit like Trent Giles had to have second thoughts about accepting it. But there was a lot of upside in it for him and very little downside. Three hundred dollars to try and nail a woman more attractive than half those he pursued on his own for free. He'd get the money, win or lose. And he'd get the girl if he won, as a bonus.

How could he say no?

I set him up to succeed. Joanne was the manager of a popular bookstore on the Third Street Promenade in Santa Monica and I had Giles go in there and ask for her help in finding a title I completely made up. Their first meeting went well; he said she laughed at all his jokes and held his gaze longer than somebody would who didn't find him charming.

For the next several weeks, he dropped in to see her every three or four days. She never shut him down or turned him away. Giles felt like she was warming to his invitations to go out, for drinks or dinner, but she hadn't yet agreed. Meanwhile, I was working on her resistance to him at home, making myself as distant and unavailable to her as possible, rigging the game so she'd have some excuse to seek affection elsewhere.

And all the while, Reina worked on me. I wanted her more than ever. The company's quarterly earnings party was coming up at the usual beachfront hotel and I knew what would happen if Reina wore a certain kind of dress that night and gave me a certain kind of look. We'd find our way up to a room and my long thirst for her would be sated at last. But I could only go there if Joanne went there first. I wasn't going to be the only one to break our promises of faithfulness to each other, no matter how desperately I wanted to be with Reina.

The agreement I'd made with Giles was for thirty days. If he couldn't win Joanne over by then, it was over. He courted her for thirty-five. He worked the last five on his own dime, because by now, his pride was at stake and he didn't want to walk away with just my money and nothing else.

But ultimately, that's exactly what Joanne left him to do, much to our mutual disappointment.

"Sorry, mac, but this isn't going to happen," Giles said at our last scheduled meeting.

I don't remember what I said in response, or if I said anything at all. I was numb.

"If this really was just a test, like you say—I'm still not sure I believe that shit—you've got nothing to worry about. The lady's passed with flying colors."

I knew there was an outside chance he was lying; I couldn't be sure he hadn't slept with Joanne at least once in the last month and just didn't want to admit it. But the look on his face was too pained to be artificial. He'd come at Joanne with everything he had and was mystified to discover it wasn't enough.

I paid him and sent him on his way.

I'm not a perfect man. I'm not always up to keeping my word, whether I've given it to myself or someone else. I am capable, however, of behaving perfectly for brief periods of time, especially as I've grown older and wiser. Time has given me the power to occasionally kick temptation in the teeth; doing the right thing is no longer too high a bar to reach.

The deal I'd made with myself was a simple one: see Joanne cheat on me first or leave Reina alone. Hold true to the vows of fidelity I'd made to Joanne, because she had proven she would be true to those she had made to me, and allow the dream that was Reina Davis to go unrealized. Forever.

As the night of the company party approached, I wasn't sure I could hold the line I'd set in the sand. I still loved Joanne and wanted to spend the rest of my life with her, but Reina wasn't going anywhere, and her draw on me was as pronounced as ever. All I wanted was one taste, a single toe dipped in the pool. After that, I could withstand the call of any other woman who might want to try me. Just one taste.

When the party came, Reina wore the dress I had both hoped and feared she would wear. I'd never seen it before but I'd known what it would look like: tight as a drum in some places and practically invisible in others. I had thought it would be red but it was emerald green instead, just like her eyes. I took her and the dress in every chance I got and didn't even try to look away, even when she caught me in the act and smiled as a way of saying, "Like it? Come and get it. I'm waiting."

For three and a half hours, Temple Synchronics' thirty-six employees ate and drank and then drank some more. And kept right on drinking. I tried to keep my own consumption to a minimum, hoping to maintain as much control over my impulses as possible, but as midnight closed in, I was drifting on my feet, seeing the world through a fish lens of intoxication. Reina and I had crossed paths several times by now, but always in the company of others. There'd been no opportunity to visit the topic we both knew was coming.

It came as I was leaving the bathroom and heading for the pool tables. Reina turned a corner and stopped me in mid-stride, a blockade I couldn't get around even if I'd had my heart in it. This time, there were no friends or co-workers nearby to force discretion upon us; Reina was free to say exactly what was on her mind, and my mind as well.

"So? Is it me, or are you looking to get your brains screwed out tonight?"

I pretended not to know what she was talking about. I played dumb and I played drunk. I made her proposition me in various other ways until there was nothing left for me to do but give her a straight answer: yes or no? That green dress and all the fine flesh encased in it filled my eyes until I thought I would weep.

I told her no.

No, I was sorry, but no. I can't. I'd love to, but I can't. It's not you, it's me. I wish to God I could, you have no idea, but no. Please, I'm sorry.

She looked at me as if I'd slapped her full across the face. And then something turned inside of her and she smiled. Like I'd gone from being detestable to pathetic in the span of a single second. Poor, poor boy. He has no idea what he's just done.

Taken the only winning lottery ticket he'll ever live to see and flushed it down the commode.

It hurt. I hadn't counted on that. I expected the disappointment but not the gut punch. Reina was now a hunger that would never be satisfied and there was no changing it. Like I said: Some women affect a man differently.

I suffered her continued presence in the office, and the benign neglect she made a point of showing me for another three months, and then it was over. She got another job somewhere in Georgia and moved away. I never saw or heard from her again.

In her absence, I slowly began to heal. I got back down to the business of being with Joanne, belonging to Joanne, and I realized all over again how lucky a man I was. Joanne was my rock, the foundation upon which I could build a long and rewarding future, and nothing was going to shake it. We'd proven that. We'd come through the fires of earthly temptation and chosen each other over the ripe, red apple we'd had dangled before us.

At least, that was my thinking right up until the day my phone rang and I found Trent Giles on the other end of the line.

"We need to talk," he said.

***

But he did more than talk. He showed me photographs. Joanne and another man I'd never seen before. At a club or restaurant I didn't recognize. The light was too dim and well-suited for quiet conversations and positions as compromising as one dared take in a public setting.

"Imagine my surprise when I looked across the club yesterday and there she was. I don't know the man's name, but I saw them together at the bookstore once," Giles said. "I didn't think anything of it at the time, but now I understand."

"What do you understand?"

"Seriously? I have to spell it out? Why she never gave me a turn. She already had somebody else in the saddle. Besides you, I mean."

He added this last with a twinge of compassion, because he felt sorrier for me than he did for himself. My reflection in the mirror behind the bar made the depth of my pain all too clear.

"Well, anyway, I thought you should know." He gestured to his phone to indicate the pictures he'd taken. "You want me to text these to you? They could come in handy."

I shook my head, sliding off my stool onto rubbery legs, then reconsidered.

"Yes. Please do."

I didn't waste any time confronting her. Roughly one half-turning of the sun, when the next day dawned. By now, I had seen a dozen versions of how this conversation would go down in my head, and none of them turned out to be prescient. Certainly, not in the way it came to a close.

She didn't insult me with any denials, which was kind, but it didn't feel kind at the time. Neither did her tears. It seemed there was nothing she could say or do to make the truth less painful. Or less cruel.

She asked me how I found out. Where I got the photos. I told I'd had her followed. Wanting to make sure she was the woman I thought she was before I popped the question.

"But I guess you aren't, are you?" I said.

She told me about the man in the photos, leaving out his name because I warned her not to mention it. His name didn't mean shit to me. He was somebody who used to date an old girlfriend of hers. They had flirted without intent back then but left it alone until three months ago, when they'd stumbled into each other at a café near the bookstore during the lunch hour crush.

Of course, because I had no choice, I asked her if she loved him. She laughed.

"Love?"

She said the word with such disdain. Like no one had ever devised or told such an absurd joke. And then I knew the nature of my grave mistake. Love to Joanne was indeed a drug, a reason for living, and a relationship built on trust and faithfulness was the ultimate goal. But drugs are a crutch and some goals are just an idea unfit for reality. Joanne believed in love the way a child, their innocence beginning to fade, believes in Santa Claus: with a desperate, hopeless sense of denial that it's all bullshit.

Sooner or later, she said, I was going to let her down, as all the other men before me had. All she'd done was take her own turn at the game of betrayal. Nothing had been broken that wasn't doomed to be broken, by one of us, eventually.

Those were the last words she ever spoke to me. People say you don't remember what happens after your mind snaps and the devil inside you is let loose because you can't contain it anymore. But that's not always true. I remember everything that came after. From Joanne's first scream to the sound of her last breath leaving her body. And I can recall seeing Reina in that shimmering green dress all the while.

Clear as crystal.

* * *

Life in a cell isn't as unbearable as you might think, once you get used to it. The key is preoccupation. Giving yourself things to do to distract your attention from the loneliness and isolation. Every man needs work, no matter who he is or what he's done.

The work I've found for myself is writing. I write every day. Or, what I should say is, I rewrite every day. Because there's no getting this damn book right. Every time I think I've nailed it, I realize I've left something important out, or made too much of something that's actually trivial. So I try again. Nobody knows the subject better than me.

As I mentioned at the start, there's no such thing as the Book of Love. It doesn't exist. But I'm going to write it anyway. If it takes five years or forty. This is how I pass the time in here without going crazy. I write.

Every day, I write the book.

WAITING FOR THE END OF THE WORLD
by Peter Blauner

The boy was standing in front of a subway window, being a hero in his own mind. He pounded his chest with his fist and held up his chin. He muttered defiant words at his reflection, and then shrugged his shoulders as if nothing the world could throw his way would faze him. Then he poked absently at his ear to keep the little white AirPod singing into his head.

Whatever fantasy he had going must be epic, Dylan McCloskey thought, watching from the corner of his eye. How sad. How familiar. He'd been like that himself until not so long ago, looking at his grandfather's war medals in a basement desk drawer. But here it was, close to midnight on a Thursday and he was on the A train heading to Brooklyn with Stephanie Stern at his side, and he sensed the great epic of his own adult life was finally about to begin.

He was no longer just a twenty-nine-year-old geek in Warby Parker glasses and skinny jeans, working under Stephanie on an ad campaign for a chain of assisted living facilities. On the eve of his thirtieth birthday, he had been transferred and made number three on the Useless Beauty cosmetics creative team. And since he was no longer Stephanie's direct report, he'd asked her to have dinner at the Ludlow Grill, and not only had she said yes, she'd smiled and laughed through the meal, and not reared back in horror when his hand touched as they both reached for the check.

Now they were side by side plunging into the tunnel under the river and there was a distinct possibility that the night might not end when they reached the transfer point at Jay Street-MetroTech in Brooklyn.

Then the train stopped.

At first, most of the passengers didn't react. They worked their cellphones like thumb pianos and stared at the ads for continuing adult education and Tinder. A group of teenagers, too young to be out this late on a school night, giggled and gossiped. A man in a long white beard and a black hat ignored them and read a prayer book. A young woman in a headscarf sewed the insole of a ballet slipper with a needle and a thread. A middle-aged white man stood reading *Zen and The Art of Motorcycle Maintenance*. An older Black man peeled an orange. A little girl sitting directly opposite Dylan and Stephanie leaned against her father and grew drowsy, sucking her thumb.

"Cursed by the travel gods." Stephanie sighed.

As the interruption continued, people began to shift and squirm. The teenagers ceased giggling. The bearded man began to rock as he read his prayer book. The little girl stopped sucking her thumb. The subway window star began to mumble more aggressively at his reflection.

A metal door between cars banged open and three young men swaggered on sloppily in collared shirts, pressed pants, and polished shoes. They were all a little red-faced with drink, breathing hard and walking as if the train was still moving, occasionally grabbing poles to steady themselves. They seemed like they were coming from a football game where their team lost or a comedy club where the jokes weren't worth the cover charge. The tallest of them stopped in front of the praying man, put his head back and made a loud high-pitched beep sound.

"This is not a test," announced the shortest of them, a bantam cock with a buzz cut and a locker-room voice. "This is the emergency warning system. We are under attack. Repeat. You are under attack."

"Fuckin' down to fourteen dollars a share," muttered the last one on the car, who was stocky with a puffy red face. "Fuckin' Spider, tanked the whole deal."

"God, I hate finance bros," Stephanie murmured. "Especially when they're drunk."

"What's that?" The short one looked over. "You say something?"

"Nope." Stephanie pulled out her cellphone and pretended to play Wordle.

The short one stumbled toward her. "Who're you texting?"

"Let her be," Dylan heard himself say.

Whatever lingering conversation there had been in the car died away. The bearded man stopped reading his prayers. The woman sewing the ballet slipper studied her finger as if she'd pricked it. The little girl who had been leaning against her father sat up as if she was being allowed to watch her first police drama. The train brakes gusted.

"What did you say?" The short one focused on Dylan.

The tall one who had been making the emergency warning sound pitched his voice higher. It hadn't been funny begin with.

"Look, we're all just trying to get home," Dylan said, eyes cast down at a Snapple lid on the floor.

"The Spider speaks." The puffy one laughed. "He looks just like, whatsisname, the fucking guy on CNBC with the glasses, doesn't he?"

"You do the Closing Bell Report, Spider?" The short one kicked at Dylan's red Converse high-tops.

"I'm not on television." Dylan tucked his sneakers under his seat. "You have me confused with someone else."

"Why is he a spider?" the little girl across the car asked in a dreamy, wayward voice.

"Spider like 'spider dick,'" the puffy one explained, as if it was only logical. "Get it?"

"Assholes." Stephanie hissed.

"You want to say that again, sweetheart?" The short one

leaned in on her.

She gave Dylan a side glance. It was so brief that he would have missed it if he turned his head. But when he saw it, it made him reconsider everything he'd ever thought about himself or been in life. Twenty-nine years old. He had never had to defend anyone, never heard a shot fired in anger, never grown anything, and had never even expressed love to anyone or anything except his mother and Trolly the cocker spaniel he had until he was ten.

"All right, that's enough." He tried to keep his voice from cracking the way it did sometimes when he was nervous or just starting to get hay fever.

"Stand up, dude," the short one said.

It was useless to negotiate. The part had been assigned. Reluctantly, Dylan got to his feet. He had always been gangly and unathletic. The last physical fight he'd had was in the third grade at a Quaker school. It had not gone well for him.

"Can we not?" he asked, making one unironic last ditch try. "Please?"

The short one shoved him so forcefully that the back of Dylan's head hit the wall and the glasses flew from his face.

Everything went white for a moment. Somehow Dylan scrambled back to his feet. The smaller man swarmed him, arms and legs and elbows and knees coming at him all at once.

Nothing in Dylan's life had prepared for him for this. His only real frames of reference for this kind of blind, bourbon-stinking fury were the vintage punk and rap records he listened to in college. He spun around, trying to duck under the punches, forearms protecting his face. But the short man grabbed Dylan by the scruff of the neck and pulled him down to the filthy subway floor.

They wrestled, with the smaller man atop Dylan, raining blows on his neck and shoulders, while Dylan rocked from side to side, trying to throw him off. He could hear people yelling and laughing. Some of the women were calling out, "stop it," like they were trying to referee badly behaved children at a birthday party. Stubby fingers were on his face, trying to gouge out his eyes. He rolled onto his side, curling into a fetal position, a cry for help building at the back of his throat, but he was wheezing too much to let it out. Why wasn't anyone breaking it up or trying to intervene? He could literally die here or get some infection from rolling around on the floor. The only good thing was that the short man's friends weren't joining in. They were having too much fun cheering their friend on.

"Dude, I'm totally getting all this on video." One of them was holding his phone up. "Get him to tap out."

Now an elbow was starting to encircle Dylan's throat, threatening to squeeze his windpipe. He felt himself start to go lightheaded. But at the same time, something inside of him was rising and surging. For once, he had something to fight for. Not just a better desk at the office, or a better job evaluation, or a meaningless two percent raise that didn't come within spitting distance of keeping up with inflation. This counted. This mattered. And he had never felt more alive in his life.

He grabbed the arm that was trying to snake around his throat. Then he bit into the short man's wrist, finding veins just below the palm.

The short man screamed. A few drops of blood spurted onto Dylan's tongue. He heard a thudding pulse and realized it wasn't coming from inside his own head. It was coming from the wrist in his mouth.

"Oh my God," one of the girls screamed. "He's a savage."

"Let him go already," shouted the man with the prayer book.

Bodies surrounded them. Hands tried to extract the wrist from Dylan's jaws even as he clamped down harder, a dog refusing to give the bone he'd fought for.

"Dylan, what's wrong with you?" Stephanie's voice urged him back toward his senses.

Dylan opened his mouth. The man he'd bitten pulled away. Several of the high school kids were pointing in horror. Dylan realized his chin was damp. He stood up. Blood was dribbling down between the little green whales on the front of his Vineyard Vines shirt. The short man was holding his wrist as both of his friends kept filming on their cellphones.

The woman who had been sewing the ballet slipper came over and took off her headscarf, offering it to the short man as a tourniquet. The older man who had been reading a prayer book turned his head in disgust. The little girl huddled fearfully onto her father's lap, sneaking looks at Dylan like he was a monster who had emerged from a nightmare onto the train.

"You sick bastard." The short man grimaced as the woman tied her scarf around his wrist. "Now I'll have to get a rabies shot."

"I don't have rabies," Dylan said defensively. "I don't even think humans can transmit rabies."

Though, honestly, he wasn't sure about that. He was more worried he could catch something from the other man's blood leaping into his mouth. He pursed his lips and tried to spit any remnants, as more cellphone cameras came out to film him. He scanned the car for sympathetic faces. But the eyes staring back at him appeared to barely acknowledge common human ancestry.

A shudder of electricity went through the car. Everyone glanced up as if they'd been abruptly awakened. The brakes gasped. The lights flickered. Wheels began to roll. The journey to Brooklyn was resuming. The motorman was trying to get the train back on schedule. The short man's friends patted his shoulder and threw dark, vengeful looks at Dylan. Some of the teenagers kept videoing with their cellphones. Dylan staggered, shame-faced, back to the seat he'd vacated.

For several seconds, as they rumbled through the tunnel, Stephanie Stern did not look at him. She sat up straight, with her knees together and her hands primly folded on lap, like she'd found herself next to a chimpanzee at St. Patrick's Cathedral.

"That was so gross," she said, barely moving her lips. "What's wrong with you?"

"What's wrong with me?" He blinked, trying to make sense

of the question. "I did it to protect you."

"From what? Jesus. You think I haven't handled situations like that all my life? You made it all a million times worse."

Coherent speech was beyond him. The cellphone cameras were still out, the short man's friends videoing him while the high school kid got up to gawk at the wound he was showing off.

"You should totally report this to the police," said one of the girls. "You were attacked."

Dylan looked up and down the length of the car, to see if anyone would contradict her. But most of the passengers had gone back to minding their business. The bearded man was davening with his prayer book again. The woman with the ballet slipper was putting her needle and thread back into a handbag. The little girl closed her eyes and leaned against her father. No one wanted to do or say anything that might further delay them from getting home.

"I don't think I want to get involved with the police," said the short man, looking at his friends. "But I got a better idea. You both got him biting me on video?"

"Definitely," said the tall one.

"We should just post that shit online," the short man said. "It'll go viral in like two minutes. We could put ads on it and make back what we lost today."

"Wait a second." Dylan rose halfway out of his seat. "What about everything that led up to that?"

"You'll be lucky if I don't sue the hell out of you." The short man checked the scarf tied around his wrist. "I was supposed to be in a racquetball tournament this weekend."

"But how did I get to be the bad guy?" Dylan asked.

"You need to be quiet now," Stephanie said out the side of her mouth. "You're in enough trouble already."

The train was rapidly approaching the first stop in Brooklyn. Dylan wondered, in a daze, how it had all gotten away from him so quickly. He pictured the video of him biting down on the smaller man's wrist going out to all the finance bros' friends and followers, and then to all of their friends and followers, like an uncontrollable virus growing exponentially to hasten the end of the world. Or at least the end of his world.

Stephanie would not be going home with him tonight. Or any other night. He'd be lucky if his roommates in Crown Heights hadn't seen the video by the time he got home tonight. His bosses at work would be aware within hours. And soon enough, his parents from Wisconsin would be calling and asking if the time hadn't come to move back home. They still had the couch in the basement. Near the desk with the medals in the drawers.

The train stopped at the High Street station and almost everyone got off. Even Stephanie, who usually stayed on until Jay Street-MetroTech. None of them wanted to ride with him any further. His eyes finally focused enough to spot his glasses lying on the subway floor. He picked them up, wiped them clean as he could on his shirttails and looked around as the doors closed and the train started up again.

He heard a thin voice trying to speak words of fortitude and encouragement. Then he realized he wasn't alone in the car. The boy with the earphones was still standing before the scratched-up window with his eyes fixed on his own reflection. A man out of time, still thumping his chest and mumbling words to music only he could hear.

LIVING IN PARADISE
by Raquel V. Reyes

"What's that look on your face?" Bill grabbed Trina's ass then bit into her meaty trapezius as she stood at the bathroom mirror applying oil to her voluminous corkscrew curls. "Your shit don't smell like roses either."

"Nah, it ain't that," she replied, shaking the air freshener before spraying a pouf of coconut jasmine over the toilet. Trina adjusted her bathing suit from riding further up her cheek. Bill had been badgering her about the number and frequency of conch fritters she enjoyed. Hypocrite. Her curves were what had attracted him in the first place. Her Bahamian-Cuban culo was what brought the boys to the yard.

"Then what is it?" Bill walked around their unmade bed to open the sliding glass door that led to the second-floor deck.

"I don't know. Just something's got me worried, you know." She wiggled her fingers through the air, making an S curve.

Bill hated *all that witchy shit*. It freaked him out. He'd learned to live with the azabache she wore on her necklace that she never took off. But the saints altar bothered him. *"That ain't Christian."*—not that he was a churchgoer. *"Giving a statue coconuts and rum is pagan shit."* Trina didn't argue with him. She knew what she knew.

Once, in high school, because his girlfriend had promised him a blow job, he'd gotten a tarot card reading at Mallory Square.

The reader had warned him to be careful around water and wind. Young Bill had laughed it off. Everyone worked on or by the water when you lived on a four-mile-by-two-mile island. Thirty-seven-year-old Bill, after tequila shots at The Wharf, would recount the story with ridicule for *"the fucking damn piece of shit fortuneteller-con-artist. Look at me now, making a killing from wind and water every fucking day."* After his braggadocious tale, he'd buy the bar a round of drinks. But Trina knew the cards had spooked him into doubling down on all warnings. Bill never took Trina's premonitions seriously.

"Smile, Trina." She hated being told to smile. She smiled all day for the tourists. Sometimes she just wanted to rest her face—be in her body without somebody judging it. But she appeased Bill and smiled closed-lipped as she joined him on the deck.

"We live in paradise." He opened his arms wide to the sunrise over the Atlantic Ocean. The warm light danced on the ripples in Cow Key Channel, making it look like diamonds were under the surface. "Another gorgeous day in the Conch Republic. Nothing to worry about except the ice melting in your drink." He kissed her. His short stubbly beard irritated her honey-brown skin.

"Do you see that weather over there?" Trina gestured with her head toward the Gulf of Mexico side of their view, where the horizon was dark and cloudy.

"Its bark is worse than its bite," Bill said.

"Still, I think I'll take the bike to Ernesto's and get some bait in case it becomes a feed the tarpons day."

"Okay, but watch yourself. I don't like the way that jerk looks at you."

"He's Mo's cousin. He's practically family."

"Yeah, well, Guillermo is a jerk, too. I gave him a chance, and what did he do? He cuts through a seagrass meadow at low tide. Doesn't trim the motor. Burns up brand-new Yamahas. Cost me six thousand dollars."

"Six thousand dollars," Trina said in sync. "I know, I know. But what could we do? He's my sister's husband. He's family."

"Your family. Not mine."

"He's your cuñado, now." Trina flashed her wedding ring set. They'd gotten married six months ago after four years of living and working together.

"Yeah, yeah, yeah. Put some shorts on before you go. You don't want to cause an accident." He slapped her ass. "I love that jiggle." He was about to tap her butt cheek again, but she pulled away teasingly. "Pour me some coffee and meet me by the boat." Bill jammed his leathered feet into the salt-caked shoes by the deck's stairs.

He took the steps in a jaunty gallop. Trina watched him descend to the cement pad below the house, where he disappeared momentarily. She heard the truck door open and close. When he reappeared, he had on his sunglasses and Miami Dolphins cap. She wondered if he also had his gun. Trina didn't want a gun in the house. Her boyfriend before Bill had been an angry drunk that liked to wave his pistol around. Bill was a "love ya, brother" drunk, but still—jealousy could turn a sweet drunk mean.

Trina had held her ground about a weapon in the house. Bill had insisted that everyone carried a gun in paradise, especially on the water. "*You never know when you're gonna find a square grouper and the people looking for it.*" They'd compromised. The gun stayed in the glove compartment at night and on the boat during the day.

She sweetened his coffee with three spoons of sugar and a glug of vanilla creamer, then screwed the lid on the tumbler. Trina slung her crossbody bag on and took the keys from their hook. Before she clicked off the lights, she tidied the saints altar, acknowledging each of the three deities. Trina gave St. Theresa a fresh glass of red wine—*to help me with the storm.*

She handed the coffee to Bill over the side of the sky-blue boat and then undid the lines from the dock cleats. As he waved good-bye to her, the sun glinted off the silver script of the boat's name. She waited until she could no longer read *Fly Boy*, then jumped on the moped—sans shorts. A wedding ring did not give him permission to mandate her wardrobe.

Ernesto's bait shop was beside his house. It was a prefab minibarn with no AC. He'd open the front and back doors to catch a through-breeze. The shed had four freezers and a cash drawer. It was a locals-only establishment. If the fish were biting, he'd leave a green export crackers can out with a notepad and pen. Everyone knew to write what they took and put the money in the can or scribble an IOU beside their name.

"What can I get you, mami?" Ernesto asked, pulling a bag of frozen squid from the cooler. He passed it to the man with a folded ten-dollar bill between his fingers like a cigarette.

Trina didn't mind that Ernesto called her mami. It was a Latin thing, not really flirting. Bill hated it. More so since they'd tied the knot.

"Thanks, Ernie," the guy said as he exited with his purchase out the back to his idling flats boat.

"Have a good one, papo. Don't get caught out there. The winds are gonna kick up later." Ernesto wiped his damp hands on his Hogfish Bar & Grill T-shirt. "Okay, mami. I'm all yours."

"You're not fishing today?" Trina asked.

"No." His lips vibrated and sounded from the huff of air he blew. "No, gracias. Been there, done that a couple of times. It's no fun getting caught in a squall. Bill's not taking parasail passengers today, is he?"

"He's the boss. I'm just the advertising." Trina motioned to the logo on her tank top. The shirt was tied on the side, but her boobs stretched the material smooth enough to read the words—Conch Wave Sports.

"That's asking for an accident." Ernesto shook his head.

"You know how he is."

"Cabezón."

Trina laughed as she nodded in agreement. Bill was stubborn. When he got something in his head, it was hard to get him to change his mind. "Let me have two bags of mullet."

"You want me to put it on your tab?" Ernesto winked.

"You know I'm good for it." Trina's voice was playful. She bent her neck and cut her amber eyes up to him. Behind Ernesto, out the waterside door, she thought she saw a light blue boat turn a U-ey at the mouth of the canal. It was too far away to see the name on the transom. There were plenty of twenty-five-foot blue boats in the Keys. She let it go. Keyhole Cut was not in the direction Bill took to work.

The flat blocks of fish were still frozen when she got to Conch Wave Sports inside Betty's Marina next to the Rum Runner Isle Beach Resort. She laid them on the dock while she unlocked the hinged panels of her kiosk. The laminated sheets tacked to the inside whistled as a gust of wind blew by. Trina smashed the metal heads that had dislodged back into place. The poster listed prices and adventure packages—snorkeling with sharks (mostly nurse and bonnet, and Lisa, the resident lemon shark, but occasionally a hammer or bull visited the reef), jet ski by the hour, parasailing, and a personal island (a floating dock with a chickee hut and a stocked bar).

Trina wheeled out the racks of life vests. Next came the mesh bags packed with snorkels and fins. Last out of the locker was Bill's harness. It was frayed from daily use. But because it had *Fly Boy* embroidered on the padded seat, he refused to replace it. She tossed it onto the dock, where it landed on the defrosting mullet. She raised the business's flag up the PVC pole zip tied to the kiosk. It whipped straight, then fluttered limp. A second later, it slapped the air in the opposite direction.

Bill strolled over from unchaining the fleet of jet skis. An employee was checking the gas levels and batteries. "What we got today?" Bill asked.

Trina turned on the tablet and checked if the resort had made any reservations. "Party of four for skis at eleven. Two for parasailing at ten thirty. Personal island has a deposit for the afternoon slot," she answered.

Bill looked at his wristwatch. "Work your magic, Trina." He pointed to a family dressed for the beach. The foursome walked from the resort's outdoor breakfast bar toward the marina. "We can get in an hour snorkel before the parasailers."

The tween kids were the same height. Trina guessed that they were fraternal twins. The girl had on a Little Mermaid shirt. The boy's was Star Wars themed and cartoonish. They were the perfect mark. Their enthusiasm would convince the parents to spend the money on an adventure experience, but the first shark would have them out of the water quickly. Trina sent "Under the Sea" to the speaker and adjusted her shirt to cover more of her chest—a little eye candy for the daddy but not enough to piss off the mom.

"Chirren, ya gun' see parrot fish, sea turtles, eagle rays, lobsters, octopus," Trina said, laying on a singsong Bahamian patois she'd learned from visits to her grandmother in Freeport. "Crystal-clear water. Only few feet deep."

The girl tugged on her mother's sleeve. The boy cupped his mouth and whispered up to the dad. "Will we see any sharks?" the father asked.

Trina knew the right answer. "You always see a nurse shark or two. Gentle creatures don't pay no mind to people." She took the man's credit card and had them sign the release forms. In less than ten minutes, she had them on the boat.

The surface water was smooth. It looked like another perfect day in paradise if you were facing east or in the water, peering down at the colorful fish zooming around the reef. The Gulf's stormy clouds were brooding in the western part of the sky but hadn't crept over to the Atlantic side yet. An occasional blast of wind whistled through the marina at altitude. Nothing a tourist would notice. Nothing Bill would let intimidate him. Maybe they wouldn't need to sell ten-dollar buckets of fish to get through the day. Trina pulled her gold necklace and amulet from her cleavage to kiss the red bead and carved jet fist.

She saw the glint of Big Mac's saucer-sized scales as it swam by then under the pier. The eight-foot-long tarpon and a dozen other tarpon visited the marina every morning. The prehistoric beasts were toothless, but their girth and muscle could injure a person if startled. They had a head like a battering ram and a body like a cricket bat. Paradise was full of hidden dangers.

Trina cut open the bait bag and took a partially defrosted fish by the tail. She let a few drops of oil and blood drip into the water. Big Mac turned and glided back to her. She wiggled the mullet so the living dinosaur could zone in on it. In a split second, the two-hundred-fifty-pound fish exploded into the air. She let go of the bait and watched it fall into Big Mac's mouth. The creature's jaws snapped shut. The gulp of air that it had inhaled left everyone breathless. A trio of men applauded and hooted behind Trina. She coyly looked over her shoulder at them. "I love the big boys," she said.

She folded at the waist and wiped the fish juice from her fingers onto Bill's gear. The men rumbled with lust. Trina had jet ski passes sold to them before she turned to face them. She continued her burlesque until they rode off in their Conch Wave Sports life vests. They passed Bill's boat as he returned to the marina. The boy twin tossed Trina a line which she hitched with a smooth, effortless crisscross.

"We saw a shark!" The boy jumped onto the dock.

The girl clutched her towel and leaned on her mother. The father disembarked and helped them off the rocking boat.

"It was so cool," the boy said. "What kind was it?" He looked at Bill.

"Lemon." Bill cut the engine.

"It was so cool. It had a big hook in its mouth." The kid was bouncing on his heels.

"Yeah, *so cool*. It could have killed us," his twin said.

"Nah, not Lisa. She's a regular at the reef. She's never bitten anyone." Bill smiled, but the girl was not convinced.

The father shook Bill's hand and thanked him. The mother shrugged her shoulders and mumbled something about an adventure to remember. As they walked away, the siblings teased each other.

"Nice job. What package did you sell them?" Bill thumbed toward the jet skiers.

"Three hours," Trina answered.

"Did you do that bend-over thing you do?"

She gave him a look.

"Triii-na, don't be mad." He put his arm around her back and clamped his hand onto her arm. "I'm not saying nothing bad, just you know, those guys looked like jerks."

"Everyone is a jerk lately." Trina released herself from his hold. "Looks like your ten thirty is here." With an exaggerated welcome, she sashayed to the couple by the kiosk.

The couple were newlyweds on their honeymoon. The husband boasted that he'd parasailed before. The woman's brave face cracked when the flag wrapped around the pole.

"Is it safe to go out with this wind?" she asked, pointing skyward.

"Safe? Absolutely," Bill said. "I'll prove it to you. I'll go up first."

Some of the tension left the woman's body. Her husband kissed her on the head and jostled her teasingly.

"Let's get you some gear, and we'll sign the waiver, and you're good to go," Trina said. She helped the woman into the adult small safety equipment when the medium vest was too loose. Trina felt the husband's eyes on her as she bent over to hold the leg holes open for his wife to step into.

"Trina. Baby. I brought you your sarong." Bill thrust the tasseled beach wrap at her.

Trina took it without comment, threw it over the rack, and then gave the male guest a coquettish once over. "I think you are an *mmmmm*—a large. But u*mmmm*, maybe we should try the extra large for those amazing thighs. I bet you play soccer," she told him before turning to the wife. "Lucky lady. Those soccer players have great stamina." She winked at the woman. The couple tittered like teenagers sharing a juicy secret.

Bill snorted an exhale. "Time to get on the boat," he said.

"Let me get you your harness, baby." Trina mashed the padded seat into the puddle of fish juice before lifting it. "Ooh, papi, I'm sorry. It's a little wet." She passed it to him. "Must have been from Big Mac's splash."

"It happens." His aw-shucks shrug was for the guests. "We're going to get a little wet on the boat anyway, right?" Bill slapped the husband on the back and moved him toward the slip. He whistled to Jack, one of their Conch Wave Sports employees, to start the engine of the parasailing winchboat.

A bluster of wind swept across the dock and wrapped the woman's hair over her eyes. She stopped like she was about to turn back. Trina went to soothe her nerves. "Sweetie, don't worry. You and your handsome man are going to have fun. You're in paradise. It's your honeymoon."

"It seems *really* windy." The woman looked at the gray clouds beginning to ink up the blue sky.

"Listen, when you get out there, if you are still worried, tell Captain Fly Boy there." She pointed to Bill and his embroidered seat, bouncing up and down with every stride. "He'll go up first and show you. And, sweetie, if you don't want to go up, you don't have to. You hear me?"

The woman nodded while tucking a strand of hair behind her ear. "But it's a two-person ride. I mean, I kind of have to go. Don't I?"

"The bar lets you ride single, tandem, or triple. You can ride together, or he can go by himself."

"Okay." The woman inhaled and held the breath.

"Listen, sweetie, if you don't think it is safe, don't let them bully you into going up. You are a grown-ass adult that can make her own decisions. Don't let any man, no matter if he is your husband, tell you how to be. Amiright?" Trina's pointer finger carved the air as she gave the sisterly advice.

"Yeah. Okay. Thanks." The woman smiled at Trina. "It's going to be fine. And if I don't want to go, I don't have to. He can go by himself." She stepped onto the boat, pep-talking to herself under her breath.

Trina watched Jack undo the lines and jump on deck. Bill puttered out of the slip. She waved and gave the woman a thumbs up. Bill stayed at the console in the back of the boat by the winch and launch platform. Jack sat on the benches with the clients to hype them up for the flight. Trina stood at the end of the dock until they'd cleared the no-wake zone. At which point, Bill opened the throttle and gunned past the "personal island" marked with the company's logoed flags. The feather flags looked like dancing flames. Trina invocated the wind deity like she did each time Bill had a parasailing trip. Accidents happened.

She ran to the kiosk to get the binoculars. A dust devil kicked up and took the sarong from the rack. It landed in the marina's water like a bait-fish casting net. Big Mac spooked and torpedoed away from it. Trina used the pole hook to retrieve it. She coiled the water-heavy fabric into a mound and left it by the equipment to deal with later.

"Sorry, Mac," she said, throwing a few mullets into the water as an offering to the sea creature. The giant ate them in one gulp and swam out into open water.

Looping the binocular strap around her neck, she went to see if the woman had gone up or not. It took a second to find the boat on the graying horizon, but she zoned in on the bobbing platform when the red chute with the pink conch shell opened. Jack was at the wheel. She tracked left slightly and saw that Bill was hooked to the chute. He gave the go-ahead, and the boat took off. Once they were up to speed, the winch was turned on, and the tow rope reeled out.

Demo flights weren't long. Jack wouldn't let Bill get to full altitude before slowing down and bringing him in. Trina kissed her azabache. Bill was above the reef when his strap broke. A gale-force gust spun the parachute into an erratic spiral as he dangled by the remaining strap. Through the binoculars, Trina saw Bill plummet into the ocean like a pelican diving for a meal.

A rescue boat left the marina before Jack had pulled in the tow rope and chute so he could turn the boat around. Trina ran over to the *Fly Boy* and turned on the radio to call Jack on the parasail boat. She listened as the channel crackled with panic and concern. They were looking, but no one saw Bill or his yellow life vest.

The chop got rougher. Jack radioed that he was taking his passengers in. He dropped the newlyweds off and went back out. The couple crumpled onto the dock in shock. They sat with their backs leaning against a mooring pylon. Pretty soon, the Coast Guard was on the scene. Trina closed the shop. She paced the dock.

The search went on until the lightning started. After the storm passed, friends and colleagues resumed looking for Bill. Ernesto heard about the accident and came to be by Trina's side.

It was four days before Bill was found. Ernesto hadn't left her. He'd made sure she ate and rested or at least tried to sleep. They talked a lot about Bill. The good times pre-wedding and then the jealous times after they'd married. Ernesto confessed that Bill had flashed his gun and threatened to shoot him. *"I'll get you when you least expect it. Some dark morning you just won't come back from bait fishing."*

When the Coast Guard came with the news, Trina was home on the second-floor deck. They told her an investigation had been launched, but it looked like the webbing around the snap hook had unraveled.

"Ma'am, I want to prepare you—your husband's body is badly bruised, and there's been some predation," the officer said.

"Predation?" she asked. "Like shark bites? Is that how he died?"

"We don't think so. The predation was probably postmortem. We will know more later. If it's any consolation, he probably died on impact or drowned while unconscious," the officer said. He voiced his condolences again before leaving.

"Mami, I'm so sorry." Ernesto opened his arms to comfort her.

Trina walked into his embrace. She looked over his shoulder at Bill's boat. "What should I change the name to?"

"Hm?" Ernesto put his lips on her warm nape and kissed her softly.

"*Fly Boy*, the boat. I'll need to change the name. I think I'll call her *Mami's Magic*."

BUSY BODIES
by Ed Lin

I brought my 2018 Lincoln Continental around Worth Street to the southern end of Mulberry Street, which is known as Funeral Row in Chinatown because a few undertakers are clustered there. I pulled over to the park on the left side of the street, killed the engine, and watched children on swings.

A man approached and knocked on the glass. I lowered my window.

"Hello," I said in Cantonese.

"Hey, you're my driver?"

"Are you Mr. Wong?" I asked. The man was about forty years old, skinny, and wore a suit that belonged on a bigger man. He smiled as if I had asked a stupid question, and adjusted his shades.

"Sure, that's me. Listen, I'm going to have to get you out of this car."

"Get me out? I'm supposed to drive you to a burial in New Jersey."

He leaned in.

"We're still going, but in another car. Pull up to the parking garage at 62 Mulberry. You tell the guy you're there for the hearse, then drive it back here."

"A hearse! Are you trying to bring me bad luck?" I had never driven a hearse before, never even ridden in one. I was born here, in New York City, but I still held some of the superstitions from the old country that my parents had handed down to me. Chinese people get funny about death.

"Bad luck?" asked Mr. Wong. "There's no such thing."

I licked my lips. "I don't have a license to drive a hearse, anyway," I said.

"Don't worry, you only need a regular license. Your boss isn't going to complain because we'll be saving wear and tear on the car."

"I don't have a boss," I said. "This car is my whole business."

"See, that's even better!"

I rubbed my knees and sighed. "I don't know about this."

"Mister," he said in an exasperated tone, "don't worry about it. I'm going to double your pay, all right? It's still the same amount of driving."

"Okay," I said.

"Good. Now let's go." He tapped the roof, stepped back, and looked away as if I were already gone.

I started my engine again and went down the street. Ten minutes later, I was back with the hearse. Mr. Wong, if that was indeed his name, now had a friend with him.

I was about to pull over to the curb when Mr. Wong walked into the street and gestured that I should follow him. He had me park just past the middle funeral home, All Blessings.

Six men carrying a coffin emerged from the funeral home and walked over. Mr. Wong lit a cigarette while his friend opened the back loading door. All the men, including Mr. Wong and his friend, seemed to be up to no good, judging by their rough appearances and unbridled youth. They certainly weren't mourners. The men carrying the coffin seemed greatly annoyed by their task, and they shoved in the coffin with little care, bumping it from side to side.

Mr. Wong tossed his cigarette, walked to the back, and chastised the pallbearers for not grooming themselves better. He shut the back door and the men got into two cars, each with "FUNERAL" cards on the dashboard.

Mr. Wong walked up and opened the passenger door. His friend slid in and sat in the middle seat, and Mr. Wong followed and shut the door.

The friend couldn't have been older than twenty, and was definitely too giddy for such a somber occasion. He pointed at me and said, "He looks like the type of guy who should be driving a hearse!"

"It doesn't matter," said Mr. Wong.

"Do you want me to drive around Chinatown?" I asked. It was customary to give the recently deceased one last ride around the neighborhood.

"Forget it," said Mr. Wong. "Let's just get on Canal and get to Jersey."

"Sure," I said.

"Steve," he said to his friend, "give the directions to the graveyard."

I spoke up. "We're still going to Mount Rose in Linden, right?"

"Yeah," said Mr. Wong.

"I know how to get there. I've driven there before."

"Great. Let's go."

I put the hearse in drive. I was surprised by how easily it handled even when loaded.

"I'm going to keep out the directions, in case he tries something funny," said Steve.

"Where else could he be taking us?" asked Mr. Wong.

"He might be trying to run up our mileage."

"He gets paid the same no matter what. It's better for him to get us there as fast as he can."

"Look, guys," I said, "Of course I'm going straight to the graveyard. I want to spend as little time as possible in a car with a dead body."

The friend giggled uncontrollably.

"Watch it, Steve," said Mr. Wong.

"There's no body," Steve managed to say.

"What!" I said.

"Nothing," said Mr. Wong. He wiped a hand across the padded dashboard. "Shit, there's no radio on this thing."

"Why did you rent one with no radio?" asked Steve.

"It was hard enough finding one with three seats in the front."

"It's probably disrespectful to listen to music in a hearse, anyway," I said.

We hit Canal Street and I turned left. Traffic was murder. We inched ahead to the Holland Tunnel. Steve and Mr. Wong buried themselves in their phones.

"What time are the services?" I asked.

"Supposed to meet up there at three," Mr. Wong said idly.

We crawled a little bit more to a stretch of the street that was under the shade of a building. I stared at my reflection in the windshield. I could see what the kid meant. I could pass for a hearse driver in a melodrama. I was in my late fifties, and not even the eternal youth that the East Asian heritage usually grants could prevent the damage from too many late nights spent working. I could tuck quarters into the bags under my sad eyes.

I rolled to a stop at a red light.

"Hey!" said Steve. "What are you doing? You could've made that light!"

"There wasn't enough room for me to make it all the way over," I said. "I would've ended up blocking traffic."

"It would've saved a few seconds."

"I could get ticketed for something like that. I don't think you guys want the cops to pull us over."

"Listen to this guy," said Steve. "Think you're calling the shots? I'll show you something." He opened the photos on his phone and held the screen to me. "You know who that is?"

I kept my foot planted on the brake and my hands at ten and two. "That's my wife," I said.

Steve swiped to another picture. "How about her?"

"That's my daughter."

"Two for two! You should get a prize."

"Steve, you don't have to rub it in his face," said Mr. Wong, who wasn't entirely displeased with his friend's actions. "He's a decent guy. He doesn't see anything, doesn't hear anything. You don't get good Chinatown people like him anymore."

"It's too bad you couldn't drive," said Steve.

"Don't have a license?" I asked.

"I do," said Mr. Wong.

"Too many DUIs, though," said Steve.

"God, shut up!" said Mr. Wong.

"What about you?" I asked Steve.

"Don't have a license. It's best to keep your information out of the system."

The light turned green and we moved on.

"We're getting nowhere fast," spat Mr. Wong.

"It's so frustrating when you can see the tunnel entrance right there," said Steve.

"Looks like there's only one lane in," I said.

Mr. Wong checked his phone. After a few seconds he said, "Accident."

"So slow!" Steve yelled.

"Aren't you glad I reminded you to go to the bathroom?"

"We should've had some food."

"You should've eaten a good breakfast. I'll bet our driver ate well."

"What'd you eat?" Steve asked me.

"Coffee, jook, and pork," I said.

"That's everything you need," said Mr. Wong.

"Your wife made it?" asked Steve.

"My daughter," I said.

"Oh," said Steve. "She can cook. How old is she?"

My left leg began shaking.

"Seventeen," I said.

"She looking for a boyfriend?"

"No."

"Hey, Steve," said Mr. Wong. "Enough."

"I've got money," said Steve, "if you're worried about that."

I kept my eyes on the road. "I'm not worried."

"When we pull this off today, I'm going to have ten thousand dollars."

"Steve," said Mr. Wong.

"That's more money than I ever thought I'd have in my life," said Steve. "I'll bet that's more money than you got in your bank right now."

I did a quick calculation in my head. "Yes, it is."

"It's so stupid, isn't it? Why should I have more money than you? You're a hard-working guy, you play by the rules, you're paying your taxes. Someone half your age shouldn't have more money. Right now, you're taking the same risk as us, but you're only getting—"

Mr. Wong hit Steve quickly in the right temple, and the kid slumped over. Mr. Wong rubbed his knuckles.

"Sorry for that," he said. It wasn't clear if he was apologizing for what Steve said, or for me having to witness the crude way he cut the kid off.

"It's okay," I said.

"Now we'll have some quiet," he mumbled.

We lingered just outside the tunnel entrance. I estimated we were about ten minutes away from entering and being able to move at a normal speed. Mr. Wong's phone rang.

He answered with a sleepy, "Yeah." He listened while unbuttoning his jacket. For a moment he turned to look at me. "It's not good," he said. "We might be a little late." Mr. Wong listened some more, said "Okay," and then hung up. "Say, driver, do we get phone reception in the tunnel?"

"Part of the way, at the deepest part, there's no reception," I said. "Probably ten minutes or so with nothing, if there are no delays."

Mr. Wong took in a deep breath and let it out with a rumble in his throat. "There's another party at the cemetery that might be impatient."

"I'll get you there as soon as I can," I said.

We eventually slipped into the tunnel to the sound of giant smoggy seashells held to our ears. No honking. That boded well for a smooth trip through.

Two minutes in, Mr. Wong nodded off, and I was driving a hearse with two criminals up front with me, and who knew how much in drugs in the back. The kid Steve was right. I was taking a huge risk for basically just my average pay.

I wasn't exactly sure what these guys were trying to pull, but things didn't seem to be going smoothly. No wonder. They seemed to be winging it.

What if something went wrong and bullets went flying? Anybody on the outside would think I was with my passengers, whom I cared about less than a professional driver should.

I sure as hell didn't want to die, much less in a goddamned hearse with these two.

I felt my phone buzz, but I didn't want to answer it and possibly disturb Steve and Mr. Wong. Another minute and we wouldn't have reception, anyway.

I entertained one scenario. Once I was out of the tunnel, I could probably find a cop or two nearby the tolls. I could pull over, jump out, and explain the situation to them.

Something could go wrong there, as well, though. The cops might not believe me. And despite all of Steve's talk, what if they didn't really have drugs in the coffin?

The original plan of driving a livery car for a little jaunt out to New Jersey was out the window, and now I just had to see this thing through.

Mr. Wong let out a foghorn belch in his sleep, and it stank up the hearse. I breathed through my mouth for a while.

* * *

As we left the tunnel, I lowered my window to remove the stink of Mr. Wong's gas. The slight breeze revived Steve.

"I fell asleep?" he croaked.

"Yeah," I said.

"God, my head hurts."

"You slept funny."

He wiped his face. "We're almost there?"

"Fifteen, twenty minutes," I said.

He tilted his head at Mr. Wong. "How long has he been out?"

"Almost as long as you."

Steve nodded. "This guy's a real untrusting piece of shit."

I shrugged.

"He doesn't want anyone in his own crew to drive him because it shows 'weakness.' Can you fucking believe that?"

"It's a personal decision," I said absently as we passed a cop car on the shoulder.

"Fuck, did he hit me? Did he knock me out?"

"I don't know."

"You have anything to drink?"

"No."

Steve touched his head lightly. "After all the things I've done for him, he still smacks me around because he's insecure. You know, his standing has slipped. He used to have thirty guys. Now we're the only ones left."

I nodded.

"He's lucky that…"

Mr. Wong's phone rang. He picked up like he hadn't been asleep. "Yeah." He raised his right hand and pressed it against the ceiling. "Wait, where?"

Steve looked at him warily. Maybe this was yet another disappointment for his crew.

"Hey, we don't have time for this shit!" Mr. Wong clicked off the phone.

"Everything all right?" asked Steve in his best servant voice.

"No, everything is not all right. We're down one car. They got a fucking flat in the tunnel, and when they got out, the cops pulled them over. This is why I don't trust you people to drive!"

Mr. Wong looked at me as if daring me to even blink. "Driver, how far away are we?"

"About ten or fifteen minutes."

"How about a free workout today?"

"For me?" I asked.

"You and Steve. I need you guys to help carry the coffin."

The day was getting worse and worse.

"What are you talking about?" asked Steve.

"We've lost three people, so now the three of us are going to have to pitch in. That's what I'm fucking talking about. I don't want to hear any lip from you guys because you're only doing what I have to do."

"You know I have bad knees," said Steve.

"How would you like to have no knees? And you, wind up the window, this Jersey air stinks."

We entered the cemetery, and Mr. Wong leaned forward to pick out where we needed to go. The left pocket of his opened jacket swung with something heavy, and it wasn't his phone.

"Left, and then a right over there, by that wheelbarrow."

We pulled into a large oval-shaped parking area shaded by tall hedges where another hearse and two other cars were waiting for us. Mr. Wong's underlings parked nearby.

"You guys stay here," Mr. Wong told Steve and me. He got out and headed to the other hearse, which was about twenty-five feet away. An Asian man stepped out of the driver's side and met Mr. Wong in the middle. The Jersey boss was going gray, but he was spritely. They shook hands.

"I don't like this deal with the Chinese in Jersey," said Steve.

"Why not?"

"Because this is beneath us. We're selling ourselves short, taking less money for less risk. The heroin we have here, we could sell for three times as much in the city for what they're giving us."

"Three times?" I asked.

"At least."

"You don't like your boss, do you?"

"I don't respect him." Steve touched the side of his head again. "Hey, tell me something."

"What?"

"He hit me, didn't he?"

"Yes, he did."

Steve lowered his head. "I don't want this kind of life, anymore," he said. "I'm tired of being treated like this."

We both watched Mr. Wong and the other boss move their hands around like they were playing a virtual reality game.

"Steve?" I asked.

"Yeah."

"I want to help you out." He laughed.

"How are you going to help me out?"

"What if I asked you to wear a wire so you can put your boss in jail?" He laughed a little harder.

"This is crazy talk."

"It's not that crazy," I said. We locked eyes, and his mouth fell open.

"Holy fucking shit!" he scream-whispered. "You're a cop!"

"I can help you," I said. "It's not too late."

"You mean, you'd put me in witness protection and everything?"

"Yeah, when it's over. You won't be able to see your friends, anymore."

"What friends? None of them give a shit about me."

Mr. Wong and the other boss began walking to the back of our hearse.

"Tell you more later," I said.

The bosses popped our back door open.

"My condolences," said Mr. Wong as he swept the flowers off the coffin. He flipped open the lid. "Go ahead. Grab any one you want." His counterpart pulled out a plastic bag.

"You don't mind if we do a quick test, do you?" asked the

other boss. He had a deep voice that was both sleepy and menacing.

"Take your time," said Mr. Wong as he closed the lid.

An underling took away the bag, and the Jersey boss crouched to get a look at Steve and me across the coffin. He had the sharp eyes of a ticket taker. The Jersey boss straightened up.

"Your driver's older than you," he said.

"That's my uncle," said Mr. Wong.

"Oh, I didn't mean any disrespect," said the Jersey boss.

"I owe that man my life," Mr. Wong said solemnly. "I hope he rubs off on my young charge here who needs a lot of work."

Steve raised his middle finger and pressed it into the seatback. The Jersey boss shook his head. "Children," was all he said.

The underling came back and said, "Good."

"Now about the rest of this…" the Jersey boss started.

"You don't have to check every bag," said Mr. Wong. "Trust has to start somewhere."

"It does," the Jersey boss conceded. "Come with me."

As soon as they shut the door, Steve said, "I'll do it."

"Good," I said.

"When do I start?"

"We have to get back first," I said.

"Then what?"

I gave him the number all confidential informants get at first, and he made a big show of punching it into his phone.

"I can't wait," he said.

Would Steve pan out? It was hard to say. We might never hear from him, in which case another undercover could take a run at him.

Mr. Wong was hanging off the back of the Jersey hearse. Somewhere nearby a sprinkler pierced the air with shushes.

"Will I get deported?" asked Steve.

"Here's what I know," I said. "If you help us put away bad guys, we'll help you out, too. We'll never hit you, that's for sure."

"Well, that's good," he said, chuckling bitterly.

"Steve, the Jersey cops are watching us right now. They're going to close in when the deal's done."

"Really?"

"Yes," I said. I checked my phone. My earlier caller had been spam.

Mr. Wong came up to the passenger window. He whistled at us like we were dogs and gestured for us to get out of the hearse. The other three guys were waiting by the back door.

"We're gonna do a coffin switcheroo," said Mr. Wong. "Once we pull this thing out, there's no breaks. We gotta carry it all the way over."

We watched the Jersey crew extract their coffin and stagger under the weight.

"Let's go, boys," said Mr. Wong. I found a position on the back right side. Steve ended up at the left front, just ahead of Mr. Wong.

The coffin had some heft to it, as much as one with a body in it. The face of my old partner surfaced in my thoughts.

We passed by the other crew, and the Jersey kids seemed younger, and their suits cheaper. They were wearing black sneakers while my side had rented shoes. I was a little wary that our side only had six while they had ten. Their boss and three other guys stood by their hearse while we didn't have anyone overseeing our side.

"Can't we put this down for a minute?" asked Steve.

"No!" said Mr. Wong. "We're getting this coffin back with the next exchange, and I have to return it pristine."

"Fuck!" said Steve.

We managed to get the coffin over and pushed it into the Jersey hearse. We backed away and sighed with relief until we heard our hearse start up. Five Jersey guys, one brandishing an AR-15, stood by as it pulled away.

"You left the keys in there!" Mr. Wong yelled at me.

"No, I didn't!" I said. I reached for my pocket when I felt something jab me in the back.

"Easy there, pops," said one of the Jersey kids. They all closed in on us and told us to raise our hands.

The Jersey boss himself frisked us. "Sorry about this," he said. "I hadn't planned on ripping you off, but I saw the opportunity. You can't blame me." Still, he tsk-tsked when he found a Glock-19 in Mr. Wong's jacket pocket.

"You shoulda brought something bigger," said the Jersey boss as he pocketed the gun.

"Shame on you," said Mr. Wong. "My mother gave me that gun."

The Jersey crew only gave him guffaws.

After he determined that the rest of us were clean, the Jersey boss said, "Now I need you to take off all your clothes. Boys, let's help them out of their jackets."

"Stealing our clothes?" asked Mr. Wong. "That's real classy."

"My boys need to upgrade their wardrobes, and they were really impressed by the way you modeled your outfits." The guy who assigned himself to me didn't even wait for me to fully extract my arms before yanking my jacket away.

"Hey," I said. "My phone's in there."

"So what?" asked the Jersey boss.

"I have Find My Phone on. We all do." He sighed.

"Leave the phones."

All of us heard a car approaching quickly. Finally, I thought. Steve looked at me and I nodded.

But I was as confused as everyone else when the stolen hearse roared past. It was followed a few seconds later by a cop car with flashing lights.

"Maybe you guys should get out of here," Mr. Wong said to the Jersey boss.

"Let's go!" yelled the Jersey boss. They scrambled and were soon gone.

We stood around in silence, dumbfounded.

Steve glared at me and I shrugged. He put his head back and yelled, "This is so fucked up!"

"I don't even care about the gun, anymore," said Mr. Wong. "But my cigs were in my jacket and I need one now."

The stolen hearse and the cop car whizzed by us again. Then another car rolled up to us. It was the three guys who'd had a flat.

One clean-cut kid who looked like an overly eager intern said, "The cops escorted us here because they didn't believe we were going to a burial. Then they saw the hearse speeding in the cemetery, and they went after it and forgot us."

"Shit," said Mr. Wong. "We need to settle this, but we have to get back to the city, first." He evaluated me and considered. "You don't want any part of this. I think you can catch a New Jersey Transit bus around here somewhere."

The eight of them hopped into the two cars and left. Steve hadn't even looked at me. He probably thought I was bullshitting him, but now I didn't even know what was going on.

I waited another minute just in case the stolen hearse came around again. Then I walked down the road, dazed. I was supposed to take Mr. Wong to the cemetery where we knew he had some drug deal planned. The car's interior and exterior cameras were supposed to record everything. Then our New Jersey counterparts were supposed to swoop in and mop up.

Everything was compromised a bit once I changed cars, but they should've been able to tell by my phone that I had still made it to the cemetery.

I came down a hill and heard a commotion. The stolen hearse was parked by the cop car, which still had its lights on. Nearby, next to three unmarked cars, cops were handcuffing several male members of a large Asian family burying a loved one.

They were arresting the wrong fucking people.

I recognized Lieutenant Connors from our video calls, but I still held up my detective shield as I slowly approached.

She saw me approaching, and shaded her eyes even though the visor on her hat must've been working.

It must've jinxed me. I stepped into a small mud river created by a leaking garden hose.

As I got closer, I yelled, "Lieutenant Jessica Connors. It's King Lum."

"Where the hell have you been?"

"I was with the criminals you were supposed to arrest—you know, the big drug deal?"

The crowd was complaining loudly, and although I didn't understand what they were saying, I knew it was Korean.

Connors waved her right hand.

"I don't know what you're talking about," she said. "We've found the money in the hearse."

"The guy who was driving the hearse, he's with one of the gangs. These other people have nothing to do..."

Connors cut me off and pointed at one of the handcuffed Korean men.

"You see that bastard with the dirt on his face? He knocked out one of my men. You're telling me he's innocent?"

I noticed two Jersey officers with shovels headed to the freshly covered grave where the mourners were gathered.

"What's happening there, Connors?"

"We've got the cash, now we're going to get the drugs that are buried in that coffin."

I got up close to her to express urgency without seeming threatening.

"Please," I said. "Do not dig up that coffin. The guy who was driving the hearse knows where the drugs are."

She smiled triumphantly at me. "He's the one who pointed out this funeral!"

"Let me talk to him," I said.

"No."

"I can't believe you fell for his bullshit, Connors."

"That's it, Lum. Go sit in the shade, you're nothing but a nuisance."

I sat on a stone bench next to a fifty-year-old headstone.

I heard the cops digging as an older woman wailed, and I buried my head in my hands.

I had thought that this case was going to finally get me good press, and that promotion to detective first grade. I didn't want to carry the rank so much as I wanted to retire at that level. Now it was looking like we'd be lucky to get one arrest out of this. And we could probably count on a civil suit or two from this extended Korean family. If they dragged the NYPD into this, I'd probably get a polite phone call telling me it would be a good time to go. I had twenty-two years in, already.

I called Hagen as a last resort.

"It's all fucked," I said.

"I know," he said. "When they found your car in the garage, they thought your body was going to be in it."

"I wish it was." I explained everything that had happened.

"We got a call from that guy," he said.

"Who?"

"The kid named Steve. Said you gave him the number. Said he knew a lot of things we don't."

I grunted.

"Look, Lum, maybe you should get back here now. Today's a wash, but maybe there's still a case to make."

I walked away from the scene until I saw the caretaker's pickup. I flashed him my shield asked him to take me to the Linden train station, and he kindly obliged.

I only had to wait about fifteen minutes before a local train pulled up. I took a seat and noticed a young couple staring at my muddy shoes and pant cuffs.

"What's wrong?" I asked. "Haven't you ever seen a guy rise out of his grave before?"

(THE ANGELS WANNA WEAR MY) RED SHOES
by Rob Osler

The can of hairspray hit the doorframe, missing Cha-Cha's perfectly painted face by mere inches. With a high-pitched shriek, she dashed into the hallway for cover. The dressing room, which moments before had been filled with shouts and accusations, now quietly pulsed with Cha-Cha's receding high-heeled footsteps and Patty's furious breaths. Patty had let the mouthy newbie wind her up. Barefoot and breastplate heaving, she stood in the center of the room, regretting her latest outburst. Not because she'd allowed her darker side to gain control—again—but because she had missed her target.

As if reflecting the room's lingering tension, the red sequins of Patty's gown, a low-cut, padded-hips-hugging Bob Mackie knockoff that had shimmered joyously on stage earlier that night, appeared now to flicker like embers. That Ricky, the club's manager, had assigned the new girl to the makeup station next to Patty, queen of all queens, spoke to his stupidity or naivete—or, more likely, his intention to stir up drama. That's what Patty thought, anyway. And when Patty was sure of something, there was no convincing her otherwise. Her latest outrage was that the wannabe fashionista had stolen her shoes, a recent extravagance that Patty had justified with signing a contract to appear in Rusted Wings, a drag show starring a group of queens calling themselves The Shady Angels. Patty had earned the lead role by lip-synching, high-kicking, and sashaying her way to crowns and cash prizes for nearly two decades. Patty was drag royalty.

And Cha-Cha? Please, she was just a baby.

But baby or not. Cha-Cha was unscrupulous. Ambitious. Not to be trusted. And so it was with the fury of a queen whose treasured Christian Louboutin heels had gone missing, that Patty had hurled a can of Extra Super Hold Aqua Net at Cha-Cha's head.

"Girrrl," Fabrique said, "I get you being mad and all. But last I checked, you weren't crazy. And that was crazy." The Atlanta pageant queen wagged a long-nailed finger. "That temper of yours is going to get your ass fired. Or worse."

The other girl in the room, Kimona, reached into her bra and removed the wet dollar bills along with each of her silicon breasts. "What those shoes cost you anyway? Must have been what? Over a thousand dollars?"

Fabrique made a hand motion, snatching a bit of air between them. "Girl. You need to double your money to get close to what Patty must have shelled out for those shoes."

To Kimona's gape-mouthed look of disbelief, Patty said, "They're SuperYaz platforms. And you'd better believe I will get them back."

"Patty! Goddamn it!" Ricky's distinctive high-pitched voice preceded his arrival.

Fabrique rolled her eyes. "Here it comes."

Still fuming, Patty set her sights on the club's young manager, who stood bristling with aggravation just inside the dressing room door. Everyone, except maybe the newbie Cha-Cha, welcomed Ricky's presence like feedback from a mic. Ricky, however, seemed oblivious to how he killed a room's vibe.

"Cha-Cha said you just tried to take her head off, Patty." He pressed his fists against the waistband of his too-tight jeans. "I've had it with all the drama. This is your last warning."

Patty had once thought the guy might be attractive if only he never spoke, lost the excessive man bling, and stopped flossing his teeth behind the bar.

With her back to Ricky, Patty faced a mirror framed in frosted bulbs and gently peeled an inch-long eyelash from her lid.

"Patty?" Ricky said, "Goddamn it, Patty, you'd better be listening."

Removing the other lash, she said, "How about you do something useful for once and get your latest conquest to return my new Louboutins before the shit really hits the fan?"

Ricky reared back as if he'd been punched. He glanced at Kimona. "Cha-Cha is not—"

"Oh, please. That might be the one thing you're actually good at around here." She locked eyes with him in the mirror. "Now, be a good boy and scurry back to your hole, will you?"

Kimona's eyes widened, accentuating her meticulously applied liner and shadow in shades of charcoal and violet. Fabrique appeared only amused; a Cheshire Cat grin lifted the corners of her glossy red lips. Moments like this cemented Patty's infamy on the drag circuit.

Patty O'Doures took shit from no one.

With legions of fans, Patty packed clubs. Most impressively, she'd commanded top billing since Britney Spears's tracks ruled the airwaves. Feared backstage, she was known to be a hot-headed diva, not to be dissed. On the other hand, Ricky was a full-of-himself twenty-something. His cute butt had landed him the manager's job—that, and the club owner's taste for gym bunnies. Patty had no time for the Rickys of the world. Still, despite him being a gold-digging twunk, he wasn't a complete fool. Knowing that Patty ensured a sold-out house—all with a two-drink minimum—and that he was outnumbered, he fired a silent glare at Patty and Fabrique before spinning his Allbirds sneakers in a one-eighty and disappearing back down the hallway.

"Next time bring drinks!" Patty shouted after him, earning a chuckle from Fabrique.

Kimona, who, like Cha-Cha, was new to the cast, looked on

with dismay, clearly unused to such barbs being thrown at the boss. She hoisted herself from one of the room's tall director's chairs. "I don't know about you girls, but I could use a vodka cran. Get you anything?"

"Stoli on the rocks, please," Fabrique said.

Patty pulled the wig cap from her head, ruffled her short crop of dark dyed hair, and then having let Kimona wait long enough for her reply, said, "My usual. Thank you, dear."

With wigs returned to their stands and sweaty garments hung, the two veteran queens went about removing their makeup and untucking with practiced efficiency. A quarter hour later, Patty was wrapping herself in a voluminous silk kaftan. "Where the hell's Kimona with those drinks?"

"Knowing Ricky, he's probably got her sweeping glitter off the stage," Fabrique quipped. "I'll go see what's keeping her."

The dressing room finally to herself, Patty relaxed. As much as she enjoyed her job and her heels, they wreaked havoc on her lower back. She'd popped a Flexeril tablet as soon as she left the stage, eager for the muscle relaxant to work its magic. Long overdue for a proper massage, she felt completely out of whack. Perhaps her CMT could squeeze her in tomorrow. Drowsiness was a side effect of her medication; she closed her eyes and, slowly tilting her head from side to side, worked the knotted muscles at the back of her neck with her fingers. Following the instructions of her phone's meditation app, she took a series of slow deep breaths and promptly nodded off.

Pop!

Patty jerked upright. What the—? How long had she been asleep? A glance at the clock told her Fabrique had been gone twenty minutes, Kimona for over half an hour. Where the hell were they? Hearing no other sound, she stepped barefoot into the hallway and cautiously followed the direction of the gunshot. It took her no time to find Kimona, Fabrique, and Ricky, standing in a close circle in the club's small office. They were looking down at Cha-Cha. Her head rested at an awkward angle, her eyes open wide. Blood seeped from a ragged hole in her cream blouse. Despite the horrific scene, the body wasn't the only reason for Patty's gasp and sudden light-headedness. She immediately recognized the shoes Cha-Cha was wearing—her missing Louboutins.

Kimona fanned herself with a hand and swayed precariously as if she might faint. "Oh God, oh God, oh God."

"B-b-but how?" Fabrique sputtered. "We're the only ones here. Aren't we the only ones here?"

"Who found her?" Patty asked, her voice frantic.

"I did." Kimona reached for the edge of the desk to steady herself. "I was passing by with our drinks when I noticed the open door."

"I never leave it open," Ricky said.

"But how?" Patty scanned the room as if expecting to find an open window or some other sign of intrusion. "Did someone break in?"

Ricky shook his head. He still hadn't taken his eyes off Cha-Cha's motionless body. "I locked up about an hour ago."

"But we can't be the only ones here. That would mean…" Patty took a long look at each of them. She fought to breathe as if all the air had been sucked from her lungs. With reality sinking in, she said, "Oh my God. One of you…? Did one of you…?"

"One of us?" Fabrique snapped. "Good God, Patty. How could you even think that?"

Kimona backed away from Patty. "Those are your shoes. You're the one with the anger issues and the drama with Cha-Cha. If it was anyone, it was you."

"Me?" Patty started to hyperventilate. Her Louboutins. The heated argument with Cha-Cha witnessed by Kimona and Fabrique and reported to Ricky. The latest episode in a long history of thrown drinks, pulled wigs, and snagged hose. The police might view such backstage drama as "a history of violence." But this? This was next level. This was so beyond anything she was capable of doing that it wasn't worth a second's thought. She knew that. But would anyone else? When the cops arrived, all fingers would point at her.

"Which one of you did this?" Patty demanded. "Because it sure as hell wasn't me."

"Yeah, right," Ricky scoffed. "Saint Patty O'Doures." He stepped forward, eyes on Patty. "I knew you were a crazy bitch, but this…" Shaking his head, he looked down at Cha-Cha and pulled a phone from his pocket. "This will end you." He started to dial.

Patty lunged, slapping the phone from his hand. It skidded across the floor and smacked the baseboard with a crack.

"Jesus. Have you lost your freakin' mind?" Ricky joined the two girls staring at her with a mixture of fear and disbelief.

"Seriously?" Fabrique gave Patty a long look. "I mean, seriously?"

"One of you is trying to make it look like I did this," Patty said, her voice, like her knees, shaking. "And I'm telling you that is not, I repeat, not happening. I want to know where you've been since Cha-Cha left the dressing room."

"You're not Colonel Mustard in the Library," Kimona said hotly. "This isn't a goddamned game. The poor girl is dead. Dead! Do you not get that? We gotta call someone!"

Struggling not to lose it, Patty slowed her breathing and squared her broad shoulders. "No one is leaving this room until you tell me where you've been."

Fabrique waved a hand dismissively, causing her half-dozen gold bangle bracelets to jangle as they slid up her thin arm. "I went to look for Kimona but got a call." She cut Patty a sly look. "From that scruffy dude in the front row. Wanting some privacy, I took it from the little girls' room. I'd just got off the phone when I heard the gunshot. I came running. Kimona and Ricky were already here. You busted in right after. There. Is that what you wanna know?"

"And you?" Patty turned to Ricky.

"Fuck you," he spat.

Patty held her ground. "You got something to hide, Ricky?"

"Unlike you, not a thing. I was closing out when Cha-Cha came crying up to the bar. She was upset, to put it mildly. Said you nearly took her head off. I tried to calm her down, offered her a drink. It was Cha-Cha, so she wanted champagne. She guzzled it, and I poured her another. I left her at the bar and went to see what you'd done this time." He ignored Patty's furious look. "I needed to check the stock in the storeroom. Usually takes about thirty minutes. When I got back to the bar, Cha-Cha wasn't there. The next thing I know, I hear a gunshot. I got here right after Kimona."

Staring daggers, Kimona fumed, "Don't even, Patty. You're not the boss of me. I don't answer to you."

Undeterred, Patty continued. "What were you doing that whole time? Are we supposed to believe mixing three drinks took you a half hour?"

"Your usual is a mojito, you stupid cow. News flash, muddling mint goes a lot faster with a muddler, not to mention the lime juice. I know for your highness it has to be freshly squeezed. Get it wrong and you'd probably throw it in my face."

Patty rolled her eyes but otherwise let the jab go. "Right. And then you found Cha-Cha...like that...but managed to set down the drinks without spilling a drop?"

Ricky stepped forward. "She didn't. I did. Kimona was standing there, too freaked to move. I took the tray and set it there." He gave Kimona an encouraging nod.

Patty pointed a toe at the champagne flute lying near the body. Despite the cement floor, the glass surprisingly appeared unblemished, intact. She considered the self-described movements of the three others: Fabrique in the bathroom on the phone, Ricky in the storeroom, and Kimona taking forever to make their drinks at the bar. Each of them had been alone long enough to have killed Cha-Cha. One of them was lying.

Patty's anxiety level was code red. She couldn't delay a call to the police for much longer. She imagined herself on the receiving end of the cops' aggressive questioning and incredulous glares. She may have a reputation for being tough, but that was Patty O'Doures, the performer. Glen Upshaw, the man beneath the beard cover and makeup, was a nerdy, overweight, forty-something guy. He couldn't go to jail. He'd never be able to defend himself from legit criminals. The thought terrified him.

"I won't ask again," Patty insisted. "I want to know—"

"No, no, no," Fabrique emphasized each syllable with a wag of her finger. "You're done asking the questions, sis. Where were you when this all went down? Huh? Oh, let me guess. You were just cooling your heels in the dressing room? All by your lonesome, right? Nothing to see here. Is that what we're supposed to believe? Need I remind everyone that you were the one who was furious with Cha-Cha? And that was before you caught her wearing your shoes. You did this, Patty. Not one of us. You!"

And there it was. Just what Patty feared. Confirmation that they'd all point to her when the police arrived. She had but one or two precious minutes left, if that.

"Why the office?" Patty tried.

"Why the office, what?" Ricky narrowed his eyes.

"What was Cha-Cha doing in here? You say you left her at the bar with a drink. So how'd she get here? Unless someone dragged her, she walked. But why? Did she hear something? Follow someone? There must be a reason for her being here in the office."

"Enough!" Kimona shouted. "I'm calling the police." She moved toward the door.

Patty stepped in front of her, blocking her path. "No. Not until one of you admits to what you've done."

"Get out of my way, Patty! We all know it was you! We should have called the police already. They should be here right now, cuffing your ass."

Patty slammed the office door closed with the same uncontrollable rage that had driven her to lash out at Cha-Cha earlier. Just minutes before, she'd been unsure and afraid. Now she was pissed.

Patty examined each of the three faces staring wide-eyed at her. She had made the situation worse for herself; she understood that. And now, the only way out was to double down. If she could find even the slightest crack in someone's story, she might figure out which of them was the killer before the police arrived and she became their prime suspect.

Patty gave a quick appraisal of the office. Nothing special. Gray metal desk, standard-issue roller chair, file cabinets. Her eyes stopped on the well-worn leather sofa. She'd been around long enough to know why some club owners had such furniture. Recalling her own promiscuous past, a thought struck with the force of a death drop. Patty whirled around to face Ricky. "Cha-Cha never dissed you the way the rest of us do. I thought she was sucking up to get more money, better numbers, more stage time. And I think I was right about all of that. But there was more to it, wasn't there, Ricky?" She paused a beat to give her next words added weight. "Cha-Cha had graduated to boning the boss."

"You know nothing."

Patty caught the look between Ricky and Kimona but couldn't read it. "Did Cha-Cha even go to the bar?" she pressed. "Or did she come straight here, looking for consolation? Knowing you'd have a drink waiting for her."

"You've got some balls," Ricky seethed.

Kimona shook with anger that appeared directed at Ricky.

"Cha-Cha or Eduardo—depending—was how old, twenty-two? Three?" Patty said. "We've all seen the boy naked, so I don't need to tell you he was—"

"Shut up!" Ricky shouted. "Just shut up and get out of our way."

"They're right," Fabrique said. "This has gone on long enough. You need to step away from the door."

Ignoring them, Patty kept at Ricky. "Oh, I've seen your AARP boyfriend. Donald, isn't it?" Sensing his impending eruption, she went there: "Comb-over, spare tire. He's no Eduardo, now is he?"

"I said shut up!" Ricky went for her. They tussled before she shoved him to the floor.

"You're right," Patty shouted down at him. "The police will determine why you did it, but there's no question you did this, Ricky. It was you. Why else lie?"

Eyes ablaze and locked on Patty, Ricky scrambled to his feet. Sensing a serious fight, Fabrique stepped between them and pushed them apart. "It's three against one, Patty. If you've got anything left to say, spit it out. Then, one way or another, we are opening that door. And we are calling the cops."

"Look at her." Patty bent down close to Cha-Cha's body.

"For Christ's sake," Kimona hissed, "we've seen—"

"I said, look at her! Look at her face. Look at her makeup. It's flawless."

"Of course it is," Kimona said. "It's Cha-Cha. What do you expect?"

"Oh my hell," Fabrique said softly, drawing a hand to her mouth. "But if she'd been crying—"

"And the champagne flute." Patty pointed. "What are you not seeing?"

Fabrique slowly shifted her gaze to the glass. "There's no lipstick. Not a trace."

"It was a setup." Patty stood, feeling taller than she had moments before. "Cha-Cha might have been reckless, but she wasn't so stupid as to wear my shoes here in the club." She jabbed Ricky in the chest. "You put them on her so it would look like I did it. Like I would kill a girl over a pair of shoes."

Kimona shook her head. "No, no, no. We didn't. You've got it all wrong."

"Shut up!" Ricky shouted at Kimona. "Just keep your goddamn mouth shut!"

"No, you shut up! This is all because of you."

"For Christ's sake, Kimona," he hissed. "Just keep it together, will you?"

Before anyone could react, Kimona pulled a gun from one of the desk's drawers. "All you do is lie!" She pointed the gun at

Ricky.

"Babe..." Voice suddenly gentle, Ricky smiled and moved slowly toward Kimona with hands raised in front of him. "Put the gun down. I know you didn't mean to do it. We can work this out."

"What?" The look on Kimona's face was extraordinary. "But I didn't—"

"C'mon. Don't be stupid. I said put it down." Now within two feet of her, he lunged for the gun.

Pop!

Ricky staggered back. He clutched his ear. Blood seeped through his fingers. "You shot me!"

Fabrique and Patty cowered, their backs pressed to the wall.

"All of you! Get down on the floor!" Kimona screamed, waving the gun wildly in their direction. "I don't want to hurt anyone. None of this was supposed to happen. I found them...Ricky and Cha-Cha." She pointed the gun at the sofa. "She was wearing your shoes, Patty!"

"Kimona!" Ricky pleaded. "You need to stop talking."

"I took your shoes, Patty, not Cha-Cha. I just wanted to try them on. See what they were like. I was going to put them back, but I didn't have a chance before the show. I left them here in the office when I was with..." She turned her attention back on Ricky, along with her aim. "This is all because of you! You and your lies!" Tears streamed down her painted cheeks. "He said we could make it look like you did it, Patty." She shook her head violently. "I said get down on the floor! All of you!"

Ricky crouched behind Patty and Fabrique. As the queens lowered themselves onto hands and knees, he bolted for the door.

"Stop!" Kimona shouted. "Ricky! No! I'll shoot!"

Ricky didn't stop. Kimona didn't shoot. She hesitated for a moment before loosing an unnerving scream and running from the room after him. Fabrique and Patty scrambled to their feet.

"Your phone!" Patty shouted, "Call 911!" Fabrique nodded as Patty chased after Kimona and, from a distance, watched her dash out the club's front entrance. Fabrique appeared, shouting into her phone and waving her free arm, bracelets jangling loudly. Relieved that the worst was over, Patty's brave front crumbled; she began to weep. Had anyone ever seen Patty O'Doures cry? Fabrique never had. Like watching a parent break down, it was disconcerting. It upset the natural order of things.

Fabrique ended the call and led Patty by her elbow to the bar. She handed Patty a cocktail napkin. "You sit tight. I'll be right back," Less than a minute later, with the sound of sirens in the distance, Fabrique returned with Patty's shoes and set them on the bar. "Better to have these on when the cops arrive. Nothing good will come from bringing up your quarrel with Cha-Cha. It never happened."

Patty nodded and dabbed the corners of her eyes.

"That was some serious Jessica Fletcher shit back there. Did you know about Ricky and the both of them? Or just guessing?"

Sniffling, Patty said, "I suspected something was up between Ricky and Cha-Cha. She refused to say a bad word about him. I'd figured she wanted something from him and thought that 'something' was my role in the show." She glanced at her heels sitting before her. "The stupid girl thought she could fill my shoes. But Ricky and Kimona? That was a surprise."

"So what the hell happened back there?" Fabrique tilted her head in the direction of the office.

"Ricky's story about being in the storeroom and pouring champagne for Cha-Cha at the bar was a load of crap. The flute, remember? All part of the ruse. I think Cha-Cha went straight from the dressing room to the office to find Ricky. Where else? That's why Kimona never mentioned seeing Cha-Cha at the bar. She was never there. And no, I don't believe it took Kimona a half hour to make a mojito. She was in the office most of the time, taking part in the shit show that ended with Cha-Cha getting shot. Then Ricky improvised a plan, starring my shoes, to direct suspicion at me."

The wail of sirens filled the club.

"There was probably no avoiding some bad blood and pulled hair, but if that stupid boy had not had a gun, Cha-Cha would still be alive."

Fabrique poured them each a drink. After a solemn moment, Patty broke the silence. "See here"—she tenderly drew the back of her finger up a shoe's heel—"the pattern's based on Turkish parquet flooring. The crisscrossed straps are Galata red suede. And, of course, the red bottoms are Louboutin's signature touch."

Patty set her empty glass on the bar before slipping a heel onto each foot. She'd thought she'd seen it all—sketchy club owners, bathroom stall romances, girls with bad habits, shade, shade, and more shade. But never had she witnessed anything close to the god-awful tragedy that tonight had served. Patty O'Doures had traveled countless miles to get here: a sticky barstool in a gay club well past midnight, sharing a drink with another queen. It might have been seventeen years ago, except for one thing. One thing that indisputably marked how far she'd come. The shoes were the real deal.

Against the sound of slamming car doors and rapidly approaching footsteps, Fabrique said, "I think I can speak for all of us when I say, should you ever tire of those shoes, you'll have plenty of takers."

Patty forced a smile. "Oh, honey. If this old queen knows anything, it's that all you Angels wanna wear my red shoes."

FAVOURITE HOUR
by Martyn Waites

Hi there, thanks for joining us once again on my Favourite Hour. And I hope it's going to be your favourite hour too. Pleasure to have you back with us. I really hope you enjoy the next sixty minutes, have a good time and like what you see, and I hope also that you'll be painting along, as a lot of you do, but if not, don't worry. By the end of the show you might just feel inspired to pick up a brush and start painting yourself. Because there's nothing better, there really isn't.

Okay, here we go.

Now, as always, the colours I'll be using today will be flashing up on the screen so you can see them for yourself. Just saves time and hey, you don't want me to keep going on about it, we've got painting to do.

Today we're going to do a winter scene. As many of you probably know, I love those Alaskan winters. Nothing more beautiful than the way the light catches a forest scene when there's snow on the ground in winter. Nothing. It's just so beautiful and so peaceful, where I can go to really feel at peace. And I want to show you how to do it, and share that with you now.

Okay. Now this here is a regular canvas that I've prepared with a base of liquid white. Always good to start with a neutral colour. Here goes. And this is number twenty-three in the series, if you're keeping count. Here we go.

Twenty-three. Ah, twenty-three…

So…I'll just get my brush loaded up good and proper here…I'm using a three-inch brush for this, and a lot of people are frightened of using such a big brush to start with but don't be. Don't be. I'm mixing up a combination of titanium white and just a hint of cobalt blue, just a hint until it's…there we go…you see that? Now load the brush with that and we're ready to go. And we put it on like this. That's right…Don't be afraid to leave brush strokes when you do it, that's good, you're filling in the sky, that's it. Get it good and filled. We can work out the details later.

You know, I get a lot of letters sent to me asking me if these places I paint are real. And are they all in Alaska? Yeah, they're all real. Or at least they're real to me. And to you, when you come to paint. Like you remember it or like you imagine it to be. Or like you want it to be in a perfect world. Which we all know this isn't. But we do what we can. We do what we can. It's your world and you make it what it is.

Okay…now loading the three-inch brush with pure white, just a hint, not too much, mind you, make your clouds. Round and round, and like I say, don't be scared of brushstrokes. Because we can always fix that later.

And then…let's see…now let's clean a little of the blue off this brush, and to do that I'm going to dip it in paint thinner and then…you know what comes next. Beat it against the frame of the easel good and hard. That's it. Beat the devil out of it, as my father used to say to me when I was a youngster. Now the crew here hate me doing this, they're always getting covered with paint. It's so funny, I wish you could see it. Beat the devil out of it.

Beat the devil out…oh yes, my father. Standing there, cupping that old watch in his hands. Looking at me, holding the belt in his other hand. I'm measuring your lost and vanished time, he used to say. You're useless. You do nothing. You'll amount to nothing. And then he'd put the watch away, and the beating would start. Beating the devil out…

Now with the clean brush we're going to push those brush strokes that made upwards. Up and round…up and round…there we go…and you see, those strokes just disappear, and there we have our clouds in the sky. Beautiful. Isn't that right? But not many because it was a beautiful day. You may want more in your painting and you can because it's your world, but this is mine and this is what I'm doing with it.

It was a beautiful day. The kind that makes you feel good about being alive. Or as good as you can be. Perfect for being outdoors. Alaska is a wilderness. Even so close to towns and cities Alaska is a wilderness. And you can set off on foot knowing no one will observe you and spend the day by yourself surrounded by whatever wildlife comes along. It's peaceful. Tranquil. Liberating. And when I feel that, that's when I'm at my most creative.

Okay…now for the mountains. I love painting mountains. They're just so bold and sweeping, such a statement. Of course, you can make your mountains different sizes and shapes than mine because that's your painting, your world, and this is mine. This is my world. And you can do anything you want in your own world.

So, we mix up some van dyke brown, some phthalo red and, okay, okay then, just a little cobalt blue, mix that up on the palette here, then you get your two-inch brush and you load it up good and well and then…okay…okay…you got to be brave at this point…and there. Make your first mark. Take it up, then down. Then along, because your mountains are going to stretch all the way along here but they're all different heights and depths, because that's how mountains are. So you take it up…then down. And along. And again…and then you start to fill in what you've done. And remember to be brave, don't worry about mistakes here, because there are no mistakes, just happy accidents. We can always put things right again.

Okay...then get your knife. And mix up some titanium white with a little cobalt blue and okay...okay...a touch of van dyke brown, and then drag it down and cut it across. See there? The edge of the knife is loaded with paint, a straight line across. And then you come to the side of the mountain, decide where your light is and...drag it down. Look at that? See? And do it again there...drag it down. And there, your mountain's starting to take shape.

The mountains were the thing I used to love to come and look at. To get away from my father and his timed beatings. It was like they were a barrier between me and the rest of the world. I couldn't see the world and the world couldn't see me. Like the mountain stone would tune out all their radio signals and get them out of my head. And I'd be left with just my head and the things in it. My own radio signals. And I could listen to them in peace and silence without anyone else getting in the way of them. And I could do what they told me to do as well.

Okay...keep doing that all the way along, remember you're putting wet paint on wet paint so it can all be changed if you don't like it. Okay...there we go...and there's a happy little mountain range sitting in front of the sky. And in front of it, what's in front of the mountains? Well, we can have some foothills here, some open land in the middle, just a little, just a little...

Because in front of the mountains you could see your own footprints. And those of any animals that came by. I used to hope that the snow would come back before it was time to go back to the town again and my footprints would be gone. But I didn't worry too much about that because I always knew that where I was no one ever came to. Or hardly ever came to. Or not often.

But just often enough. Someone would come along, some hiker or climber on their own, enjoying the mountains and the forest for the same reasons I was there. The tranquility. The silence. The peace.

But I didn't like anyone sharing my peace. Anyone.

Okay...now we're getting somewhere...because this part here is...maybe scrubland or foothills...whatever you want it to be. It's your world. And in front of that, well we get to that now. Let's put some bushes in front. Two-inch brush, mix up some phthalo red, van dyke brown...and then...maybe, maybe...here. Here it goes...and make these curling motions as you go, again don't be scared to let your brushstrokes be seen, there are no mistakes, only happy accidents. Right along here and down here...that's the way, all the way along...curling, curling...happy little bushes...

That's when I saw him. Coming over the ridge. I glimpsed him through the bushes. And I knew he was for me because I felt that feeling again. That same feeling. Familiar feeling. Like it's calling me home again. To a home I've never been to but always wanted to live there. To the home in my mind. The world in my mind. The one I'd live in all the time if I could.

And he was coming with me.

I waited until he approached. Then I made out that I'd been there all along and hadn't seen him. Positioned myself so I was sitting on a rock looking at the frozen stream in the distance, just reading a book. All on my own in my own little world.

He jumped, startled by my sudden appearance. I pretended to be startled by his. He said hello. Apologised for making me jump, even though it was him who'd actually done that. I told him not to worry. Said the usual things that humans say to each other when they meet each other by chance in the wilderness. The weather, obviously. The scenery, and also what effect it has on a person. I had a flask of coffee next to me. Asked him if he wanted to share some. He said that would be fine and sat down next to me. What's your name? I asked him. Ray. And he accepted a cup of coffee.

And that's how it began.

How it always begins.

Okay…time for some trees. Now I know from your letters what a lot of you think. That I get this far with a painting and then spoil it by putting these lines in there for the trees. Well, I know you've got to brave when you do that, really make your mark in the right place. So here, get the knife loaded up with van dyke brown and phthalo red, that's it, mix it up, but not too much, remember to let those colours come through. And…a little bit of black, not too much though, because a little touch of black goes a long way. And we don't want to overpower the tree with darkness. So there we are…pull down, across…loaded all up there, see it? And, and, and…here. Make the line here.

Yes, it looks black against the blue sky but it won't be for long. Bring the knife down, down…there we go…down…okay. And we don't want him to get lonely so let's give him a friend right next to him. If he goes…maybe, maybe, maybe…here. And down again…down, down…there.

And quickly load the knife once more and let's do some branches. Not too much, not too much, go all the way down, down…there we have it.

Quick glance at my watch…we're doing well. We're right on time. You know, a lot of people ask me why I still wear such an old-fashioned pocket watch and I have to tell you, it's a family heirloom. I wear it and I think back to my late father, God rest his soul.

FAVOURITE HOUR

* * *

My father was the first. I came home after the army and he thought he could pick up where he left off. I soon showed him he couldn't. The army was good for me. Took that rage that was running through my veins and turned it into ice. So when I killed him I felt the rage and when I got rid of the body I felt the ice. That's how I got away with it. And I took his watch as a memento. Still wear it to this day. And I still see his face, every time. Every time.

Give that a little clean on this cloth...now. Take your two-inch brush and mix up some red, with a touch of yellow and just a hint of black. And then move along these branches in these circular motions, that's it...not too much...you want to let the sky come through behind...that's right...there...and the other tree...there we go. There we go.

Now into the thinner and we beat the devil out of it once more...really beat it...and then taking the white, mixed with yellow and just...that's it. Just a hint of snow on the leaves. That's it...not too much, just a hint...there we go.

And...okay...what do we need...let's have a cabin here.

I didn't touch the coffee. I never do. I know what's in it. And it didn't take too long to have effect on him. Ray. Although soon he would have another name. When I was sure he was all the way out, I stood up, looked down at his slumped body. Knelt down beside him and picked him up. I would say he was heavier than he looked but they all were. Even the skinny ones. Even the women. I started dragging him along. I knew exactly where I was going. Where I always went.

The cabin.

I love painting cabins. I could do them all day. And this one here...black and van dyke brown mixed...then get the knife, load it up and...there. Down at the sides, the roof goes this way and then...there.

With the same knife, don't clean it, take some brilliant white and then drag it across the roof. And there's the snow. Beautiful. Then we need some more van dyke brown for the sides, and the front...then take the knife and up there, along, down again...there's the door. And the planking, go along, big strokes. It's an old cabin. Nothing modern, nothing smart.

You know, people often ask me why when I paint a cabin, I don't put a chimney on and have smoke coming out of it. Well, maybe the guy who lives there doesn't have a fire. Maybe he doesn't burn logs. Or why don't I ever put lights in the window. Maybe he doesn't like to have the lights on. Maybe he prefers the darkness. And maybe he's got a generator all of his own but only puts it on when he needs to. That's my world. You can do it differently in yours.

Okay...

It's exactly as I left it. No one's been here. I like to think no one knows about it. They probably do but they don't think about it. Just explore if they're passing. It's too far from the city for kids to come here. And it's not far enough into the wilderness for some Grizzly Adams type to make his home. I chose it well. But even so, I keep my tools hidden. Just in case. Because you can't trust people. Any of them.

I get my tools from the place I've hidden them. Lay them out in front of me. The three-inch, the two-inch. And the small knife, ready to pull through and across...

Now, maybe we need some bushes in front of the trees. Right at

FAVOURITE HOUR

the side of the cabin. Don't want anyone looking in, now, do we?

The generator still works. As it should. I come out here from time to time and service it. Let that anticipation—that frisson—build up inside me. Get prepared for the next one. And now the next one's here.

The bench is where I left it. I heave the body up on to it, use my knife to strip it. Then I stop, look at it lying there. Wait for that feeling to come over me. That of the true artist. When it does I smile. I'm ready now.

Ready to have my fun.
Ready to murder and create.
Ready to enter my own world.

Okay...now let's put another one of these bushes...here. Don't want the first one getting lonely. Needs his friends around him. There...and remember once you've done that, get your knife and...there. Make these lines right on the canvas here...pull back...and down...and across...not too much, just to, just to give, to let the bushes see what's inside them. There.

Now, all we need is some kind of path to the cabin, leading away...and we do that by mixing a little van dyke brown, a little alizarin crimson, here, like that, and then with your two-inch brush sweep that along like this...that's it...don't be worried if it goes over the side, that's okay. That's okay. And there we are.

And there we are. Another masterpiece. I can look at what I've done and see it as something else, something transformative. Firstly for me. I've had this work inside me, waiting to escape, and now I've been able to make that happen. And also for the subject of the work. In fact this is the most transformative aspect, where the subject of the work becomes—literally—the object of it.

It's the beauty of creation once again. Immersive. Wonderful. Cathartic.

At times like this I feel like the most powerful person on the planet. No, it's more than that. I have created. I have made my desires, my imagination, become real. Become flesh. I am God.

So now I'll do what I always do. Admire my work. Stare. Until that feeling disappears and it's time to dismantle it. Set the stage, leave a blank canvas for the next one.

I don't always work here though. I go all over the country. Wherever there's beauty. Wherever I'm inspired to create art.

And I still keep mementos. Not as obvious as the watch, though. These paintings I make. Each one is numbered. Each one is what I suppose you might call in your prosaic language a crime scene. Not to me, obviously. To me each one is a work of art. And when I want to relive it I just go and look at it, replay the events in my mind. Or if I want to experience it all again I just paint it again.

Well, I think we're just about ready for me to sign my signature in the corner here with my special red paint…there we go.

Oh, and the watch that I cup in my hand is telling me that we're just about done for this session. Our Favourite Hour is up and it's time to go. So thanks for watching and a special thanks to those of you painting along at home with me. I sure love what I do and hope you enjoy it too.

We'll be back next time with number twenty-four in the series.

Ah, number twenty-four…

So until then, God bless and be kind.

I WANT YOU
by Alex Segura

Miami. June 11, 2022.

Christina Mendez was on the hunt.
She could feel it. The ideas whirring in her brain. The buzz of energy surrounding her every movement. She was onto something. The call with her editor in New York—a gentle, bespectacled man twenty years her senior named Adam Skolnick—had confirmed it all for her. Had cemented this idea was more than just an errant thought in her head. The worn-out reporter's notebook in her back pocket. A collection of ideas on a Word document on her computer. No, it was a book. Well, it could be a book. Christina had to make it happen. She swallowed the last gulp of her cafecito and scanned the parking lot of Versailles on Calle Ocho, the Miami heat boring down on her like a giant, sopping-wet towel. Her blouse was already sticking to her tan skin and she could feel the sugar-coated coffee spread over her entire nervous system. But it wasn't the coffee. It was something else. Something big.
She looked around. The cheap white tables and chairs situated outside of the Versailles ventanita were empty. It was midday, right before the lunch rush, but most people were working. Christina felt like she was melting, but the real heat hadn't kicked in yet. She remembered why she left Miami. Why she hadn't been

back in years. Why she couldn't come back. Then she scanned the parking lot again.

He wasn't here yet.

"It's a risky book, but you can make it sing, Mendez," Skolnick had said, his nasally voice even tinnier over the phone. "You just need that one, homerun source. That one person that'll blow the lid off the whole thing."

Mendez had that person. Or thought she did. She fell back into one of the flimsy white chairs, facing the lot. She felt her sweat-damp blouse start to stick to the chair. Felt her body spasm slightly from the superpowered fuel she'd just downed with a gulp. Two older women exited the tiny bakery annex, which was adjacent to the much larger Versailles restaurant—a sprawling, opulent love letter to Cuba, Cuban food, and everything in between. At least this hadn't changed, Christina thought. Some things stayed the same.

The ladies were chattering about something they'd heard on the radio. Something stupid the governor said or what was happening with a primo in Cuba and what might happen next. Christina didn't care. She was waiting. He was ten minutes late.

Normally, this would be her cutoff. But she wanted this. She couldn't just up and leave. She needed this meeting. It could literally change her life. If she got stood up—the entire idea might as well slide into the shredder that is publishing. Onto the pile of ideas that were never completed. Christina didn't want that. She wanted to work on this book. Wanted to immerse herself in this idea that felt so damn perfect it couldn't be real.

"¿Quieres algo más?"

The question shook Christina. She turned to see another woman, a few years older than her, hair tied back in a bun, peeking through the half-open door to the bakery. She was checking to see if Christina wanted anything else. She didn't. But she knew this wasn't a library. She ordered two pastelitos de guayaba. The woman smiled and stepped back into the air-conditioned cool of the bakery. The idea of the flaky pastry and its sweet sticky filling in her mouth made Christina's stomach turn for a minute, especially after the glucose IV that was the cafecito. But she couldn't just sit here. But she needed to just sit here.

Christina pulled out her phone and scanned the notifications. No texts from him. Just a few group chat WhatsApp notifications. One from her FIU college crew, bemoaning something the mayor tweeted. Another from her New York writers group, sharing the latest gossip about who was a creeper and who might be a creeper. She scrolled some more. New York Times alerts. The Heat were in the playoffs again. A handful of Substack newsletters. An email from her brother. But nothing from him. No "I'm running late" or "can we reschedule?" Nothing.

She slid the phone back into her purse and looked out onto the lot again.

He was coming, she thought to herself. He had to come.

Christina Mendez was tired of the churn. She was a writer, yes. But the stuff she wrote was exhausting. Or had become exhausting. After years working the police beat in Miami, she'd moved up to New York with big dreams and even bigger debt, desperate for a fresh start, new set of friends, and thousands of miles between her and her parents. But it hadn't worked out exactly as planned. Did it ever? She was still in debt. She had cobbled together a half-decent career writing about celebrity gossip for whatever website or tabloid would pay her and had managed to write and sell one book—a true crime page-turner called *Tropicana Terror: The Crimes of Rex Whitehurst*. It got some minor buzz, a few decent reviews—then disappeared. It was the worst kind of moment, Christina thought—because she could've handled acclaim. She could've even handled it being panned. But no one cared. The book fell flat, despite—in Christina's opinion—it being some of her best writing ever. She'd spent two years interviewing the families of Whitehurst's victims. Had spoken to the PI who'd taken down a copycat killer a few years back, Pete Fernandez, and even retraced the killer's steps to point to some potential murders that could be tied to him. Despite all that, the book was a blip on the radar. Just one book lost in a sea of them. Her publisher dropped her. Her agent dropped her. Next thing she knew, she was writing about royal fashion, the assault trials of midlist celebrities, and whatever was trending on Twitter that afternoon. The immediacy of it all made her sick to her stomach.

"C'mon, bro," Christina said as she checked her phone again. Nothing.

Christina was pragmatic. A realist. She figured she'd had her shot, did her best—and that was it. Now it was back to the coal mines to figure out next steps. But then her college bestie, Desi Cabanillas, had emailed her an article from *The Miami Times*. Barely an article. A short news item that could've been generated by AI for all Christina knew. If Christina still read the print copy of, well, anything, she knew this particular piece would've been buried on the fourth page of the local section.

FORMER MOB HEIRESS STILL MISSING FORTY YEARS LATER

Relatives remain mum on status of so-called 'Daughter of the Don'

Elena Vidal, daughter of notorious Miami drug kingpin Osvaldo 'El Monstro' Machado, remains missing—over four decades after being last seen at the height of a drug war that threatened to envelop the entire city.

Vidal, who was a law student at NYU just a few months prior to returning to Miami in 1983, was rumored to have not only come back to the Miami area to help her family recover from the brutal murder of Machado—but also to take over the family business. According to various sources from the time, Vidal—who changed her name to distance herself from her father and younger brother's criminal exploits—ran the remnants of her father's crime family with a cunning and vengeance that even surpassed her father, and led the family into a new golden age of criminal success. Thanks to Vidal's financial and legal savvy, the family was able to maximize its relationships with the Latin American drug cartels—cementing the pathways for illegal drugs to enter

Miami during the so-called "Cocaine Cowboys" era. At the same time, Vidal managed to funnel enough of her family's fortunes into legitimate businesses, while ruthlessly eliminating those that dared oppose her—including Los Hermanos Guzman, two Colombian drug overlords who'd allegedly murdered her father.

But at the height of her so-called power, with the Machado family firmly entrenched as the most vicious and feared gang in South Florida and beyond, Vidal did the unthinkable: she disappeared.

Or did she? Some true crime junkies assume Vidal was murdered—the body hidden in the Everglades or destroyed. Others—including some notable former law enforcement officials—suggest she may have carefully built an alternate identity, allowing her to fade into the shadows once her work avenging her father was complete. The sad reality for followers of Miami history and its criminal undercurrents is more mundane: we may never know.

The words had screamed at Christina as she read them while scrolling through the painfully mediocre *Miami Times* website.

WE MAY NEVER KNOW.

Desi's email had been harmless. Hardly a call to action. Desi was a store manager at El Dorado in Hialeah. She wasn't trying to find Christina a new book to write. She just thought the story was interesting enough to share with her high school best friend while she was on break between shifts. But it was so much more to Christina. It felt like a door opening. But she had to walk through fast.

That had been six months ago, Christina realized as the woman from the bakery stepped back out into the scalding heat and placed a small, white paper box on the table in front of her. Christina handed her a five and waved off the change. She didn't even look at the box. Couldn't even fathom biting into the pastry. Not yet. But maybe later.

Six months ago, thanks to that email, Christina thought there might be hope. Hope for another book. Hope for another chance.

Hope for Christina to pull herself out of the journalistic doldrums and actually write something people would read. Not a listicle that someone would scroll through to complain about what wasn't there. Not a puff piece about an actor with a middling part in a summer blockbuster. Not a crime blotter story about a sex cult featuring actors from a comic book TV show. The kind of book people would read and put on their shelves, between *A Stranger Beside Me* and *In Cold Blood*. She would find Elena Vidal, and she would figure out just what kind of damage she did in Miami forty years ago. Christina would dig up the bodies and present a picture of a city in turmoil—in the wake of the Mariel boatlift, the McDuffie Riots, a post-Watergate America, and firmly in the shadow of the Cuban devil, Fidel Castro.

It felt almost too perfect, Christina recalled. She'd Googled and researched other books that seemed to touch on the topic. But none went deep—and none asked the question Christina couldn't get out of her head: where was Elena Vidal? What had happened to this woman who had, allegedly, taken over a male-dominated criminal organization and not only waged war on her father's enemies—but cannily reshaped it to become something else? Something legitimate and real?

Christina had immersed herself in documents. Newspaper clippings from the era. Books about the Cuban exile community. Salacious stories about the criminal activities happening in her hometown. The Dadeland Mall massacre. The murder of Osvaldo Machado, the decorated Bay of Pigs veteran who'd parlayed his military knowledge into a criminal empire, as he stepped out of his bulletproof-glass-plated Oldsmobile to embrace his comandante, a man only known as El Leon. A burly, swarthy man who would do anything for his jefe. And who may have betrayed him, too. But secondary sources could only get Christina so far.

She put together a pitch. She wrote some sample chapters. She even mocked up a cover and started strategizing her reporting. Christina knew this was barely scratching the surface, but her work had started to suffer. She was too obsessed. She was running behind on her work—usually producing a baker's dozen of stories each week, the number had dwindled to four or five. Her editors were annoyed. But Christina didn't care. She sent the proposal off to a handful of agents and reeled one in. A young, hungry woman named Liz who was based in L.A. In a few weeks, Liz had brokered a deal with a mid-level publisher. Skolnick bid high and fast. Christina was all for it.

But now comes the hard part. Writing the damn book. And to do that—to write something sweeping in scope, something that not only painted a picture of a city being torn apart, but also solved a decades-old mystery—Christina needed more than hours at the library. She needed sources. She needed people who were there. And she needed them to go on record. She wanted this so bad, she realized. She could visualize herself. On the dais of some fancy literary award, accepting the plaque—looking out onto the blinding lights, imagining her friends and family, her editor, her agent, in the audience, looking on in rapt attention. She would be humble and brief, but also glib and funny, as if this was all part of the big plan. Christina licked her lips for a moment. She saw the battered Ford Taurus enter the parking lot and almost jumped out of her seat, her movement shaking the plastic table, sending the box of pastelitos sliding away.

Christina righted herself and sat back down, back straight, her entire body on alert.

He was here.

Osvaldito Machado was here.

In every multi-child family—royal, criminal, or otherwise—there's the eldest. The heir apparent. The firstborn. The one who will take over. Take care of the parents in their old age. Make sure their younger sibling is okay. It rarely worked out that way, but the traditions and symbolism of it all creates expectations, and from the research Christina had spent the last few months swimming in, she knew Osvaldito Machado had had plenty of expectations on that fateful night in 1984. The night his father was gunned down and a three-year-long gang war kicked off, sending the city into an even deeper state of chaos and bloodshed. Turning Miami from international nexus point to the frontlines of an internecine war that had no end in sight.

But Osvaldito's expected rise to run the family hit a speed bump. One he hadn't expected. At least, that's what Christina had been led to believe. But now she would hear it for herself, from the lips of Osvaldito. She could almost picture the conversation. Could see him shuffling over to her table, perhaps with a walker—or an aide helping him along. Osvaldito Machado was not in the best health. Despite being barely seventy years old, the years had been tough on him. Cancer. The loss of his parents. The disappearance of his sister. And the gutting of the one thing he loved—the one thing he wanted: his family's criminal enterprise. Now, Machado Holdings Inc. was a global company, with a board of directors, public stock, and offices in Miami, New York, Madrid, Buenos Aires, and Toronto. Elena Vidal had taken her father's Miami empire and gone global, leaving her little brother in the dust.

Or had she?

She heard the creaking of a car door and watched as a slim, older man stepped out of the driver's side. This was no frail cripple, Christina thought. This man was older, certainly—but he was fit, strong. Osvaldito walked with a confidence that Christina longed for. His tailored gray suit looked like it'd been just pulled off the rack, not a hint of sweat, not a wrinkle in sight. Osvaldito was stylish, she thought.

Their eyes met, Osvaldito granting Christina a slight, knowing wave as he walked across the gray asphalt, the sounds of Calle Ocho pulsing between them. The car horns. The loud salsa music drifting out of speeding cars. The soft hum of Spanish from inside the bakery, louder as the door opened, dulled when it closed. It all felt so natural, Christina thought. She felt her senses dulling. Felt a calmness wash over her as she waited for the big fish to arrive.

She felt a drop of sweat slide down her back. Felt a dryness in her mouth as Osvaldito made it to the bakery's outdoor seating area. Felt a breath catch in her mouth as she stood up and took his leathery, dry hand in hers. Felt her chapped lips pucker as she leaned forward to kiss his cheek. It was happening, she thought. He was here. She'd wanted this so bad. Not Osvaldito, not him in particular—but this. The precipice. Being so close to what she'd envisioned, as if by some great power, she'd manifested it.

Osvaldito Machado held all the secrets. Osvaldito Machado could tell her where Elena Vidal was. Osvaldito Machado was her ticket to fame and immortality.

He smiled as he sat across from her, wincing slightly as he settled into the chair, the first sign of frailty. His invincibility broken.

"You didn't tell me you were beautiful," he said, his voice silken and confident—as if he'd used the line many times before, to great success. His eyes looked relaxed, lived-in. His gray hair and mustache neat and well-kept. Osvaldito Machado looked like he slept and ate well, and was taken care of.

Christina smiled at the compliment and leaned forward, pushing the box of pastelitos over to her subject.

"I got you a treat," she said, a soft twinkle in her eyes. Was she flirting with him? Maybe.

Osvaldito looked at the box but didn't reach for it.

"Not hungry," he said, like a child. "But thank you. I've got to be down on North Beach later. But I wanted to make our appointment. I don't like to break plans."

Christina started to respond, but Osvaldito leaned forward, elbows on his knees, his eyes locked on Christina's. He cleared his throat.

"The questions you're asking—the reason you want to talk to me…it worries me, linda," he said, a wistful look on his face—almost like a disappointed parent. "It could be very problematic for you. And for me, if I talk."

Christina felt the wind slowly escape her body. Tried to retain some oxygen to not only speak, but to survive the rest of the conversation. But she knew things could've gone this way. That

Osvaldito would give her the polite goodbye. She hadn't expected it. Once the reclusive gangster had agreed to meet with her, she thought he'd at least give her something. She hadn't anticipated this. She felt stupid. She'd let her desire—her desperation for the story—cloud her reality. What had her papi told her when she'd pitched the idea to him? Her papi, who'd spent years as a reporter at *The Miami Times*, who'd never written a book. Who'd never moved to New York. Who'd only dated his wife and had only spent money he'd earned fair and square.

"Sometimes things are secrets for a reason, mi cielo," he'd told her over the phone, a few days before she boarded a plane back home to Miami. "It's not someone making a mistake. There's no secret to success. People don't talk about something because they don't want to. And it isn't some conspiracy. Those are the kind of things you leave alone. No lo toques. Because if you do? If you rattle the cage—something might come out and bite you."

She knew he was right now. As Osvaldito Machado leaned back in the rickety chair outside of the Versailles bakery. But she wanted this, she thought. She wasn't going to just give up.

"I want you," she blurted out, and she could see the older man's eyebrows pop up. She pressed on. "I mean, I want you to talk to me. I want you to feel comfortable talking to me. I know that's going to be a journey. But a lot of good can come from this. We can really tell your story, explain your past and how your sister was involved. We could find her."

"Find her?" Osvaldito said with a dry, humorless laugh. "Who says she's even missing, niña?"

Christina opened her mouth to respond, her entire body frozen with shock. Despite having said nothing, Osvaldito had managed to say so, so much. Had he just confirmed that his sister was—

The screech of tires. The familiar creaking and slamming of car doors. The rushed patter of rubber soles on hot, jagged concrete.

Christina turned to her left. She saw the black car—she couldn't make out the model, much less the year—sloppily pulled up in front of the bakery, the back tires sticking out into the street. *They're going to get a ticket,* Christina would remember thinking in this moment, even as she noticed the three men, dressed in black from head to toe, running toward them. Three men wearing black balaclava masks. Three men holding guns. Big, long guns.

Christina didn't move. She heard the awkward scratching sound of the cheap plastic chair grinding against the floor as Osvaldito stood up, turning back toward his car. He moved fast for an old man, she thought, her mind still in stasis as the three men got closer, not saying anything, the only sound their footfalls as they approached. Then they stopped. The sounds stopped. And she watched as Osvaldito froze, too, midstep, his body turning to look at the three invaders, his eyes wide, mouth agape. The look of a deer on a darkened road, as headlights strafed over its brown body. The sense of looming death. The certainty of what was to come. Christina felt it, too.

Then the silence was broken by the sound of machine gun fire, and Christina felt herself being yanked to the floor, her hands scraping the hard, broken floor. Her head slamming into the concrete. She felt her body curling into a ball. She watched Osvaldito, still standing, still frozen, too—except now he looked like he was being pelted by berries. Red splotches on his light gray suit. Little dots that got bigger, shaking him violently each time they connected. She watched, dust and rocks, sound and panic spreading all over her as she watched. He shook violently now, his knees buckling. Christina watched as Osvaldito Machado fell to the floor, like a stained napkin being tossed aside, no form or function anymore. She could feel her heart beating inside of her—screaming to be let out. Pounding on her chest like a monster desperate to escape. She felt her nails digging into her arms, her entire body clutching itself, and Christina knew she had gone somewhere else—had forced her mind to experience what was happening from a distance, because what was happening was too bad, too terrible, to think about in the moment.

And as quickly as it started, the noise stopped—the soft, gruesome thud of Osvaldito's bloodied head hitting the floor with a hollow *skrunk* sound. His eyes—still open. Staring at Christina, curled into herself. The pattering of feet—growing distant. The slamming of doors. The screeching of tires. And, in the background, faintly—the sound of sirens.

The tears came now. Warm and dirty, sliding down her face. Christina waited a long time to get up. Didn't move until she felt a hand on her shoulder. Until she looked up and saw the police officer standing over her, cursing to himself. She couldn't make out what he was saying to the other man—the ringing in her ears thick and dense. She didn't want to hear. She didn't want to know. She got up shakily, her legs bending at weird angles, unable to do their jobs. Unable to prop her up. She felt hands under her arms. Heard someone talking to her, asking what happened—if she was okay. She felt a cushion under her. The lights from an ambulance. The sounds of shattered glass scraping on the pavement as the men propping her up walked her away. But all she could see, burned into her mind, was Osvaldito's face. Handsome and well-aged. The nicely trimmed mustache. The sleepy eyes. Not so sleepy, no. Not anymore. Wide with fear. Mouth open in surprise. The look of death on his aged face.

Christina had wanted this. Had wanted answers. Had wanted this book. This moment. But instead, she'd gotten this. Scrapes on her hands and body. Blood running down her leg. Breathing ragged and desperate. Christina leaned forward on the cot in the ambulance, ignoring the EMT personnel trying to poke and prod her and ask her if she was okay. She was not okay. She was not okay.

If you rattle the cage—something might come out and bite you.

WATCHING THE DETECTIVES
by Mary Anna Evans

I should have seen the truth on the children's faces. The facts of the case should have been obvious from the moment I edged through their front door, loaded gun at the ready. But who is at their best in a situation of utter chaos, listening in darkness to voices tuned for intimidation and waiting for the sound of doors being battered down? And, maybe, listening for the sounds of gunfire and death.

I remember my partner Dan bellowing from his position at the house's side door, just out of sight. "Police! Is anybody home?"

He got no answer but morning birdsong and the sound of my voice repeating his question, "Police! Is anybody in there?"

My backup, Marvin, covered me. With his knees flexed, he held a picture-perfect stance, torso square to the target and feet spread. Only his wispy gray hair and soft middle kept him from looking as deadly as he was. Marvin's partner Pedro was covering Dan. Pedro had no gray in his hair yet, but he was just as soft and just as deadly. Voices in all directions told me that we had the house surrounded. Everything was in place. It was time to go in.

I'd been here before. Not to this house, no, but I'd been to fifty other houses like it, where neighbors had called in something disturbing enough to trigger this kind of response. This time, we'd received reports of a woman's scream, loud enough to freak out multiple insomniacs as they brewed their pre-dawn cups of joe.

That's all anyone had heard, a single scream. Just a long, wailing "He's dead" and no more. No answering voice. No gunshot.

Nobody had reported an assailant fleeing the scene, but they were all honest enough to say that they hadn't looked. In that neighborhood, showing your face at the window when a criminal was on the run was a good way to die.

I shouted, "We're coming in!" and then all hell broke loose.

For a good solid minute, it swirled around me as I stepped through the door and looked up into four faces that drew my eyes like magnets. For a long heartbeat, it was just the five of us, four children and me, motionless and bathed in the urgent shouts of my fellow cops. Perhaps I should say there were six of us frozen in the tumult, as there was a dead man to my right, sprawled in his own blood.

The children stood eight feet above me at the top of a flight of stairs. Three of them had faces as pale and still as moons, framed by dark hair that blended into the dimness. Their pallor should have told me something. The fourth face was golden-tan. Crowned by dark curls tipped with gold, it was oddly asymmetrical but still beautiful. Dan and three of my colleagues had their handguns trained on those faces, one muzzle per kid.

None of the children moved, not even when Dan called out, "Show me your hands. *Show me your hands.*" I'm not even sure any of them blinked.

"All of you," Dan barked. "You've got to show me your hands. Now."

The golden-curled adolescent boy let go of the banister, slowly reaching for the ceiling. Toddlers are mimics through and through, so his little brothers hurried to copy him, thrusting their hands up so quickly that I would have laughed if there hadn't been an unholy number of loaded guns pointed in their direction. The fourth child—and she was a child, despite the fact she'd had the care of both two-year-olds for their entire lives—couldn't, or wouldn't, let them go.

I'd call a seventeen-year-old in those circumstances a child, wouldn't you?

Instead of setting the children down so that she could raise her hands, she left them where they were perched, one on each hip, carefully peeling her fingers off their little torsos. Clenching them to her body with her elbows, she raised her hands to the level of her ears and displayed their palms. That was good enough for me.

"Okay," I said. "Okay. That's good. Keep your hands where we can see them. Okay. Is anybody else in the house?"

By this, I meant, "Is anybody else in the house besides the dead man over there with a knife in his chest?" But those children knew what I meant.

"Just...the people that you see." Her voice was wavering, but the girl clutching two toddlers with her elbows made it clear that she was the family spokesperson. "You can search the house if you need to be sure. And I guess you do."

"Do it," I said with a jerk of my head intended to be commanding. It was 1977, and none of the other officers were used to taking orders from a woman, but I give them credit. They always treated me like one of the guys. Saying this rankles now, because a person shouldn't have to be a "guy" to merit respect. But in 1977? I was just glad that the other officers followed my order to leave the room with no hesitation other than a quick, "You okay, Greta?" from Dan.

I dismissed the question with another jerk of my head. They fanned out, going room by room through the creaky old house. Our forensic science was laughable back then, but we weren't stupid. My colleagues eyeballed the living room, saw that the spindly-legged 1960s furniture offered no place for a killer to lurk, and left the body for the lab techs to handle.

As they moved away, I studied the room, trying and failing to imagine the sequence of events that put a corpse there. The furniture was shabby but neat. The carpet was clean, except for a few threads scattered around the dead man's feet. Through an open archway, I could see a tidy, yellow-painted kitchen, where a washer/dryer combo sat next to the stove. The first shafts of sunlight had started to shine through the windows, so bright strips lit up the floor. The house smelled like death, with an incongruous tinge of sunshine. Nothing about this murder scene made sense.

I've often wondered why I chose to be the one who stayed with the children, rather than demanding a chance to lead the search for danger. I think it was simply because I had lived forty years in a world that thought I should be good with children because I had a uterus. This "rule" was ridiculous on the face of it, and yet, on that day, I obeyed it.

Dan was a father of two. Martin had three children and four grandchildren. Even young Pedro had a baby girl. I, on the other hand, was a lesbian (closeted and loveless, of course, because it was 1977 and I was a coward), and I wasn't just childless. I wasn't remotely interested in children. Nevertheless, here stood four children who appeared to have no adult protector, and I stepped into that role without giving it the first thought.

"Who's the dead man?" I asked, pretty sure I knew the answer.

"Our father." The girl's voice was quiet and cool as she continued in her role of family spokesperson.

"Where's your mother?"

"We haven't seen her in a long time." Still quiet. Still cool.

"Grandparents? Aunts? Uncles? Godparents?"

All four of them shook their heads.

"Friendly neighbors?"

Nope.

This complicated the logistics of the day to come. Once the house was clear, I needed to get these kids out quickly, leaving as few footprints to confuse evidence collection as possible. They couldn't be allowed to contaminate each other's testimony, so I couldn't leave them alone with each other, and I really needed to separate them completely. To do that, I needed three patrolmen free. Three plus me would put each officer one on one with a kid, until we could get them back to the station and let the detectives find out what they knew. I hoped to God that this happened before one of the toddlers needed to go to the bathroom, because I had no idea how I would pull that off.

Actually, I did. I could see a bathroom tucked under the stairs. If nature called, my plan was to let the girl take the kid in to do his business, while I stood in the door and simultaneously watched the bathroom proceedings and the other two children standing just outside the bathroom. As it turned out the little kids were still in diapers, so I was spared that experience, but I was ready for it. At all times, I try to be ready for anything, but nobody avoids every last surprise.

The girl's name was Lydia. When things were calm enough, I handed the boys off to three officers, taking charge of Lydia myself. (Why her? Because we both had uteruses? Probably, but it was a point in her favor that I wouldn't need to change her diaper.) It was hard for Lydia to let the toddlers go, but she did. Dan and Marvin exuded the confidence of experienced fathers, which helped her.

"What's his name?" Dan asked, cradling a little boy who had clapped both hands over his eyes to block the light of the morning sun.

"Kevin. And that one's Kelly." She pointed at the crying child in Martin's arms. "They're two years old. Twins."

Pedro was a young officer then, twenty-eight or twenty-nine, so it made sense to assign him to Lydia's other brother Jimmy. At eighteen, Jimmy was older than he looked. He would look up to someone Pedro's age, or so I hoped.

Pedro held up two cups. "C'mon, kid, let's go find a place to drink our coffee in peace."

Lydia's eyes darted from me to each of her brothers' faces. And then she turned her head, distracted by things that shouldn't have been attention-getting. A broad oak tree. A particularly fluffy cloud. Even the sun, which she stared at until her eyes watered.

I should have known.

Oblivious, I said, "Lydia, these gentlemen are going to take care of your brothers. You and I are just going to sit in this car and relax."

I gestured toward the passenger door. She fumbled with the handle until I swooped in and opened it for her. I hadn't spent all those years on patrol without learning what it looked like when somebody was going into shock. It might have been early morning, but we were in Orlando and Lydia shouldn't have been shivering in July.

I snatched a coffee out of Pedro's hand and held the cup to Lydia's mouth as I called out, "Somebody get me a blanket. Hell, get blankets for all the kids."

Lydia was gulping the coffee, still shaking.

Martin tucked the crying Kelly under his arm like a football. Already on the move, he said, "There's a diner down the street. These kids need breakfast."

"Then go. Get something substantial. Bacon. Eggs. More coffee."

He grunted to say he was on it.

"Wait. Is the diner open already?" I asked.

"They never close."

The coffee, bacon, and eggs put some pink in Lydia's pale cheeks. And they were pale, my God. I have never before or since seen such pale skin on a person so apparently healthy. She didn't have so much as a freckle. If she'd been anemic, then the eggs would have been an excellent idea, but I didn't think she was. Her lips and the rims of her eyes were pink, and her nail beds looked good.

I had sent somebody to K-Mart for clothes for all the kids, so Lydia had changed from her shabby nightgown into a purple T-shirt and stiff new jeans. She was eating a piece of buttered toast as she watched a parade of strangers troop into her home. A photographer passed, lugging both a Polaroid camera and a chunky thirty-five-millimeter beast with a tripod. Technicians followed with equipment to collect blood samples and fingerprints. Most important of all were the detectives in their sober suits.

The detectives paused. They conferred. They instructed the technicians. Eventually, they disappeared through the open door, but still they weren't out of sight. Lydia's father's body lay in a chair backed up to what my mother called a "picture window," so whenever the detectives stood near him, we could see them.

The glare of sun on glass obscured details, but we could make out the shape of them. Lydia and I waited for hours for approval to take her to the station. All the while, we watched the detectives work in silhouette.

Early on, I flipped the key and put the car in auxiliary mode. Twiddling with the radio, I asked, "What kind of music do you like?"

She shrugged, marking her as the only teenager I'd ever met who wasn't interested in music. My tastes leaned toward Elvis, who still had a month to live, but I found a Top 40 station.

"Where do you go to school? You must be—what?—a junior?"

"We don't go to school."

That set me back on my heels.

"I know Kelly and Kevin aren't old enough for school, and maybe Jimmy has graduated, but you're only seventeen. Did you finish early?"

"We haven't been to school since our mother left."

"When was that?"

She took the tiniest nibble of toast. "A long time ago."

"The twins are only two. Or maybe they have a different mother?"

"They do." Another nibble of toast. "They're so sweet, but they're a lot of work to take care of. There's been nobody but me doing it for a long time, at least in the daytime."

I didn't know what she meant by "a long time," although I did know that she hadn't answered my question. Feeling as I did about diaper changing, a month would seem like a long time. Maybe a week. But I didn't think Lydia was talking about a week.

"This is a nice car." She patted the dashboard vents.

It was getting a little steamy, so I thought she was hinting for me to turn on the air conditioning. I flipped the key again to crank the car, and sweet cool air wafted into the cabin.

"I don't remember ever seeing a car with air conditioning," she said.

This prompted me to check the house for window units. I was relieved to see two on the first floor and one on the second. I remembered Orlando before widespread air conditioning, and I didn't miss those days. Then I noticed the brand-new Monte Carlo in the driveway, cherry red.

"Surely your dad's car has air conditioning."

"Maybe," she said, polishing off the toast. "Never been in it. Never seen that new house down the street, either." She pointed at a house with a well-established lawn and overflowing flowerbeds like a person who really wanted me to see something.

I felt it in my stomach, a hard clench that was like a physical blow, when I realized what the sum total of her oddities meant. Her innocence of modern music and cars, even car door handles. Her wonder at the sight of trees and clouds. Her eye-watering stare straight into the sun. Her pale, pale skin, unmarred by a single freckle.

"Lydia."

Her eyes darted to and fro, looking for more things she'd never seen before.

"Lydia, when did you last leave the house?"

"I think it was—well, I was nine, so it must have been 1969." She blotted her lips daintily with a paper napkin. "And I was eleven the last time I came downstairs, so that would have been 1971."

"The twins?"

"Not since they were born."

"Jimmy?"

"Once he got big enough to work construction, our father started taking him to work with him. Double the money, you know. But he stopped keeping all the money about two years ago when Jimmy hit him and broke his nose. He turned around and broke Jimmy's nose, but he started letting him keep a little of his own money."

So the outdoor job explained Jimmy's sun-kissed skin and hair, and his father's fist explained Jimmy's asymmetrical beauty. But where was the twins' mother and when did she leave? I desperately wanted the answers to those questions to be anything but, "Right here," and "She never left." And I wanted the reason for the dead man in the house to be anything but, "This time, he pushed Jimmy one step too far."

Small talk had become impossible. I couldn't ask her about school. Questions like "What's your favorite subject?" or "Are you in any clubs?" or, dear God, "Do you have a boyfriend?" were now officially obscene. I couldn't ask her about hobbies, because people who spent their waking hours locked indoors to care for twins in diapers had no time for hobbies. And I couldn't ask her anything about the monster who had locked her away for most of her life because those questions should be saved for an official interview.

And so I floundered until I noticed her draining her coffee. I pointed at my radio and asked, "Would you like me to call for somebody to get you a soda?"

"What I really want is a cigarette. Menthol, if you can get it."

I called for a pack of Newports. Somehow, the cigarettes made it easier to sit in silence. Lydia and I spent the rest of the morning puffing on our cancer sticks and watching the detectives.

I spent the afternoon watching children answer detectives' questions. I perched, nervous, on a hard desk chair outside a one-way mirror, listening to the proceedings through an intercom that made voices harsh and screechy.

Lydia didn't have much to tell them. She didn't know what time her father died. She only knew that Jimmy had gone downstairs to get ready for work and called for her. She'd come downstairs and screamed at the sight of the dead man.

The detectives, Stephens in a brown suit and Bronski in gray, had asked her to describe the scene. Then Stephens had gotten to the point. "Tell us the condition of the body of—"

He checked his notes as if he really didn't remember the victim's name.

"Tell us about the body of Wilford Tompkins."

"I saw a knife. In his chest. And I saw blood, but not nearly as much as I would have expected."

Most likely, most of her father's blood had filled his chest cavity instead of spraying back on his attacker or splattering onto the floor. Chest wounds worked that way sometimes.

"You didn't see anybody?" Bronski asked. "It was just you and your brother Jimmy?"

She nodded.

"Did Jimmy have any blood on him?"

"Just a little on the palm of his hand. He had checked to see if our father was dead. He washed it off in the downstairs bathroom. You're not trying to say Jimmy killed him?"

I could see the blood leave her face, showing me that I'd been wrong. She *could* be paler.

Bronski pressed Lydia further while Stephens watched, silent. "Do you have any idea who might have done this?"

"A thief? It was payday so he may have had a lot of cash. Everybody he worked with would have known it. Did you check his pockets?"

Neither of them answered her question.

"We don't have anything else worth killing for," she went on. "Or maybe somebody just wanted him dead. I doubt my father's ever had a friend in his life."

"Are you saying he's a difficult person?" Stephens asked, and I knew him well enough to know that his caring tone was fake.

"I said nobody liked him. Isn't that pretty much the same thing?"

Bronski tried a new tack.

"Where's your mother?"

"I have no idea."

"I guess that means she was one of those people who didn't like him," Stephens said. "Could she have been the one who put that knife in his chest?"

"I doubt she's come within a hundred miles of this town since she got free of him."

"Are you glad to be free of him?" Stephens's eyes were black and they glittered.

"Am I? Free of him? I guess I haven't had time to think of it that way."

"You didn't hear anything before your brother called you?" Bronski asked. "Not even a slamming door?"

"No, I didn't hear any noise until Jimmy called for me. When I came down, the back door was standing wide open, so no. I didn't hear it slam. Wasn't it still open when your officers got there?"

It had been, but neither detective conceded the point. They also didn't say that her father's blood had been smeared on the doorknob, and also on the latch of the gate leading from their overgrown backyard to an alley too well-traveled to yield footprints.

She put her hands flat on the table between them, leaned forward, and said, "My father is dead and you're questioning me like...like you're completely coldhearted. Does that mean you think I did this? Because I think I might need a lawyer."

"No no no, you're not a suspect," they both said, waving their hands in the air as if smoothing rough water. "We're just looking for information.

"What kind of information did you get from Kevin and Kelly? Did you really need to take them away from me and separate them from each other, just so they can show you how well they play patty-cake?"

I had watched the interviews with the toddlers. The detectives had asked, "When you woke up this morning, did you hear any noises?"

Kevin had burst into tears and said, "Leelee crying." Then he had refused to say anything more.

Kelly had said, "Kev farted," and laughed until he fell out of his chair.

"Well?" Lydia demanded. "Are you finished torturing us? Jimmy and I need to take two little boys home."

"We can't let you do that, miss," said Stephens. "The house isn't...clear."

By this, they might mean her father's stone-cold body was still overseeing the work of the fingerprint techs. But they also might mean that, although the body had been collected, the folks at Child Protective Services weren't wild about putting three minors in the care of an eighteen-year-old in a house still defiled by their father's blood.

"We've made arrangements for you and the younger boys to stay at a children's shelter. Kevin and Kelly are already there." Bronski said this so smoothly that it was possible to miss his actual meaning, which was "We're putting you in an institution."

"And Jimmy?"

"Jimmy is of age. He tells me that he has enough money for a hotel room tonight, and we have every expectation of clearing the house for him to go home tomorrow."

"And we'll go, too?"

"If the folks at Child Protective Services say it's okay." Stephens' smile was as chilly as a bulldog's wet snout. "Now, if you don't mind, let's go over what you remember about this morning again. It may jog your memory to hear the questions a few more times."

I was proud of her when she said no, she wouldn't be doing that, and she might actually like to talk to a lawyer.

I was less proud of my career-long ambition to be a detective.

My progress toward that goal had been slow, which was only to be expected back then when one was a woman, but I was almost there.

By the time Lydia dismissed her tormentors, I had lost any desire to be the one doing the tormenting.

Jimmy, in contrast to his sister, was positively garrulous with the detectives. He described in detail how he had turned off his alarm clock, taken a shower, and headed downstairs for breakfast, just as he did every morning. He'd found his father dead and called upstairs to Lydia. She had come down and screamed. He told this story again and again, and neither Stephens nor Bronski could shake him into changing it.

He was equally free with his words when it came to their family situation, in a way that Lydia emphatically wasn't.

"My father liked women. They liked him, too, but only for a little while, because he wasn't nice to them. My mother stayed long enough to have me and Lydia, but not long enough to see us lose our first teeth. The twins' mother—Sally was her name and I don't know her last name—didn't even stay that long. That stung because I liked her."

"What was your mother's name?"

"We called her Mommy."

"Who took care of you when your father was working?"

"Sometimes, it was our father's woman-of-the-month. Sally stayed longest, because she got pregnant. Once the twins were born, she was gone. When there wasn't a woman around, our father locked us in our rooms with food for the day. Then he'd go to work and to wherever he went after work. He always came home drunk and went straight to bed, so we had to make sure we didn't eat all our food too early. He'd wake up the next morning hungover, but he was usually sober enough to leave us another day's worth of food. Once he started letting me go to work, things were better. I had my own money to make sure everybody ate."

Even Stephens and Bronski lost their poker faces at this. This showed that they believed him. I, on the other hand, did not. At least, not all of it.

Lydia never told much of the story. She told a version of the truth that was thin, and there were holes she never patched, but I don't believe she ever lied.

But Jimmy? I believe he embroidered his fictions over the holes in her thin story, and as awful as his version was, I believe the truth was worse.

I visited him once at the home where their father had died, while he was waiting for the others to be released from the youth facility. We sat on the spindly-legged 1960s furniture and tried not to look at the spot where the recliner had been. I was angry at myself that it hadn't occurred to me to come help Jimmy. He shouldn't have had to clean up his own father's blood. He saw where I was looking, and he was a sweet enough young man that he tried to make me feel better about it.

"It wasn't that bad. Cleaning everything up, I mean. I'm not a naturally neat person—"

Bottles of empty cleaning products scattered across the carpet, dropped right where he'd finished using them, said that he wasn't lying.

"—but I had a good teacher. Lydia really suffered when we didn't keep our space upstairs clean. She'd say, 'This is our whole world. If it's filthy, what does it say about us?' And then she'd mop the floor again."

As if Lydia were standing there, pained by the clutter, he picked up the bottles. "Once I started bringing home a salary, I could buy diapers, laundry detergent, dishwashing soap, whatever Lydia needed to make our space nice. There was this lemony floor cleaner that she just loved. It was expensive, as floor cleaners go, but it made her happy. And bleach. She liked to bleach things, because you could be sure that bleach got them clean."

I was barely listening. I was trying to imagine how hard those years would have been if Lydia had been depending on her father for diapers. Honestly, my brain had stopped working when he said, "Lydia really suffered."

"I have to find a place to stay soon," Jimmy said as he tossed empty bottles in the kitchen trash. "I can't cover the mortgage, and it's not like the bank's going to let me stay here for free. I figure I've got days before they kick me out."

We both knew that he couldn't afford anything that the Child Protective Services people would consider suitable for the other children, but I had it covered.

"I've started the paperwork to be a foster parent, but you're of age. You don't have to wait for permission from the state. You can come live with me now."

He didn't say yes, but he didn't say no. I figured I'd ask him again after the bank had done what banks do. When that happened, he was going to need a roof and a friend.

Stephens and Bronski spent fruitless weeks looking for Jimmy and Lydia's mother, a nameless woman who'd had ten years to hide. They had no better luck finding another woman named simply "Sally," who had evaporated immediately after giving birth. The funny thing was that Lydia never called the missing woman "Sally." She called her "the twins' mother." If you parsed her words as carefully as a Victorian schoolmarm teaching English grammar, you could see that everything Lydia ever said about the twins' mother could just as easily have applied to her.

"The twins' mother was young."

"She was afraid."

"My father wouldn't take her to the hospital, so she had the twins at home."

"She was scared of my father, but it was hard for her to leave her babies."

Stephens and Bronski were good detectives, but they were not infallible. Given the chance, I would have been a good detective, but not this time. There was no way in hell I was going to tell them what I knew. It was Lydia's secret. I wasn't going to tell it for her, and neither was Jimmy. Lydia never uttered anything but the truth, but Jimmy lied his ass off. I just kept my mouth shut.

When the lab report came back, we learned that their father's blood had been mostly liquid Quaaludes, which explained why he'd lain there so relaxed and let somebody stab him. The knife that killed him, according to his children, was his own, and nobody had any reason to disbelieve them. His fingerprints were on it, and nobody else's, so the killer had worn gloves. This suggested premeditation, but you can't level a murder one charge on thin air.

Wilford Tompkins had been a hard man, living in a hard neighborhood, working in an industry run by hard men. It only made sense that he'd carry a switchblade, and it only made sense that the time had come when it didn't save him from the hard death he'd earned.

It eventually became apparent that Stephens and Bronski were going to fail to find either mother. Thank God there was no DNA testing in those days to help them. They also failed to identify even a suspect among the army of day laborers and drug dealers who swarmed Orlando as it grew into a major city. The time came when nobody wanted the case closed more than they did, especially since they'd found no way to pin it on the kids either.

Well, I guess I might have wanted it closed more than Stephens and Bronski, and Jimmy probably did, too. It's anybody's guess what Lydia wanted. While the investigation dragged on, I spent my evenings visiting her at the facility, where she sat calmly on a settee, smiling while the twins crawled all over her and kissed her and pulled her hair. Every time we talked, she was counting the months until she was eighteen.

"I could get a job," she said, every time. "Do you think I could get a job? Nothing much, just a checkout clerk at the grocery store. I bet it would be enough to pay for a little apartment for the boys and me. And Jimmy, if he wanted to live with us."

"I bet it would be enough," was my answer, every time. "In the meantime, you could live with me while you got your money together."

I had to lead them by the nose, but Stephens and Bronski finally assembled a theory of how the murder came to pass. Wilford Tompkins was an addict and he'd run afoul of the dealer who sold him his pills. The dealer had followed him home, found him stoned out of his mind, and stole his payday money out of his pockets. He was presumably very, very angry at Wilford, prompting him to stab the man to death. This was not so farfetched, as the investigation showed that Wilford Tompkins was widely known to be a terrible man. Being a very prepared drug dealer, he had been wearing gloves, which were unfortunately never found. And neither was the drug dealer, who had vanished into the same hole that swallowed the children's mothers.

This theory was not solid enough to close the case, but it was enough to get the detectives to lay off Jimmy, who hung around town until he was sure his sister was out of legal trouble and safely moved into my house with Kevin and Kelly. Then he disappeared. Perhaps he fell into the same hole that seemed to swallow everyone in Wilford Tompkins's vicinity.

I spent the rest of my career distracting anyone who displayed an interest in cold cases, burying the unsolved Tompkins murder deeper and deeper in our files by the year. I only retired when the department made me go, because I was that dedicated to keeping the Tompkins file out of the hands of people who were smarter than Stephens and Bronski.

I wrote this all down for Kelly and Kevin. It seemed like they should know the truth, now that they're middle-aged men. After what happened last night, though, I've decided to burn it before I do something stupid like give it to them.

I've known who killed Wilford Tompkins since Stephens and Bronski were busting their balls on this case, and I'm pretty sure I know how they did it. My theory can't be proven, and airing my suspicions would have ruined lives, so I didn't. The only person who deserved to have his life ruined was Wilford Tompkins, and ending it was sufficient ruination. Killing him was an act of justice, and it's not my job to knock the scales of justice off-balance again.

Here's what I think: the murder of Wilford Tompkins started hours earlier than anybody ever guessed. I think Jimmy did something to make him overdo the Quaaludes. Maybe he used his own money to buy stronger pills. Or maybe he ground up some of Wilford's stash and stirred the powder into his drink. Or maybe he just sat drinking with his father, egging him on to take just another pill. And another and another. His method is immaterial, and maybe Lydia helped him. The results are what counts. Long before Lydia screamed, her father lay in that chair, unconscious, unresponsive, and perhaps even already on the edge of death.

Perhaps that had been the original plan. If they could have gotten their father to overdose, then they would have been rid of him with little or no action on their part. But the man was too mean to die.

Imagine them watching him for hours, hoping each ragged breath would be his last. As dawn approached, they had a decision to make. Let their father awaken from his bender and resume his abuse, or end it forever.

It was a simple matter for one of them—Jimmy? Shall I say it was Jimmy?—to put on a pair of their father's work gloves, rifle through his pockets for his knife, and stab him through the heart. (If I can be so bold as to presume that the man had a heart.) He would have used a bloodied glove to open the back door and run through a backyard so overgrown that his path through the shaggy grass showed, but not the footprints that might have incriminated him. Again, he used a bloodied glove to open the back gate, and that is where the killer's trail petered out for Stephens and Bronski. Or maybe there never were gloves. Maybe he kept his fingerprints off the knife with a simple kitchen towel, bleached white again after the fact.

Jimmy would have backed his way along the line of disturbed grass and into the house. This is when he would have called Lydia to come back down, just before putting his soiled clothing (unless he very intelligently stabbed his father while nude) and gloves (or towel) in the wash. A trip through the washer and dryer with a goodly portion of Lydia's cherished bleach would have defeated the forensic technology of the day, especially since the detectives didn't expect the evidence to be hidden in plain sight. Why pay much attention to Jimmy's T-shirt drawer if you really don't think he did it? He would then have ducked into the bathroom below the stairs to shower away the evidence.

But Lydia gave herself away—to me, at least—by what she did while Jimmy was in the shower. Think about the years she'd spent making a safe, clean home upstairs for the four of them. Do you really think that Wilford Fuckin' Tompkins kept a neat house and a tidy kitchen? While Jimmy was in the shower, Lydia vacuumed the house's ground floor, except for the blood-spattered area around the body that she didn't dare touch. This is why I saw stray threads at the corpse's feet and only there.

She surely encountered a sink full of nasty dishes and she just as surely washed them, dried them, put them away, and wiped down the counter. She must have mopped the kitchen floor with the lemony cleaner that Jimmy said she loved, and that is why a room with a dead man in it still smelled like sunshine to me. When Jimmy came out of the bathroom and saw what she'd done, he must have thought he was going to prison, but he stuck with the plan. He waited until the dryer cooled, then he gave her the signal to come downstairs and scream. Despite her potentially fatal compulsion to clean, he stuck with his story and he kept his freedom. They both stuck with the story, with the difference being that Lydia never said anything that wasn't true.

On the day we learned that Jimmy had disappeared, I told Dan what I was going to do. To his credit, he didn't say that I was nuts. He just said, "Do you ever watch old movies? The ones they call noir?"

"She's no *femme fatale*, Dan."

"You're not just adopting her. You're adopting the twins, too. Is there such a thing as a *them fatale*?"

"They're children, Dan. They've done nothing wrong."

"You're sure about that?"

I wasn't, but unlike Lydia, I can lie. "I'm absolutely sure."

After Lydia and the kids came to live with me, I took a desk job at the station, so that I could work a nine-to-five. Lydia was home alone with the twins all day on weekdays, but she always knew help was coming at five thirty. When you're feeling alone, it helps to know that it's temporary. I think Stephens and Bronski were glad when I gave up my quest to be a detective. It would have stung for them to be shown up by a woman, and oh, how I would have shown them up.

Even now, in her sixties, Lydia's not comfortable going places, although she goes when it's important to her. The twins' high school graduations, their college graduations, their weddings, the births of their children—these things were worth stepping out into unfiltered sunshine. She prefers the swing on our shady back porch where she can feel the warm sun on her face, while still hiding from its light. Fortunately, Kelly and Kevin live nearby. They come to her often.

They were here last week. In their innocence, they almost up-ended the life that Lydia has spent more than forty years building for them.

Kevin was waving a plastic tube around. "So I spit in one of these things. I mail it in. Somebody compares it to a DNA database, and boom. We've found our mother. Leelee could do it and find her mother, too."

Kelly had his own plastic tube. "Maybe we can even find

Jimmy. I sort of remember him. He'd be over sixty by now, and our mother would be older than that. If we're going to find them before they die, it's time."

Lydia said nothing. I wouldn't have expected her to, so it took me a moment to notice that she wasn't just silent. She was gone. The twins, still irrepressible in middle age, were busy yapping about their new toy, so they hadn't noticed when she left the room, either.

I found her in the bathroom, methodically poking a nail file into the blue-veined white flesh of her inner wrists.

"They can't know," she said between jabs.

I didn't bother asking her what they couldn't know. If she hadn't been able to say it in the forty years we'd known each other, she wasn't going to suddenly start being able to say it.

Here's what they can't know. They can't know that the woman they believe to be their sister is their mother. They can't know that their father was also their grandfather. They can't know that he kept their mother a prisoner for years, forcing her to birth twins alone at fifteen. They can't know that she freed herself by helping her brother kill him. They especially cannot be allowed to consider what this genetic heritage means for their own children, who were born because neither Lydia nor I could bring ourselves to tell them the truth.

I made sure that her wounds weren't dangerously deep, then I tenderly bandaged them as I said, "They won't know. I promise you. I'll make sure of it. Will you promise not to do this again if I go out there and stop them?"

She promised, and Lydia doesn't lie. I helped her to her bed, then I went back to Kevin and Kelly and delivered a speech that would have won an Oscar for Best Performance by a Deceitful Faux Mother in a Supporting Role, if such a thing existed.

"Why do you want to find your mother?" I shrieked. "What does she matter to you? She's gone." I lowered my voice to a hiss and said the most hurtful thing possible, except for the far-more-hurtful truth. "She left you. You mean nothing to her."

Then I stuck the landing by slamming down the guilt card. "*I'm your mother.* Me. I'm the one who has always been here. If you do this thing, you'll break my heart."

"But Jimmy..."

"Leave Jimmy alone. He left his family. Let him stay gone. If he wanted to come home, he would. It's not like we're hiding."

I held out my hand and they put the DNA spit tubes into it, as dutiful and obedient as they had been when they were seven. They were always good boys, such good boys.

"Promise me that you'll forget this. Your family is in this house. You don't need another mother."

They promised, so this will be the end of it.

I know this is true, because they're just like their mother. They never lie.

OPPORTUNITY
by Reece Hirsch

Hal Pynchon was in the USC Film School Library on a warm Southern California afternoon, hiding. The film library was across a dappled courtyard from the law school, and he liked to study there to escape the ambient stress of being around his ambitious classmates. As usual, what had begun as a study session with his torts casebook had ended with him sitting in a carrel watching a Sony U-Matic cassette copy of *Seven Samurai*.

The Pynchons of Santa Barbara, a tribe of doctors, lawyers, and the occasional banker, were more than willing to fund his law school education at USC, but they refused to pay to send him to the film school next door. In 1971, the purpose of the film school wasn't even entirely clear. No film school graduate had ever been hired to helm a major studio picture.

Hal had enrolled in USC Law hoping that it would provide a more pragmatic entrée into the film industry. He became an avid reader of the school library's copy of *The Hollywood Reporter*, with its cryptic, slangy headlines. But as he entered his third year of law school, Hal was beginning to realize just how long the odds were. Many of his classmates wanted to work for one of the cadre of powerful entertainment law firms in Century City or a studio legal department, but there were very few openings, and they were reserved for those with the very best grades or connections. Hal had neither.

His concentration was disrupted by a reflection in the monitor and a looming presence over his shoulder. He tried to ignore the figure, focusing on the silvery visuals as Toshiro Mifune prepared villagers for battle.

After another long minute, Hal slid the headphones down around his neck and turned to face a hulking man, at least six foot three, with a black beard and mustache. There was a red cord around his neck, from which hung a large sombrero, giving him a humpbacked appearance. The man was wearing a short-sleeved guayabera shirt with a button that read, "Apocalypse Now."

"I don't know you," he said.

"Hal Pynchon. And I don't know you, either."

"Are you a film student?"

"No, I'm from the law school."

"So what are you doing over here?"

"I come here because some days I'd rather watch movies than study law."

"Can't argue with that. But what I'd really like to know, Hal, is whether you're a villager or a samurai."

Hal considered the question for a few seconds and, frankly, he wasn't sure of the answer. But he already knew what this gringo Zapata wanted to hear.

"I'd have to say that I'm a samurai."

"Good, Hal. That's good. It's good to be a samurai, isn't it?"

"I suppose. If you don't mind me asking, what's with the button?"

The man looked down at his chest. "Oh, this? I saw some peaceniks around campus wearing these buttons that read, 'Nirvana Now.' And I made this because I believe in war, Hal. Any good thing that man has accomplished throughout history has been achieved through combat."

"That's not a popular opinion on campus these days."

"I don't give a fuck whether it's popular or not. It happens to be true."

Hal peered up at the man. "What's your name?"

OPPORTUNITY

"John Milius."

"And, you, I take it, are a samurai?"

"Goddamn right." He leaned down as if to study him more closely. "Do you surf, Hal?"

"A little, yeah."

"Then come with me. We're going to Zuma."

"I don't have a board."

"I can get you one."

Milius strode across the small film library. The other students didn't seem to take much notice of his new acquaintance, like carny workers who were accustomed to seeing the elephant rumble past. He paused in the doorway.

"Well, are you coming?"

Hal turned off the Kurosawa and rose. He never would have considered himself an adventurer, but he felt like some sort of portal had briefly and miraculously opened before him. If he didn't step through it, he knew that he would always wonder.

He followed Milius to the parking lot, where he climbed onto a khaki-green motorcycle with a sidecar. "Get in," he said, nodding at the bike's precarious-looking appendage.

"You expect me to ride in that?"

"Yes, I do, Hal."

"It doesn't look safe."

"Life is not safe, my friend. But this beast survived two wars. It can handle an L.A. freeway."

Hal gingerly stepped into the sidecar, which dipped under his weight. As soon as he sat down, the motorcycle jerked forward onto Exposition Boulevard.

Milius handed him his sombrero, saying something that sounded like, "Damn thing is like a kite."

Soon they were speeding on I-10 across the city, headed for the ocean. Milius was right, the sombrero caught the hot wind whipping past and struggled to break free of his grip like a writhing animal. Hal wrestled the sombrero the entire way to Santa Monica, then down the incline to Highway 1, and then north through Malibu. It was a standard-issue, bright and hazy April day in Los Angeles, with the San Gabriel Mountains rising softly in the distance through a light smog.

The motorcycle finally came to a stop in the parking lot of a surf shop across the highway from Zuma Beach. Milius seemed to have some sort of standing arrangement with the proprietor, because he soon appeared shirtless and in garish orange and green Hawaiian swim trunks, a longboard under each meaty arm.

Milius leaned Hal's board against the wall of the shop and handed him a pair of trunks. "Put these on in the bathroom out back. You can leave your clothes at the counter inside. Just tell them you're with Milius."

They walked barefoot to the ocean across the nearly empty beach. The sand was scorching, but he resisted the impulse to dash for the surf because Milius paced steadily forward, seemingly impervious.

Milius belly-flopped onto this longboard and paddled out through the chop. Hal followed his lead.

When they reached the break, Milius sat up on his board and they looked back at the hills. The traffic and strip malls of L.A. seemed far away. There was no sound except for the slap of the waves against the board and the timpani crash of the surf. Hal could feel the pale skin on his back already beginning to redden in the sun.

Milius ran a hand through his wet hair, sweeping it back off his forehead. Beads of water clung to his beard. "From here, it looks like Eden, doesn't it?"

"I can see why you like it."

"I come out here to tap into something pure. Because there sure as hell is nothing pure about that place," Milius said, with a dismissive flick of his hand toward the shore. "It's full of talentless studio executives, industry toadies, and development execs who wouldn't know a good story if it crapped on their Italian loafers."

"That sounds a little cynical for someone just starting out in the business."

"It's important to know your enemy, Hal. You have to define the rules of engagement. Otherwise, the enemy will co-opt you before you've even fired a shot." Milius began to paddle away from him as a swell rippled toward them.

They spent the afternoon surfing. Hal got off to a rocky start, but by late afternoon he was catching waves more consistently.

Milius was surprisingly graceful on his longboard. As might be expected, he had an aggressive, slashing style that led to quite a few wipeouts. But when his timing was right, he commanded the waves, standing astride the board like an emperor with his belly thrust forward.

Hal and Milius surfed until the sun approached the horizon. A cool breeze began to blow in off the Pacific, which felt good on his sunburn. Every muscle in his body felt rubbery. After two years largely spent in the law school library, Hal had forgotten what it felt like to be so physically tired.

As darkness began to descend, Milius waded out of the surf and plopped down in the sand to watch the sunset. Hal sat down next to him.

After the sun had been reduced to a white-hot pinpoint on the horizon and then extinguished, Milius said, "I'm curious. Why do you want to be a lawyer?"

"Because I'm not talented enough to be a filmmaker, and I want to be near the movie business."

"And you weren't just bullshitting me with the Kurosawa?"

"No. I've loved movies ever since my mom took me to see *Lawrence of Arabia* when I was fifteen."

Milius shrugged. "Then maybe you just might be the best of a bad bunch. At least that's something."

Hal wasn't so sure that he would even be able to join the ranks of that bad bunch. For a person with Hal's temperament and interests, living in a company town like L.A. produced a kind of constant ache that arose from proximity to a glittering world that he suspected he would never inhabit. He knew that over time, when the last of those hopes had dissipated, the ache would likely metastasize.

Milius seemed to sense the downturn in his mood. "I'm going to a party tonight in Nicholas Canyon. Want to come?"

"What sort of party?"

"It's a little house on the beach that's being rented by two actresses, Margot Kidder and Jennifer Salt. They're both gorgeous, but do not hit on them. The place is kind of our clubhouse, and for some reason they tolerate us."

"Who's going to be there?"

"Some buddies of mine from the film school."

"Am I dressed for it?"

"Well, we'll need to get out of our board shorts."

They changed back into their street clothes in the bathroom of the surf shop. When they returned to the parking lot, he felt slightly less ludicrous climbing into the sidecar. Hal was relieved that he no longer had to wrestle the sombrero, which had been left behind at the surf shop. He had no doubt that to observers he still looked every bit as ridiculous wedged into the sidecar as they took PCH north from Zuma, but he was beginning to adapt to the reality distortion effect of being with Milius.

The effect was enhanced when Milius lit up a large joint at a traffic light and handed it to him. It flared in the breeze as they took off. He quickly realized that it was the strongest pot he had ever smoked.

The sky over the Pacific still had not completely darkened, displaying a little sunburn pink. Hal held out his cupped hand so that he could feel it slicing through the night air.

"What is this?" he finally asked.

"Oaxaca." Milius took his eyes off the beach access road for a moment. "Keep it together, Hal."

They pulled up in front of a slightly off-kilter A-frame at the base of the foothills across from a white-sand beach. There was a flagpole in the front yard, from which a tie-dyed flag flew. The house glowed warmly in the darkness, all of its lights on. When

OPPORTUNITY

the growl of the motorcycle engine died, Hal could hear the distant thunder of the surf at Nicholas Canyon Beach behind him and the low roar of a party before him.

Inside, the large living room was covered in worn shag carpet with a brick fireplace at its center and benches along the walls. Almost as soon as they were through the door, Milius hailed someone across the living room and promptly abandoned him. Hal made his way to the kitchen and took a can of Falstaff beer from the refrigerator.

He leaned against the counter and tried to look like he belonged there as he eavesdropped on conversations. A small, animated man who looked too young for his beard and mustache was holding court in the breakfast nook about *McCabe & Mrs. Miller*.

Hal wandered around the party. The room seemed to be growing warmer, but he wasn't sure whether it was the body heat of the crowd or his still-expanding high.

As his eyes roamed around the room, Hal found himself gazing blankly for a moment at a man standing a few feet away.

The man helpfully broke the awkward staring match. "I don't think I've seen you here before."

"Hal Pynchon."

He had an unruly mass of curly dark hair and the slightly rearranged face of a boxer, and was wearing pressed jeans and a green polo shirt. He extended his hand. "Don Ermey. So, Hal, what brings you here?"

"I'm in the law school at USC."

Ermey continued to stare at him because this did not answer the question.

"I met Milius today."

"Ah," Ermey said, "Milius." There was a note of commiseration in his voice, as if Hal had just told him that he had been ripped out of his apartment window by a tornado and deposited there.

"So are you a film student?" Hal asked.

"No, but I'm going to be a producer someday."

"Good luck," he said.

"Oh, I don't need luck. Not with the talent in this room."

"Really? They don't look like much," Hal said, surveying the assortment of scrawny and acne-pocked twenty-somethings drinking beer, laughing and jousting.

"You just don't know what you're looking at," Ermey said. "George over there is working on this sci-fi thing called *THX 1138*. It's incredibly ambitious for a student film. I think Warners is actually giving it a theatrical release. Milius has already sold several scripts, including one I really like about this mountain man guy, Jeremiah Johnson. Marty, who's next to the fireplace, was one of the editors on the Woodstock documentary and Cassavetes is kind of his mentor. I have a little trouble understanding him because he talks so fast, but he seems really smart."

Ermey pointed at a young man on the other side of the living room. "And Steven over there might just be the most talented of the bunch, even though he didn't have the grades to get into SC. You know how he caught on with Universal? He got a three-day pass onto the lot and then he just kept coming back. Sid Sheinberg seems to have kind of adopted him. They're letting him direct a TV movie called *Duel*."

"But they're just a bunch of kids. When has going to film school ever been a real career path?" Hal winced at the realization that he sounded like his father.

"I think that's gonna change. The studio system is tired. And that's why some of the people in this room have a bright future."

"And you want a piece of it."

Ermey nodded. "Hopefully, more than a piece."

Hal surveyed the room again and it no longer looked like an off-campus beer party.

"Do you surf, Hal?" Ermey asked.

"Yeah. That's the second time today somebody has asked me that."

"Well, when you're at the break and you see a wave starting to swell, you either make a move or you don't. Am I right?"

OPPORTUNITY

Ermey's eyes locked on a tall woman with blond, Peggy Lipton hair who was stepping out into the backyard through a sliding glass door. "Now, excuse me, but there's someone I need to speak to."

Hal wandered around the living room, tuning in to a series of fragmentary conversations like he was spinning an AM radio dial.

He stood on the periphery of a group that was engaged in a heated debate. A woman wearing octagonal, gold, wire-rimmed glasses was critiquing Hitchcock, and a bearded guy in an army surplus jacket named Brian was not taking it well at all.

"Hitchcock is pure cinema," Brian proclaimed. "No other director has so much control over the content of every frame. Everything is intentional."

"I agree," said Octagonal Glasses, "that's what makes his films so airless. Hitchcock has so much control that it flattens everything else, from the performances to the screenplay. If there were more women directors, you'd see more collaboration on film sets. The obsession with control is so male."

Hal was familiar with this form of nerd-on-nerd violence. Denigrating influences was the preferred mode of attack.

He wanted to join in the conversation, but it was hard to find an opening, and it didn't help that he was really feeling the Oaxaca. Pot always made him quiet and mildly paranoid.

Deciding that he needed some fresh air to clear his head, Hal made his way across the room to the back door.

As soon as he stepped out onto the small concrete patio, he felt better as he breathed in the cool air with its tang of sea salt. Hal sat down in a folding chair next to a grill and felt the sea breeze drying the perspiration on his forehead.

Bone-tired from a day of surfing, and the beer and the pot, Hal zoned out for a few minutes. He was roused from his stupor by a sound that he couldn't quite make out. It might have been a dog or a bird, but whatever it was there was an abrupt violence to it.

He rose and followed a dirt path in the direction of the noise.

When he crested a hill, he saw Don Ermey hurrying toward him on the trail in bright moonlight. There was a new expression on Ermey's face—panic, mixed with something else.

"Is everything okay?" Hal asked.

"I wasn't here, okay? I just wasn't here. Understand?"

"What's happened?"

Ermey's pinballing eyes focused on Hal for a long moment, and then the words came out in a torrent. "I was talking with this girl, this actress, I think her name is Vivian. Then I went for a walk and this guy Beau, some pissant, would-be screenwriter, followed me out here and told me to leave her alone. I told him to fuck off. Then he shoved me, and I hit him. It wasn't even that hard, just like—"

Ermey made a soft, indistinct motion with his hand through the air. Hal did not believe it for a second.

"Don, what happened to the guy?"

"He fell and hit his head on a rock. I think he might be hurt pretty bad. He might even be dead."

"But you're not sure?"

"I tried to check for a pulse, but I was so freaked out that I'm not sure I did it right."

"So you just left him there?"

"I was coming back to the house to get help."

"Is that why you told me you were never here?"

"I'm not thinking straight."

"Clearly." Hal made a "stop" motion with his hand. "You stay right here, and I'm going to go and take a look."

"If he says anything about me, don't believe him. Fucking screenwriter."

"I'm just going to go and check, okay?"

Hal turned away to follow the trail toward the ocean. When he had taken a couple of steps, Ermey said, "Make this go away, Hal. Please."

Hal turned to look at Ermey, whose features had hardened. Ermey's eyes were now sharp and focused; fear had burned away the effects of any intoxicants. "What did you say?"

"I think you heard me."

He walked down the narrow dirt trail as it gently inclined toward the ocean. When he came around a bend, he saw a hillside of scrub brush and beyond that the Pacific, dark, serrated waves tipped with silvery moonlight. About twenty yards ahead, a pair of legs blocked the trail from the brush.

Hal approached slowly and saw the body of a man lying face-up. He was not moving or making a sound.

He bent down to get a closer look. Beau looked to be in his early twenties with longish brown hair, wearing jeans and a Triumph Motorcycles T-shirt. Earlier, Hal had seen him sullenly drinking in a corner of the living room. Near his head was a large rock with a dark blotch on it.

"Beau! Can you hear me?" He patted his cheek.

His eyelids slowly rose. "My head feels weird."

"I'm going to look at it, okay?"

"Okay."

Hal cupped his right hand under Beau's neck and lifted his head. There was a lot of blood, and a fracture that had matted the hair at the back of the skull. Hal was no doctor, but it looked very bad.

"You need to see a doctor."

"Don Ermey did this."

"I'm sure it was an accident."

"No." Beau drifted off again into unconsciousness.

Hal stared at the screenwriter, and a kind of calm clarity came over him. He knew what he had to do.

He placed his left hand over the man's mouth and with the other hand he pinched his nostrils shut. After a few seconds, Beau's body began to jerk and his eyes opened.

Hal could feel him trying to draw in air through his nostrils and mouth. It reminded him of the sensation of placing his hand over the hose of a vacuum cleaner with very weak suction.

A powerful surge of fear shot through Hal. He was afraid that he wasn't going to be able to finish what he had started. But then how could he explain himself, what he was doing?

There was no explanation that he could admit to himself, much less anyone else.

Hal looked away from the eyes, which were wide open now, and kept his hands in place.

He had trouble sealing Beau's nose and mouth because he was weakly twisting his head from side to side. This was taking far too long, but Hal did not want to put his hands on Beau's throat because then it might not look like an accident.

Desperate to end the struggle, Hal grabbed Beau by the ears and smashed his head down on the rock in roughly the same spot as the existing wound.

At last, Beau stopped moving. Hal didn't want to repeat Ermey's mistake, so he placed two fingers on Beau's carotid artery and took his time confirming that there was no pulse.

Hal stood up and felt so lightheaded that his knees nearly buckled beneath him. He examined himself for any bloodstains but saw none.

Then he studied the body to see if he had left any marks on the face where his hands had been. Beau looked much the same as when he had found him, except there were scuff marks in the dirt where he had kicked. Hal spread some pine needles and brush until the marks from Beau's desert boots were no longer visible.

If Don Ermey had never been there, then neither had Hal.

He walked back up the trail in darkness to the house. Don was still standing where he had left him.

"What did you do?" Don asked.

"Let's go back inside. We were just outside smoking a joint, okay? We never went any further down the trail."

"Okay."

"But first, you need to tell me the truth about what was going on between you and that guy."

Don paused. After looking at Hal's face, he seemed to decide that he was going to need to give him something in the vicinity of the truth. "Okay, I fucked his girlfriend. I suppose that makes me the asshole?"

"Probably. Did you hit him first?"

"He was threatening me. If I didn't do it, I could have ended up with my skull bashed in on a rock back there."

Hal grabbed Don by the elbow and led him up the trail to the patio. "Whatever you do now, don't turn around."

"You know I owe you," Don said, as he walked a bit unsteadily up the back steps. "You're my lawyer for life, okay?"

Hal shook his head. "I'm not your lawyer. I'm your producing partner."

Don nodded and slid open the sliding glass door. "I need a drink."

As they were again enveloped into the warmth and noise of the party, Hal felt the same way he had earlier in the day at Zuma Beach in that moment when he was flailing to catch a wave, and then felt the powerful dark tide rise from the ocean floor, take him in its grasp, and propel him forward.

MY AIM IS TRUE
by Gary Phillips

Ridley walked into the Park N Shop grocery store a little past ten in the morning.
To one side of the entrance-exit, an elderly woman wrestled to right her utility cart brimming with her just-purchased groceries. Somehow it had tipped, canting awkwardly. Loose avocados spilled from a precariously placed bag atop her box of Tide, the deluxe size on sale. She huffed to get the cart upright. An eye on the dual swing doors to the rear, Ridley scooped up the three avocados rolling around on the floor. She put those back in the paper bag and set the cart.
"Thank you, dear," the older woman said to her. "Lord, don't get old." She shook her head from side to side.
"You have a blessed day," Ridley said as she resumed her trajectory.
"Child, let your light shine," the oldster replied, humming a gospel song as she wheeled her cart out of the market and along the sidewalk.
The mom-and-pop-sized store had three checkout lanes but only one was open at this hour. A bored clerk was at the register, three customers in line. Past them and a display of green cleaning products, Ridley went and pushed through one of the rear swing doors. She entered a cooler area where there were stacks of various cardboard boxes of produce along with racked plastic pallets of

sundry items. There was a teenager here busy applying prices with a label gun to some cereal boxes. He looked over at her.

"Sorry, but Mr. Treadmore says the bathroom isn't for use by the public."

"He said that, did he?" Ridley was on her way to the closed pine door marked "Manager." "Let me ask him about reconsidering his policy. I mean, when you gotta tinkle, you gotta tinkle."

The teen hunched a shoulder and resumed tagging boxes. Ridley knocked on the door with the middle knuckles of two fingers. This hand wasn't wrapped but the other one, her dominant hand, was encased in neon-green stretchy material. Wrapped nice and snug.

"What is it, I'm busy," came the reply through the door. The manager assumed his employee was the one on the other side.

Ridley tried the knob; the door wasn't locked.

"Hey," Treadmore blared as the door swung inward. "The fuck's wrong with you, Tony? I said I was busy."

"Watching porn on your computer?" Ridley stepped into the office. "Girl on girl?"

"Who the hell?" Treadmore said. He was a middle-aged, heavyset white man with a balding pate and a thin mustache. One side of his unshaven face was pockmarked due to a childhood bout of chicken pox. He remained seated, glaring at the intruder. Carnality wasn't cavorting on his monitor. He was in the middle of playing online poker with a few others. He had a full house. "What do you want, lady?"

"Tell Dobbs I want my goddamn cut."

His body tensed, shivers of apprehension edging into the corners of his eyes. "I don't know what you're talking about."

"Like hell you don't."

Treadmore was easing a drawer open on the right-hand side of his desk, where there was an unruly stack of file folders and invoices. He hoped his attempt was blocked from view.

Ridley was around the desk and slammed the open drawer shut on his hand.

"Motherfuck," he exclaimed.

The younger women hit him flush in the face and he reeled back in his swivel chair, the front wheels lifting off the floor. For whatever reason, this triggered a flash in her head; the two bullets slamming into her back and her tumbling down the rise into the dark brush below. As Treadmore shot forward again, all the wheels back on the floor, he used the momentum to get up, grabbing for her. His reactions brought her back to the present and this time when she struck him with her wrapped hand, she buried her fist in his substantial gut. Air whoofed out of him in a gust of breath laced with coffee and this morning's breakfast burrito. His hand to his stomach, he sagged into the chair.

"You a boxer or something? You hit hard."

"Or something." Ridley jabbed a finger at him. "You tell Dobbs I better see my end. Tell him don't make me work my way up the chain to him."

"He doesn't take kindly to threats."

"Yeah? I don't take kindly to bitch-ass bullshit." She let a silence descend then added, "He knows how to get a message to me and I'm sure as fuck impatient to hear from him. He best get me my motherfuckin' money." She leaned in. "Now can you remember all that? You need me to write it down?"

Treadmore blinked at her. "No, I got it."

"Good." Ridley opened the drawer and took out the Glock he'd been reaching for earlier.

"Come on, take it easy. I swear I'll give him your message." He gestured surrender with his hands, eyes locked on the weapon. Because he hadn't responded to a raise, his session timed out in the online poker game.

She ejected the bullet in the chamber and pulled the magazine free. Then she tossed the gun onto the desk and left the office, taking the magazine with her. The door was ajar and Tony the teenager watched her walk out of the rear of the Park N Shop. Outside at the curb she got in her aging RAV4 and drove away, passing the nearby Plaza Mexico here in Lynwood.

Treadmore was at the open doorway to his office and told Tony, "Go up front and help Teresa out."

"Okay," the kid answered.

Treadmore watched him leave and closed the door when Tony was out of earshot. Pacing about, he called a number on an encrypted phone he got out of another drawer in his desk. When the line connected, he said, "It's me, Dobbs. This chick was just here. Black, tough. Torn jeans, leather coat, heavy boots. Maybe a dike, I don't know. But she thumps like a motherfuckah." He continued to tell the man on the other end what had happened and what she'd said. Finished, he listened for a few moments, walking around his compact office. He stopped and said, "The fuck I know how she knows about me. What I do know is she wants what she says she's owed. You the one that must'a tried to pull a fast on her."

Dobbs said more on the other end of the call. Treadmore spoke again when he was done. "Of course I didn't say shit to her about you and me. She didn't ask but she knows enough to show up here and that I'd get in touch with you. But I don't want her coming back around here swinging like Mike Tyson with tits. Shit. You got to freeze her out." He listened to Dobbs's response, relaxing some.

"Right, okay, great. Yeah," he was nodding as he talked, "for sure." The call over he put the burner back and sat down. He wanted to get back to his poker game but was too keyed up to concentrate on virtual cards. Rolling over what to do next, he settled on brewing a carafe of fresh coffee. Thereafter he attended to the business of running his market, including dealing with an irate customer who insisted the floor wax she'd bought the other day was not the name brand as listed on the bottle, but an off brand he was selling for more as if it were the expensive version. Eventually he was out back, tearing down carboard boxes and putting the flats in the dumpster.

"Your work ain't never done, is it, Treadmore?"

The manager looked around. The man before him was dressed

in a designer dark blue tracksuit with gold piping and a floppy hat. It took him a moment to recognize this guy out of context. He'd only seen him at the club. The sunlight glinting off the blade that now flicked into place took him aback.

"Wait, no, come on, tell Dobbs I'm cool. I'm not talking," Treadmore protested.

The second of the two quick stabs into his body drove the blade into a lung. Treadmore gaped. The other man held him as Treadmore collapsed, his breathing becoming labored as his lungs filled with blood. The killer in the tracksuit gently set him on the ground beside the dumpster and walked away. The life wheezing out of Treadmore, he fixated on water dripping from an outdoor faucet. If he'd been so inclined, he might have taken this as being symbolic.

The three in scuba gear swam through the waters off the western coast of Saint Kitts. The sun had set, the turquoise clear sea now a shimmering ebony. The built-in headlamps of their wetsuits illuminated their way. So as not to rely on radio and its frequency possibly being intercepted, each wore a small whiteboard bordered in black around their necks. A grease pencil was attached to the board to write brief messages. The thieves came up under an anchored superyacht which had two saunas, a Gold's-worthy gym, heli-deck, and racquetball court among its amenities. They were under the boat's tender bay. Attached by cable there floating before them was a cylindrical container the size of two fifty-gallon drums stacked together. Should the cylinder be removed from the cable, an alarm would sound. Should the cylinder be breached, an alarm would sound. The three unlimbered the equipment bags each had towed along. Two of them began assembling the underwater torch and the third one clamped an apparatus that looked like a parolee's ankle bracelet around the cable. This instrument would, when calibrated properly, reroute the signal from the alarm. Essentially loop it back on itself. They'd brought along something similar for the canister. The flat tender blocked the light of the torch once they got busy cutting their prize loose.

A hand in the pocket of her thrift-shop-purchased nylon windbreaker, Ridley walked down the aisle of used cars on the Prestige Motors lot. The business was located on Washington Boulevard at the demarcation between Los Angeles and Culver City. She wore oversized sunglasses, a cloth cap, and a wig of straight hair underneath. She strode past one of the salespeople, a woman with a vine-and-snake tattoo running the length of her arm. She was sweet talking an older couple into test driving a two-year-old Dodge Charger. Ridley went up the short flight of steps leading to the office, an old-fashioned freestanding wooden structure with its windows overlooking the cars.

"Yes, what can I do for you today, ma'am?" a man in a dress shirt tight across his muscular chest asked from behind a desk.

"Get the fuck out of here, you and whoever else is in this office."

He rose, several inches taller than Ridley's five-eight. And far broader. "The hell you talking about?"

Ridley took her hand out of her pocket. She was holding a grenade.

A gasp came from beside Ridley. From an inner office a woman in red and black had stepped out to see about the commotion. She stood aghast.

"Let me say it again. Get the fuck out of here. Clear everyone out," Ridley said.

"You're confused," the man said, his tone softening. "Look, I've been there, okay? You get back from the sandbox and nothing seems like it should be, like how you remembered it was. Nobody to talk to, no one understands." He took a step.

"Homeboy," Ridley began, "another time, another place, I would have appreciated your concern. But today I'm gonna blow some shit up." She pulled the pin, holding the grenade's safety lever in place. "Get out of here."

"How about we do as she says," the women in red and black said. She went toward the man and took him by the elbow. "Come on," she urged.

His pleading expression at Ridley gave way to resignation and he accompanied the woman out of the office. Through the window, Ridley could see them talking to the saleswoman and the couple. The woman in red and black was on her phone, a mechanic who must have been in the service area next to her. Soon the police and their bomb squad would arrive. She put the pin back in the grenade. Back outside she went behind the office which overlooked a short wall bordering a narrow passageway. Up over the wall she stood in the passageway and tossed the grenade back into the used car lot. It struck the side of an SUV and bouncing off of it, rolled under the car next to it. The grenade exploded, igniting the car's gas tank and the rear end bucked into the air like a bronc. The blast took out the windows of the SUV and another vehicle, a Lexus.

Ridley understood the protocol the police would undertake. First they'd cordon off the lot and surrounding area then evacuate people to make sure if any other explosive devices were detonated; civilians would be relatively safe. Down the passageway and a turn at the corner brought her to a cinder-block wall. She jumped up to take hold of the top and got herself over this too. She was now in an alley that was unoccupied given everyone was out in front of their shops and what have you to see what had happened.

Ridley had previously checked out the area for her escape route. Soon she was walking on Venice alongside what was once the Helms Bakery complex long since turned into spaces for trendy furniture stores and restaurants. Sirens were fast approaching. People were gathered and buzzing excitedly. She blended in with them, having ditched the cap, wig, and coat she'd been wearing. Police cars, fire trucks, and an ambulance roared by. She stayed with the crowd for more than forty minutes.

Making sure she offered her ideas on what happened along with the others. Eventually as some began drifting away, she was merely one of many who did so.

The Chemical Syndicate was a two-story nightclub in Koreatown. The L-shaped club dominated a corner and wing of a strip mall at the intersection of Ardmore and 7th. Inside the establishment was a boba lounge, bottle service, and three bars including one in an alcove in what was called the Exclusive Retreat. The club's playlist ranged from hip hop, Top 40, EDM to R&B. At the moment a rendition of "I Second that Emotion" was playing. Couples slow danced to the song. Above them suspended from three sections of the ceiling were faux vats like out of a 1940s-era movie serial depiction of a chemical factory. The vats were tipped. Each one contained built-in padded seats upon which sat two women and a man in sexy outfits of leather, latex, and feathers. They all wore platform thigh-high boots. Regularly one or the three might lip-sync to a song, shimmy up the telescoping pole the supposed vats were connected to, or sometimes jump down to waiting arms.

In the VIP area on the second tier overlooking the dance floor, Dobbs sat with three others. One of them was his enforcer, Hakeem, who favored tracksuits.

"Bitch is getting to be a real problem." Hakeem took a puff on his dark-hued cigar, blowing smoke toward the ceiling. He had more of his Bache-Gabrielsen cognac.

"Tell me something I don't know," Dobbs said. He was a tallish, light-skinned black man rummaging in his forties. He had a small hoop earring in one ear and worked out regularly. He'd made money producing music, including K-Pop. While the club drew heavily among an Asian clientele, a whole swath of folks from the Southland's various neighborhoods also frequented the night spot.

"Can't you settle with her. Pay her what she's owed?" Ryan Hong said. He was a man in his mid-thirties, trim in a tailored suit and wearing tortoiseshell glasses. He was an investment banker—a crooked one if such was not an oxymoron in terms. Hong was drinking a Moscow Mule and rattled what was left of the ice in the copper cup.

Dobbs answered, "I have the feeling she won't be satisfied just getting her money."

Hakeem nodded in agreement, touching his temple with an index finger.

"But she's making waves," the remaining VIPer said. She was a quaffed blonde with dark eyes. "And I don't need to preach to the choir, but we don't need this kind of attention now." She was a real estate developer, Aquanetta Barrows. Many were surprised on initially hearing that name then meeting her that she wasn't black. Her parents were Lutherans from Iowa. She too smoked a cigar.

"We got money out on the street," Hakeem said.

If Dobbs was irritated his muscle was talking as if it was his money being used to prime the snitch pump, he didn't show it. "Ridley won't be interfering for too much longer."

Barrows took a long pull on her cigar and let the smoke out slowly, watching the trail drift upward.

The ballad over, the next cut to play was a bumping deep house number that had folks filling the dance floor. As Hong and Dobbs watched the cavorting patrons, Barrows and Hakeem eyed a woman with a curly mohawk with zig-zags designed into the close-shaved sides of her head. She ascended the steps to this level. The woman was darker than Dobbs and dressed in a hip-hugging mid-length dress and low heels. The lower part of a tattoo peeked from below the short sleeve of her dress. There was a cuff-type bracelet as if from the times of the Roman empire on a wrist.

"Hey, Gee," Dobbs said as she came over to sit on the arm of the club chair and gave him a peck.

The woman, Grace Alison, crossed her legs. "Your boy Freddy texted. I called him back."

"What he have to say?" An encrypted texting app had been

set up to receive tips about Ridley.

She smiled sweetly. "That he knows where Ridley lays her head at night when she ain't fuckin' with you."

Dobbs exchanged a look with Hakeem. The latter said, "I'll check it out."

"Got an address." She produced a Post-it. "According to Freddy she's squatting in a granny flat." She leaned across and handed the address to Hakeem.

Studying it he said, "The hell is this?" He showed the paper to Dobbs.

She cocked her head to the side. "Santa Clarita. I looked it up."

"What the hell's her redbone ass doing out there?"

Dobbs regarded him. "Doing good at not being found."

Hakeem frowned. "Freddy hardly goes west of La Brea. How he tumble on this?"

"Think it's a setup?" Dobbs countered.

"Maybe I'll ask Freddy."

Dobbs's head dipped. "Can't argue with that."

Hakeem stubbed out his cigar and left.

Alison took his seat. The waitress appeared and handed her a fresh glass of cognac. As the server left, she and Barrows locked smoldering looks.

Hakeem drove his low-slung BMW to Freddy Hughes's salvage yard that was in the city of Vernon, fronting southeast L.A. County. He was listening to one of the life coach podcasts he subscribed to. Achieving and believing were states of mind and Hakeem had big plans. The roughneck work he did for Dobbs was a stepping stone to the future he'd mapped out. Not long from now he'd be the one giving the orders. Hughes, a widower in his sixties, actually lived in a small-frame house behind the yard. Hakeem drove his car onto what remained of the dried, yellowed lawn. The sidewalk only existed on one side of the house. Momentarily he chewed the inside of his cheek as the wellness guru went on about the five steps to thriving. The old man's pickup truck wasn't in the driveway.

Nonetheless, the enforcer notched his light to high beam to shine through the dingy, diaphanous curtains on the barred front windows. In this way he hoped to lure the older Hughes outside. Hakeem watched from the driver's seat but there was no movement of a curtain, and no one appeared on the porch. He shut off the lights in the car and got out. He closed the driver's side door quietly. His gun was tucked in his waistband at his back, his loose top covering the grip.

Up on the porch he knocked on the security screen and called out. No response. "Fuck," he said. He knocked again, harder, banging on the metal. "Freddy," he said loudly, "it's Hakeem. Open up."

The good thing about Vernon, he reflected, was that during the day, the industrial-oriented town was heavy with trucks, workers, and diesel fumes. During the off hours, there was a low residency of inhabitants so he wasn't too worried about attracting attention. No Freddy. Back at his car's trunk, he removed a flashlight and prybar and went around the far side of the house, out of sight from the street. He was at a bedroom window, the shade up. There was shrubbery to his back. His light shone in on a threadbare room including a dresser he estimated must be from thirty years ago. Probably everything in Hughes's house was secondhand, he concluded. Before he got down to the business of breaking in, he called Dobbs.

"He don't seem to be around," he told him after his boss answered.

"Get on in there and take a look. Could be Ridley found out he dropped a dime and smoked him."

"What if she did?"

This time Dobbs didn't hide his irritation. "Then we can get the law on her. Get the fuck in there and see what you can see."

"Okay."

Perpendicular at the end of the passageway was a width of chain-link fencing. He climbed over this to find himself in a backyard also of yellowed grass and patches of dirt. Darker still shapes against the night loomed about. Gun in hand, Hakeem's light swept across these forms. Situated in the backyard were various homemade metal statuary. Not the old cars he expected, though there were a few engine blocks around too. But these seemed to be purposely arranged, not just left around haphazardly. Illuminated were representations of humanoid and animal figures hammered, cut, and welded out of the shells of cars and other recovered material he saw. No critic of the arts, Hakeem had to admit he was surprised at the old man's initiative. The old boy was now able to finally express himself after a life of just getting by. You just never know about people, he reasoned.

Hakeem was at the back door with its security screen. He inserted the wedged end of the prybar between the heavy gauge screen and the wood and grunted as he leveraged to tear the lock free. After several attempts, sweat breaking out on his brow, he was successful. The inner wooden door wasn't much to get through. Thereafter, Hakeem, with the aid of his flashlight, was looking into a spare kitchen. Dried dishes sat on a rack next to the sink. No flies zipped around, so maybe no dead body decomposing. Tense, he stood before the threshold, gun back in his other hand. But no junkyard dog came scampering across the aged linoleum, streaked black from wear. He made to enter, his heel landing on a pressure plate. Guillotine-like, a saw-toothed blade the width of the inner doorway descended into the trapezius area of his upper back.

"Oh fuck," he screamed as the impact drove him to the floor. The flashlight was dropped, its light going out. The blade was embedded deep in the muscle. Hakeem was unsure of what to do, the pain dominating him. But he called upon those many hours of devouring positive aphorisms—all that couldn't have been in vain. He lowered his head, gathering his strength. A light shined and he looked up. The disembodied head of the perpetually grinning life coach Tony Robbins floated before him in the center of that light.

"You can do this, Hakeem," Robbins said, his too white and too big teeth gleaming. "Obstacles are opportunities."

"Obstacles are opportunities," the trapped enforcer repeated. He tried to rise.

"There you go," Robbins encouraged. "Come on, you can do this."

Hakeem had to get on his feet then twist around so as to hold the blade in place and try to pull himself loose. But to do that, he'd shred the wounds worse in his back. Would he pass out from the agony and bleed out until death? His shirt was soaked with blood. His phone chimed in his back pocket.

"Let go," Robbins said. "No time for self-doubt. Rise, Hakeem, rise. Rise," Robbins encouraged.

Hakeem cried loudly like a stuck pig, his grandma would have said. Inch by agonizing inch, he rose. He had to do this; he had to get to a hospital.

At the Chemical Syndicate, Barrows and the waitress had gone off to spend time in one of the suites in the Executive Retreat. These were accessed behind the bar in the alcove. The wall of bottles swung outward to reveal a passageway lined with polished cherrywood doors. Banker Hong drank alone. Dobbs and Alison were in his office. He was at the window, the Venetian blinds slightly open. Her legs under her, Alison sat on the couch having more cognac. Dobbs turned from the window and regarded the iPhone on his desk. He picked it up to stare at the screen.

"Should have heard back from him." He texted and called Hakeem.

"Maybe Freddy is tougher than he looks."

"Shit. That fool would fold at the sight of a nosebleed on a napkin."

"Maybe you should take your mind off your troubles for a

while. Relax." She sat her glass aside and undid her legs from under her. Feet flat on the floor, she pulled her dress up, opening her legs wider.

"Yes, ma'am," Dobbs said, grinning. "You sure are something in that party dress."

He came over and got on his knees. Dobbs leaned his head in between her thighs.

Alison sighed, "Nothing lasts forever."

Her tone gave him pause. The cold muzzle of a pistol to the back of his head dissipated his lust. He looked around as Alison moved away to stand by Ridley and her gun.

"You two." Deflated, Dobbs sat on the floor, his back against the couch.

Ridley chucked the end of the gun under his chin, yet Dobbs's attention wandered. Before him, the room and its occupants disappeared. Filling his mind was he and Alison, her breath hot on his neck when he aimed upward and shot Ridley in the back atop the mound of dirt. She fell down into the dark. She must have had on a Kevlar vest under her jacket, he realized. They'd met at the construction site, the project he'd bought in on through Barrows and Hong, to divvy up the swag—the cash realized from fencing the haul of Klemmer's gold bars. Hakeem wasn't there that evening to allay any suspicion on Ridley's part, who'd come strapped.

"It was all a con," he declared. He'd believed Alison was double-crossing Ridley for a bigger cut and to be with him. "Fuckin' fool," he groused.

"You're not the first man to be led by his dick," Ridley cooly observed.

He'd met Alison at the club, which wasn't unusual. What was different was she had smarts along with her looks. She wasn't about being a singer or becoming an influencer. Among her attributes, she was the manager of several women MMA fighters, some of them ex-service members like Ridley.

"We were angling to rob you," Alison admitted.

"Until you brought us in on your score," Ridley added. "A much better takedown."

"Ain't that some shit?" He almost laughed.

Among the regulars to the club was a Silicone Beach tech CEO Egil Klemmer. It was during one of Klemmer's excursions to a suite behind the bar with two others, a man and woman from the overhead vats. Dobbs later heard a tidbit from one of the performers that the high Klemmer had let slip. Dobbs followed up, making sure not to show his moves. Sure enough, Klemmer was hiding gold in space, secreted away on a few of his satellites. He'd helped finance the launch of several private space flights from Saint Kitts toward a populated trek to Mars. But as had been rumored in some quarters, as Klemmer was of white South African descent, there was a family fortune from before the apartheid era extracted by the sweat and lives of Black labor. What better way to continue to keep this treasure secret but in space, he apparently had speculated. Klemmer was a proponent of various conspiracy theories and looked to eventually establish a space station for him and his family when Armageddon came.

Ridley was talking. "Stealing is one thing, double-crossing your partners is another."

"This is on me," he groused. To Alison he added, "You had my nose wide open, girl." Alison knew his operation and had told Ridley.

She regarded him clinically. It was Ridley she'd brought in on the score – Ridley, who got wary when pulling off the job got closer. Hakeem overplayed it being solicitous with her. Klemmer's boat made regular trips to the island, and they'd figured out that was how he was transporting the gold. Ridley knew how to scuba from the service and taught Alison and Hakeem.

"If there was any other way," Alison began, then choked. "We'd just go our merry ways."

Ridley appreciated her girl did have feelings for Dobbs. She was no trick. "But there isn't." She grouped two in Dobbs's chest. Alison flinched. Ridley lowered the gun, which had a suppressor on the end. She wiped off her prints and left the gun on the floor. Time would pass, the police investigation would drag on as there would be a number of suspects to consider in the murder of the shady Dobbs. The two would approach the banker and the real estate developer about taking over Dobbs's investment in the redevelopment deal. They might balk but what could they do but agree? They were crooked but they weren't gangsters like these two. And as Ridley had pointed out, they were owed. Dobbs had used the swag derived from the gold to buy in on the deal—including what would have been Ridley's cut. The one going by the name Alison was a willing investor.

"Come on, Alison, let's get out of here," Ridley said. Holding hands, they walked away from the club and into the night.

ACCIDENTS WILL HAPPEN
by Naomi Rand

Marty and Bill are sitting on their regular stools at the far end of the bar. Retired, they come in early and stay late. The two of them have that gone-to-seed, grizzled look. Bill's wife died last year and Marty's long divorced. They're cousins and drinking buddies. Bill's a Fox News junkie who's sick and tired of those freeloaders wanting a piece of his ever-shrinking pie. Marty's a Bernie guy who loves to point out to Bill that if his grandparents hadn't gotten on that boat, he'd never be sitting here at all and besides, does he want to work for minimum wage at the meatpacking plant and lose a limb?

They get into that argument pretty much every night. It resolves itself two ways: either they agree to disagree, or it leaves them sputtering and breathless. But that doesn't change the ritual, first in, last out. They may disagree on everything else, but they'll defend each other's right to drink themselves into a stupor.

Lila's met guys like this in every bar she's ever worked in.

Alcoholics? Definitely. But who are they hurting other than themselves, she thinks.

"Sweetheart, can I get a refill?" Marty calls out.

"Sure thing," Lila says, grabbing the bottle of Wild Turkey and heading over to give him a generous pour. Kentucky bourbon's his drink of choice. Bill's more of a slow burn, downing draft after draft of Milwaukee's finest. Putting the bottle back, she catches sight of a girl with spiky platinum blond hair.

For a moment she doesn't recognize herself.

The door opens and she feels a blast of cold air.

It's Drew and two guys from his construction crew.

"You're here early," Lila says.

"The snow," Drew explains.

Through the plate-glass window, Lila sees the evidence, white flakes floating down.

They slide into their regular booth and Lila grabs three menus, then heads over.

"Can I start you gentlemen off with a beverage?" she asks.

"Why not?" Drew says, giving her that slow-burn smile.

A pitcher of ale with three frosty mugs. Lila's back at the bar, filling it when the door opens again. It's Manuela with her two young children trailing behind her.

"Sorry," Manuela apologizes, ushering them through the bar and into the back.

Her ex, Eddie, is a piece of work, Lila thinks. In the four weeks she's been working here, he's flaked out three times. There's always an excuse. And as for child support? It's nonexistent. Instead, he bribes them with gifts. Like those iPads they'll be spending all their time on tonight, while they wait for her shift to be over. When Lila suggested suing him, she laughed.

"With what money?"

All hers has gone to the immigration lawyer and she's still waiting on her green card.

The door opens and there's another blast of cold air. In come more familiar faces. Manuela emerges from the back and grabs menus, heading to the booth they've taken. The bar slowly fills up. The first snow of the season isn't going to deter people from going out. Not up here in northern Wisconsin.

Lila falls into the familiar, soothing rhythm. Drinks mixed and poured. Beer steins and glasses filled with the foam flicked away. Manuela works the floor, moving with calm efficiency. And in the back, Ralph, the short-order cook who retired from running the high school cafeteria and then signed on here because he was bored, turns out a steady stream of fried chicken, meatloaf dinners, and burger platters. As for salad? Ralph's version is a slab of iceberg lettuce and a few wan slices of a tomato served up in one of those faux-wood plastic bowls. The packets of Russian, Italian, or blue cheese dressing sit out on the table, next to the bottles of catsup and mustard.

On the radio? Classic rock.

On the TV? The Bucks game. Glancing up, Lila sees they're ahead by eleven. Still a lot of time though. It's only the third quarter.

Turning, Lila sees Manuela emerging from the kitchen, carrying a platter. She sets it down in front of the man sitting at the high-top to the left of the bar, then turns to go.

"Hey!" A voice booms out, cutting through the ambient noise. It's the man at the high-top. "That's not right."

"No?"

"You gave me the wrong fucking order!"

Manuela reaches out to lift the platter and he grabs her arm.

"Sir, I need to..."

He's a big man, at least six feet, with broad shoulders and a gut. Manuela's what? Maybe five-four?

"You people. You're all the same," he spits out.

Lila ducks under the bar flap.

As she walks up, Manuela extricates her arm.

"Don't you understand English!" he rants.

The conversation's died down, leaving the soundtrack. The Stones complaining about how hard it is to get satisfaction. Like they'd know, Lila thinks, the ones who are still alive are old and insanely rich.

"What's the problem?" Lila asks.

Up close, his face is florid. A heavy drinker, with a nose to match, bulbous, the unattractive red lines crisscrossing it. "She tried to cheat me." Pointing to the offending plate, a hamburger deluxe with fries like it's been poisoned. "Are you the owner?"

"No," Lila says, "But…"

"I want to speak to them."

Manuela shoots her a panicked look. That's the last thing she needs—Frank, the owner getting involved. What if he comes down here and sees Manuela's kids in the back? What then?

"I'm very sorry, sir. I truly am," Lila says, her voice saccharine sweet. "We so apologize. How about we comp you for the drinks?"

Three, so far.

"I don't know."

"And throw in a free dessert?"

"I guess."

"Let's get that order going for you now. What was it?" Then Lila makes a show out of heading to the kitchen to place the order herself. Leaning in, she quietly regales Ralph with the abridged version.

"Extra sauce?" Ralph asks with a mischievous grin.

As in, spit?

"That's up to you."

Walking back out, she passes Drew's booth. He gives her a sympathetic smile and shakes his head.

People.

She shrugs.

What can you do?

That's it for excitement.

On it goes. Gin and tonic. A gimlet. Tequila shots, salt on the glass, lime. PBR, Miller, bottled craft beer from the local small-batch brewery. And on the evergreen soundtrack, the hits from bands that her parents were too young to listen to.

Fleetwood Mac, Journey, Foreigner.

Her parents who called today and left that happy birthday message.

She didn't pick up. Knew better than that.

What are you doing with your life, Lila?

That's always the subtext.

"They just changed the forecast again," a man at the bar announces.

It's up from six to a foot. A serious storm now.

"Why they even bother," another one grumbles. "They always get it wrong."

Still, it sets off the general trend. People dropping their money and grabbing their coats. Clearing out. Heading home.

Manuela goes to clear the prick's table off.

"*Maldito!*"

She holds up the single dollar bill to show Lila. Balancing the dirty dishes in her arms, she heads for the kitchen.

"Manuela?" Drew stops her. "I'll cover it."

"No, no."

"I insist." Reaching out, he tucks the bill into her apron pocket.

"You don't have to…"

"I know I don't." But he's firm.

Off she goes, relieved. And Lila gives him an appreciative nod. Drew nods back and smiles. His eyes crinkle up when he does. Not a bad looking guy that Drew. His friends have their jackets on.

They throw down money and head off.

Not Drew. She's aware of that. Of him, settling up but still sitting there. Of him watching her.

It happens fast. Down to him and Marty and Bill.

Marty and Bill leave together and as they walk past, she catches Bill in the mirror leaning in to say something to Drew.

"Night, Lila," Marty calls out.

The door closes and Drew gets up and slides onto a barstool.

"You're not going?" Lila asks.

"Should I?" he asks.

"Up to you."

"Is it?" he asks.

Coy.

"I won't be long," Lila says.

His smile widens. And charmingly enough, his cheeks redden. A blusher, even at his advanced age.

Who would have thought?

Lila takes all the cash tips and stuffs them into the envelope. Then she pulls out her wallet and adds even more. Licking it shut, she heads into the kitchen. Ralph's in his coat. The big black garbage bags are waiting at the door.

"Did Manuela leave?"

"I'm taking her home," Ralph says. "That car of hers. I told her I didn't trust it."

"This is for her," Lila says, handing him the envelope.

"Get home safe," Ralph says.

"You too."

Lila pauses for a moment. What if he's gone?

Then he's left, she tells herself pushing the door open.

There he is, sitting where she left him.

"What can I get you?" Lila asks.

"Whatever you're having."

She reaches for the Dewars and grabs two highball glasses.

"How do you take yours?" Lila asks.

"Neat."

Neat and tidy. Lila pours two fingers into each glass and lifts hers.

"Happy birthday to me."

"It's your birthday?"

"It is indeed," she says.

"And you spent it working here? Shit. I'm sorry."

"Don't be," Lila says. "I've had worse ones."

"I'm sorry for that, too," Drew says.

Lila leaves that one alone, clinking.

"Happy birthday to you, Lila!"

"Happy birthday to me," Lila agrees. "Where do you live, Drew?"

"Just out of town," he says. "What about you?"
"At the Sunrise."
"You're at the motel?"
"It's what I could find," Lila says.
"You're not from around here."
"I'm not," Lila says, lifting the bottle. "You're not going to make me drink the rest of this all alone in my motel room, are you?"
"Definitely not," Drew says.

Last one out locks the door. Done. Walking to her car, her feet sink into the freshly fallen snow. Drew's already in his, a dark blue pickup truck. Lila wipes the snow off and gets in, turning the defrost on high. Pulling out, she follows his red taillights.

They head down Main Street passing the shuttered hardware store, then Annie's Dress shop, then Hong's Chinese, all dark and shuttered.

Not far at all.

He lives just out of town in a one-story ranch with an attached garage. There's room for his truck inside. Getting out, he gestures for her to come in through the garage. In the hallway there are jackets and coats hanging off the hooks on the wall and work boots and sneakers on the floor. Lila adds her own to the mix.

Drew's in the kitchen.

It's pretty much what she expected. What does a single man in his late twenties need? Not much. Thus, the drab dark wood cabinets and the basic amenities, a stove, a fridge, a dishwasher.

"What can I get you?" Drew asks.
"I'll fix us both drinks," Lila says.
"I can do that."
"You go get comfortable." Shooing him away.

Lila guesses right, opening the cupboard with the glassware in it on the first try. It's a mismatched assortment. The kind you'd find in a frat house, Lila thinks. The free promotional glassware with brands logos on them.

She picks the two highballs courtesy of Johnnie Walker.

His is neat.
Hers, on the rocks.

Carrying the glasses out, she finds Drew perched on the couch, a sectional made out of dark brown pleather.

Drew looks up at her expectantly.

"Here you go," she says handing him the glass. She perches catty corner from him on the L-shaped couch. Their knees abut. "To snow days."

He grins, then lifts his to his lips.

Dutch courage. He sets it down half-drained, then reaches for her. One smoky kiss. His hand moves under her shirt, caressing her breasts.

Lila pulls away. "The bathroom?"

"Second door on the right."

First is the bedroom. Inside, a queen-sized box spring and mattress set with a tangle of sheets, and one lonely dresser. Nothing at all on the walls. No personality in evidence other than the lack of one.

Who is Drew?

Impossible to say.

Someone in desperate need of a Queer Eye makeover.

She should nominate him.

Inside the bathroom it smells like mildew. The shower curtain's pulled back, revealing a squat pink tub that looks in need of a cleaning, as does the sink with its crusted remnants of facial hair and shaving cream. Is he waiting for his mother to come and clean for him?

Some men really never do grow up.

Lila opens the drug cabinet. Inside, the usual selection of grooming products and toiletries. Nothing more dramatic like an array of prescription drugs. Not that it means he doesn't take them. Maybe he's discreet, hides those in his top dresser drawer.

Shutting it, she finds her face oddly bisected. There's a faint crack in the mirror. Drew looks at himself in this every morning. Like Two Face. But which side is the good Drew and which pure evil?

Now there's a question for the ages.

Walking in, she finds Drew draped across the couch. The glass in front of him is empty. Drew looks up. "You find it okay?"

"I did," Lila says, plopping down in the easy chair.

"Sit here," Drew says, patting the couch next to him.

"I'm a little hurt," Lila says.

"Hurt?"

"That you don't remember me," Lila says coyly.

Drew searches her face, looking for a clue. "Where?" he asks, puzzled.

"That would give it away. Sure you don't remember?"

Take a closer look. Lila leans forward to help him. Drew studies her.

"I don't," he admits. "I'm…" His tongue flicks out of his mouth, wetting his lips. "I don't…"

"It's not very gentlemanly of you," Lila pouts.

"What did…" Out comes his tongue again.

"I'd think you'd remember. You did try to kill me," Lila says. "Madison, in front of the statehouse? I was the one holding the 'Hate Has No Home Here' sign. I guess you were going for the irony."

That hits home.

"You can't…" Words fail him. He lurches to his feet and sways, shaking his head like an angry bull. Not that it clears his head. Drew tries to take a step and fails, collapsing back on the couch.

Lila walks over, standing above him.

He looks up at her. "What did…"

"You were gunning for me, but Cory saw you coming. He shoved me out of the way."

And took the full brunt.

"Your lawyer argued that you felt threatened by us. You were trying to get away and lost control of the vehicle. A total lie, but the judge was on your side. He let you off with a warning. And Cory got to spend the rest of his life in a hospital bed. He never woke up."

Drew's eyes dart around.

"A permanent vegetative state," Lila says. "You're getting a little taste of that now. How it feels when you can't speak or move. It sucks, doesn't it? That's what you gave Cory. That's all he ever had. His parents kept hoping for a miracle, but it never happened. When he died, I came here. I'd been keeping track of you all this time. Livefreeordie112? Couldn't you come up with something more original?"

"Fuck you."

A full thought. His last. Drew's tongue flicks out. His eyelids flutter. Then, he's out, his body slumping. His chest rises and falls rhythmically.

Lila gets to her feet. Pulling the rubber gloves out of her bag, she dons them. Then she checks the windows, making sure they're all securely closed. Carrying the glasses into the kitchen, she washes and dries them, then she takes the baby wipes out of her bag and wipes everything she touched down. Then she removes the printout of Cory's obituary from the plastic sheath and walks back to Drew. She takes his flaccid fingers and pushes them down on the piece of paper, then she lays it on the coffee table.

Some things you can't predict. Like the gas stove, bonus points there. Lila snuffs the pilot light then turns the knobs to the highest setting. In the hallway, Lila dons her boots and coat. Then she lifts his keys off the hook on the wall.

Lila props open the door between the house and the garage. Then she rolls down the windows in the truck and turns it on. She clicks the remote and ducks underneath the garage door Then she inches her way around the house until she gets to the side where the pine trees form a barrier. She takes a path through them down the hill to where she parked her car. Getting in, she makes a U-turn and heads back through town. Main Street's had its makeover, the snow covers everything. It looks like the backdrop on a Christmas card.

First snow.

Then, too.

Sophomore year. She and Cory sitting at the kitchen table in that ramshackle wooden house. They were roommates first, then friends, and then…he was so easy to talk to. That tall, lanky frame. The shock of light brown hair that hung over his eyes. Every so often he'd brush it back.

What had they been talking about?

She can't remember.

Only that she looked up and the snow was falling. They had the same thought and acted on it, pulling on their shoes and walking down the rickety stairs into the backyard. Magical. It always was. Opening her mouth to let the white flake falls onto her tongue and melt.

"Is it okay if I kiss you?" Cory asked.

"Is it okay?" Laughing at how polite he was, then reaching for him. Tears roll down her cheeks. Lila wipes them away.

It won't bring me back.

I know.

On the drive to her room at the Sunrise Motel, the snow turns to hail. By the time she pulls into the parking spot in front of her room, the road is coated with icy pellets. Trapped inside, Lila is left with the obvious. There were witnesses who saw them together tonight.

If you leave, it'll make you look guilty.

And if I stay and they'll figure out who I am?

You'll deal with that tomorrow.

Sitting cross legged on the bed, she holds her own private wake. When she finishes the Scotch, she raids the minibar.

The roar of an engine wakes her. Getting out of bed, she lifts the slat. A truck with a snowplow attached is clearing the lot. Wincing, Lila backs away. Her mouth tastes like chalk and her temples pound. A beast of a headache.

Coffee.

That, and a double dose of painkillers.

Dressing, Lila heads out. It's a short walk to The Daily Bean. And it's open. Just up the road on the opposite side, the neon sign's lit.

Start Your Day Right.

Doing my best, Lila tells herself, trudging through the snow. Checking for traffic, Lila starts across. She's almost to the double white line when she hears the car coming. Swiveling her head, she sees the dark blue pickup truck barreling at her.

Is that Drew at the wheel?

Impossible.

But it is. It's him. He's alive.

Lila takes off. Or tries to. Her front foot slides out from under her and she goes down hard. Getting up, she sees it's too late.

Turning to face him, she girds herself.

Above her, the sun bursts through the clouds. The asphalt in front of her shimmers.

Black ice.

She thinks that just as the truck's tires hit. It veers away, missing her by inches. As it flies past, she sees Drew's face contorting.

The squeal of brakes. The acrid smell of burning rubber.

It's oddly balletic, the way the truck flips, end over end. There's a horrific crunch as the cab slams into the road. The metal roof pancakes.

Did that just…

Yes.

As Lila crosses the street, a car pulls over. The driver runs over to the wreck. Peering in, he pales. Turning her way, he shakes his head.

Lila lifts her phone.

Nine-one-one. What is the nature of your emergency?

PERMANENT LENT
by Peter Spiegelman

Deirdre tells me to let it go.

"If you were Irish or a woman, you'd have more feel for vengeance than you do. But you're neither, so take it from me: there's nothing here for you. Let it go. Move on."

Two of many things I'm no good at.

I know enough to know she's smart—smarter than me, anyway. I want to take her advice but still it picks at me like a crow at a carcass. Peck, peck, peck—that black beak again, right in my ribs.

Anyway, there's a maple come down in the storm, still flush with scarlet leaves, and it's lying over half the main drive like a crime scene. If I don't get it cleared before her majesty is up from the city, I won't hear the end of it. I load the chainsaw and a gas can into the back of the Jeep and drive over from the tractor barn.

She shows up on Thursday, but his lordship doesn't follow as planned on Friday morning. He's off to London or wherever instead—a business emergency or some such, and he'll make it when he can. Her highness is plenty pissed.

"That's four menus in the garbage," she yells at the kitchen girls, as if they had anything to do with it. "Friday dinner! Saturday lunch! Saturday cocktails! Sunday brunch!" She counts them off and with each graceful finger raised, her voice is louder and more brittle. If she was a nun there'd be bloody knuckles next, but she's no nun.

There are punishments, though. She tells the kitchen girls to empty the two big fridges in the butler's pantry and watches as the catering is carried outside and heaved, platters and all, into black garbage bags, the bags are loaded into the back of her Range Rover, and the whole mess is carted off by her driver to the town dump. The entire time she's taking pictures on her phone and sending them to London or wherever. Before she dispatches the driver, a white-haired ex-cop with a whiskey nose, eyes like dried beans and skin like a basketball, she gives instructions.

"I want to see everything—every fucking bag—on that trash heap. You don't leave there till you send me the photos."

Her driver looks tough but he's a pussy, and he's nodding and looking at his shoes while she's talking.

She sees me watching from the greenhouse and she glares and waves me over. So then it's my turn.

"The horses are in Florida," she says.

I nod. "Trailered down on Tuesday," I say.

"So the stables are buttoned up for the season?"

"Not yet," I answer.

"Well, they will be—today."

"Manny's not back till Monday." Manny runs the stables and travels with the horses.

"What is it—fucking brain surgery, and only Manny can operate? I think you know how to use a shovel."

"You want me to do it? I have a list of other things—"

"It's my list that matters, and the stables are what's on it. But don't worry, you won't do it alone." I squint at her. "Orla and Donal will help you." Orla and Donal are her stepkids, from his lordship's most recently terminated marriage. I squint at her.

"What's wrong with you? You look like you're going blind. Orla has a field hockey game over in New Canaan, and Donal has soccer in Darien or someplace—Nanny knows where. Go pick them up and give them shovels. It's their goddamn horses—they can deal with the goddamn shit. Teach them something about responsibility."

I draw a breath to speak but Deirdre catches my eye and shakes her head and I let it go.

Her ladyship comes to inspect early next morning. She stalks around the stable—hands jammed in her fleece vest, questing for problems and disappointed when she finds none. Her blond ponytail is so tight it makes her blue eyes bulge, and her boots sound like a nail gun as she paces the floorboards. I half expect her to pull out white gloves and start running her fingers over things. Instead, after her walk-around, she stands outside one of the stalls, folds her arms across her chest and stares at me. I'm looking for Deirdre but nobody's around. It makes me nervous.

"The kids do their parts yesterday?" she asks.

I nod. "They did fine."

"Which is bullshit. Donal told Nanny you let Orla drive back, you bought them ice cream, and the most work they did was to sit around stuffing their fucking faces while they watched you shovel shit."

I don't say anything, but stare back.

"You think I'm the evil queen or something? And you're—what—the kindly woodsman? You think this is a fairy tale—that there's a happy ending coming?"

I shrug. "Those stories are pretty dark, actually. But maybe you're not much of a reader."

The smooth skin on her cheeks and long neck redden. "You know I can fire you." I don't even shrug at this, and the red patches darken. "You think I can't, just because he likes how you take care of his fucking toys? You think you're the only one who can wax a car?"

I shake my head. "For sure, there are plenty of Ferrari-certified mechanics around. Might take a while to find one checked out on restoring classic models, of course, and you might have to pay them a signing bonus, or relocation from Florida or wherever. Assuming they're willing to move. But for sure, we're easy to find."

Her fists are white stones. "You're so damn clever," she says, and her voice is tight. "But if you knew anything you'd know things change, and things change hands. What's his today could be mine tomorrow—including that fucking car collection. You'd know how to help yourself, if you were really smart."

"No one's ever accused me of that," I say, and leave her in the stable.

Saturday dusk, some parts come in from Maranello—original dash gauges for the '71 Daytona I'm working on. I'm headed back to the car barn after jawing with the FedEx guy when I hear her. I stop on the path.

"I swear, Marty, you say prenup to me again I will slit your goddamn throat. How many times do I have to tell you—I had no choice but to sign. He wasn't gonna go through again what he went through the first two times—he made that plain. And stupid me, I thought it was giving me protection too—that he couldn't do me the way he did them. But I didn't know shit, and that lawyer of his ground me down and made it clear if I didn't sign there'd be no wedding—and never mind the invitations and the announcement in *The Times*."

She's on her phone, pacing the brick courtyard between the big house and the guest house, still in her down vest and boots. The last strands of daylight cling to her hair and pale face, and her left hand carves through the shadows like a white blade as she speaks.

"So now here we are—with me trapped in this pile of stone and horse manure with his sad sack kids, him shacked up in London with that M&A cunt, Veronica—in my fucking suite at the Mandarin, by the way, plus you giving me agita over the goddamn prenup. I know what it says, Marty, but I'm telling you—it's not gonna be a problem. There are things he'll want me to keep to myself—which I'm happy to do so long as he meets my number. And believe me, Marty, it's a very large number."

I don't know if Marty—whoever he is—has anything to say, but if so she doesn't listen. She pockets the phone, sighs deeply, and yells "Fuck" loud enough to send something clattering out of the hedges and through dry leaves. It startles her and she looks around. Maybe she feels my gaze, because the pale face turns toward me and I know those blue eyes are searching the shadows. I keep very still and hold my breath and finally she goes inside.

One of the kids comes to my place that night. I hear footsteps climbing the stairs that run up the outside of the garage to my apartment, but the knock still sends a jolt through my limbs—which is not good for fine work or anybody's health. I take a few slow breaths, put down my tweezers and soldering iron, and fold a drop cloth over my project. When I open the door, Orla barges in without an invite. She's in sneakers, jeans, and a fleece jacket with an owl on the breast and the name of her school on the back.

She's never been up here before and because it's new and strange, her eyes bounce around the place: the pocket kitchen, the spavined sofa, the pair of creaky chairs, the door to the bathroom, the door to the bedroom, and the long table under the hanging lights, now covered in tools, wires, manuals, schematic drawings, some gauges long past use, and others just out of the FedEx box.

As she scans the space, I'm struck by how much she looks like her mother—the pale skin, the freckles, the eyes like wet green stones, the thick auburn hair that falls in waves below her shoulders—but with an overlay of fifteen-year-old uncertainty and awkward bravado. Her nose crinkles up, which makes her freckles more prominent. "It smells like you're cooking metal."

"Soldering."

She doesn't know or care what that is. She looks at the sofa and at the chairs and can't decide what's worse. I pick up the stool I was sitting on and bring it to her. She sits and her knee starts bouncing. I can see her pulse throbbing in her pale neck. She's rehearsed something but now that the moment is here, she doesn't know how to begin. She swallows a few times, opens her mouth, but nothing comes out.

"It's late for a driving lesson," I offer.

She nods. "I heard her talking tonight," she says.

"Your stepmother?"

She flinches and rolls her eyes. "Maybe that's what you call her. I don't."

"But you listen in on her conversations."

"You should be glad. She was talking about you tonight."

"Oh yeah?"

"To Marty."

"Who's Marty?"

"I dunno. Her lover maybe." She hits the word hard—makes it at once ridiculous and shameful. She looks at me when she says it, to measure my shock. I disappoint her.

"So, what did she have to say to him about me?"

"That she's going to get rid of you."

"What's that mean?"

She shrugs. "Murder you, maybe."

I laugh. "You want a soda or something? Orange juice?"

She shakes her head. "She could do it. Don't think she couldn't."

"She talks a good game. How about toast—I could make toast."

"I don't want toast. Actually, she said she was gonna have my father get rid of you."

"So now he's going to murder me?"

She snorts. "Lucky for you, he's busy with other things."

"Like?"

"Like cunt Veronica." I squint at her and she blushes deeply.

"Hey, I didn't give her that name," she says.

"Who's Veronica? And why does your stepmother call her that?"

"She works for my father."

"And the name?"

"Take a wild guess," Orla says, and shivers. "The whole thing's just gross."

"What whole thing is that?"

"Everything—my whole fucking life. My father and Veronica, my stupid-ass brother, her." She tosses her thumb in the direction of the big house. "And let's not forget the part about my mother being dead." She tries for nonchalance with the last bit, and lots of irony, but she can't pull it off. Her chin quivers and tears track down her pale, freckled cheeks. She wipes a sleeve across her nose.

"Fuck," she whispers.

I get paper towels from the kitchen and hand them to her. She wads them in her lap. I walk around the table, pick up a manual, pretend to study it while she composes herself. I hear sniffling and whispered curses. After a while she speaks.

"She liked you, you know—my mom. She said you were a good guy, despite the fact that you're so into cars."

"Cars are my job. If I was a fisherman, I'd be into fish." I force a little smile onto my face and try to otherwise keep still. "I liked her too, your mom."

"Yeah—so did I." I nod. "You know she's sending us back to the city tomorrow, me and Donal, with Nanny? She says she's tired of having us underfoot." Orla shakes her head. "She has exactly nothing to do with us."

"You'd rather stay here?"

"God, no. This place is extra gruesome when Manny and the horses are gone. They're the only decent people around." I laughed. "Besides you, I mean."

"Nice recovery."

She smiles. "I'm just counting the days till I'm out from under them."

"How many left?"

"I'm sixteen next month. So a month and two years till I come into my money."

I nod. "It'll go faster than you think."

She looks skeptical.

When she leaves, I heat up the soldering gun and get back to work.

"It hasn't been easy on her," Deirdre says. "On either of them."

I nod.

"She's a good girl," she says.

I nod again. "She drives pretty well," I say.

"The boy's good too."

"Despite the fact he sold me out?"

Her green eyes glisten and she touches her thick hair. "They don't have a lot of grown-ups in their lives. Not many they like or trust, at any rate. They're looking for friends. Allies."

I nod.

She looks at my work. "Is all this going to help them?" she asks.

"It's addition by subtraction."

Deirdre shakes her head.

The kids go back to the city in the morning, but her majesty stays behind and comes to the garage. I'm in the Daytona installing the gauges and while I work she walks up and down the aisles of cars, running her hands over their curves as if they're horses—as though they might quiver or buck at her touch. When I'm done, I towel the sweat from my face, put away my tools, wash my hands, and get out the chamois mitts. She's watching me.

"Busy, busy, busy." She's wearing snug jeans and a tight black top unzipped to her sternum. I see a vee of pale flesh, the curve of her collarbones and the swell of her breasts. Her straight blond hair is loose and falls below her shoulders.

"Skin oil isn't great on these finishes," I say, and start to rub out the smudges on the burgundy skin of the 1960 250 GT Cabriolet.

She makes a show of inspecting her palms and long fingers. "I'm moist," she says, smiling. "I don't apologize for it."

"Your husband doesn't like fingerprints."

"So you wipe them off and no one's the wiser."

While I buff she opens the door to the next car over, a blue '62 GTO, and climbs into the passenger seat. "Do those mittens work on leather? If these seats get wet, for instance?"

"Jesus," I sigh.

"He isn't here," she says softly. "But I am, and I'm talking to you." She smiles at me from the shadows of the passenger seat and tugs the zipper of her top an inch farther down. "You hear me, or should I speak louder?"

"What do you want from me?" I say.

She shrugs. "Maybe I want what little Orla's been getting. Maybe I want to learn to drive stick too."

"I don't have time to teach you and, besides, I don't think it would work out well."

Her smile widens. "You're telling me no?"

I shake my head. "Actually, I'm telling you fuck off," I say. "Maybe go find some puppies to drown."

Her laugh is deep and smoky. "Suit yourself," she says, and climbs out of the GTO. She zips her top up and strides off, whistling.

Orla calls from the city very early the next morning. She's in a dark room and her face floats on my phone like white mist on the sea. She's pissed and she's crying.

"Tell me you didn't—not with her!" Her voice is like breaking glass.

I swing my feet to the floor and rub a hand over my face. "Girl, it's like four a.m." My voice sounds like a stone in a hole.

"She came back here after dinner and she had a video. She made me watch it. Then she told me how it would look to everyone—what everybody would think when they saw it. Girls at school...everyone."

"Orla, I have no idea what you're saying. Are you talking about your stepmother?"

"She's a fucking monster."

"Which is why you can't believe anything that comes out of her mouth. What was on this video?"

"It...it was me, from last night. Me going to the garage and up the stairs to your place, and me leaving a while later. I think my asshole brother took it. He's always creeping around, and always wants to get on her good side—God only knows why."

"That's all that was on it? Just you, climbing up the stairs and climbing back down?"

"That's what she showed me."

"If that's all, then so what? What's supposed to be so horrible about it?"

Orla swallows hard and turns the phone away from her so that all I see is a pillow like a blurry gray mountain. I hear her blowing her nose. She returns after a while, or at least her forehead and eyebrows return.

"She said people would think that you and I...that we...She said anyone who saw it would think that, and especially if they knew what went on between you and..." She disappears again and her crying is louder.

"Between me and who, Orla?"

"Between you and...my mother. She said that you and my mother—"

I cut her off. "That's bullshit, Orla, don't even think it. We never—"

But Orla can't stop. She spits words as if they're burning her mouth. "They fucked in every one of those cars—that's what she told me. She said you thought it was a perk of the job, like getting to drive all my dad's Ferraris—you get to screw the lady of the house. She said now people would think it's my turn."

"I promise you, it's bullshit. Your mother and I were friendly, friends even—I thought of her like that, anyway. But as far as anything else—your stepmother is full of shit."

"You swear?"

"Yes!"

"Say it, then."

"I swear, Orla—nothing happened between me and your mother. Not a thing."

She's quiet for a while, sniffling, trembling. "You okay now?" I ask.

She shakes her head. "She said other stuff about my mom. It's like she couldn't stop shit-talking her. She was so proud of herself, telling me."

"Telling you what?"

"About Mom and you. But not just you—about other people too. Other people she...How everyone thought Mom was such a saint, but they had it all wrong. How she had everyone fooled, and no one knew she was batshit crazy."

"You can't let her—"

"Maybe she's right—maybe my mother was batshit crazy. Her accident—some people say maybe it wasn't an accident. Maybe she did it on purpose."

"You can't listen to her, Orla. She wants to get into your head—to hurt you. You said it yourself: she's a monster."

Orla rubs a white hand at her eyes. "I'm not stupid," she says. "I know that. I'm just pissed she saw me cry. I fucking hate it."

"I get that," I say.

"But I couldn't help it. She just kept saying it over and over again, in that fucking singsong voice she does."

"Kept saying what?"

Orla swallows and does the singsong voice. "St. Deirdre. St. Deirdre. St. Deirdre."

There's moonlight through the windows of my place, so I can walk around without lights. Everything is silver—the floorboards, the kitchen counter, the water in my glass, my bare feet, my eyes in the mirror.

I feel bad about lying to the kid, but what was I supposed to say? The truth is: something did happen. Yes, it was just the once—but how many times does it take? Is there some magic number? The truth is: I loved her mother. The truth is: she loved me, or said she did, even if it was just the one time and her clothes reeked of weed and later she said she was probably mistaken.

But if I told Orla any of that, what good would it do? It would just complicate things for her. And if I told her those truths, where would it end? How much more truth could she bear?

Should I go on to say that her mother's death was neither accident nor suicide? That her father orchestrated it, and that her stepmother—not her stepmother then, merely her father's latest mistress—encouraged it? That there was a deliberate campaign to make Deirdre miserable and frantic—denying her alimony, denying her child support, denying her a roof and four walls, denying her even her children, and entangling her in legal proceedings that stripped her financially? That the campaign worked, and an already fragile soul expired in a ratty cottage, attended only by a bottle of Irish whiskey, handfuls of barbiturates, and a cigarette in bed, engulfed in her last moments by flame and choking smoke? That the fire marshal noted suspicious spread patterns on the charred bones of the cottage, suggesting the presence of an accelerant, but that those observations never made it to his final report? That that same marshal retired immediately after filing his report, decamping to Arizona, the beneficiary of an unexpected inheritance from a previously unknown relative?

That was four years ago, and it took me all of that time to put the pieces together. Together enough for me, if not for the cops. And what would cops do, anyway—the lord of the manor has more money than God, and all the lawyers and well-placed friends such treasure always buys. Even stacked one on another, all my truths weighed less than air. Not enough to change things for Orla, and certainly not for Deirdre. And so, addition by subtraction.

In the mirror, I run a silver hand through my silver hair, rub my silver eyes and sigh. Though she often turns up now, just before dawn when I'm so often sleepless, Deirdre is nowhere to be seen. It's the emptiest part of the night, and very quiet. Outside only birdsong—a nightingale or a lark.

The royal couple is due back here in a day, which is fine with me. Her majesty sends a text to remind me and tells me his lordship has things he wants to discuss, and I should make myself available. I smile. Make myself available—I wonder if somebody helped her with that. She doesn't say what things he wants to talk about, doing her best to make me sweat, but I don't care. Everything's in place and ready for the final hookups. I text back that I've finished the restoration of the Daytona; it'll be ready and waiting for his lordship to drive when they arrive. I copy him on that one.

Which gives me a day to kill. Which is always tough for me—idle hands and so forth. I go downstairs and check on things again, not because I'm uncertain but for the comfort of seeing everything in its place. It's like a hand on my cheek, or a compress over my eyes. After that, I climb in the Jeep and drive the bridal paths around the grounds. The property is tucked away for the season—the trees bare, the ornamental shrubs bundled in burlap, the lawns brown and still, waiting. In a few weeks, the tree guys will be here to string the Christmas lights. Or not.

I drive to the top of the hill, a mile off, and to the folly his majesty's first ex built there. It's basically a living room with a big veranda attached—red tile roof, louvred doors and shutters, ceiling fans, hemp rugs and bamboo sofas with canvas cushions.

Deirdre called the style Neo-Colonizer. From the veranda there's a long view of the property—the fields, the barn, the paddocks and stable, the garage and outbuildings, and the main house and its gardens. Nobody visits the place, and I used to come up sometimes to read and have a nap. I especially liked it in the rain.

It was raining the afternoon I found Deirdre here, smoking weed and singing along to the music she had going. She didn't ask what I was doing—just seemed to accept my presence as the way of things, like the rain. She saw I had a book under my arm and wanted to know what I was reading. I told her: *Under the Volcano* by Malcolm Lowry. She looked at me for a while, quiet, then she nodded.

"Order in your life, but chaos in your stories," she said at last. It was a pronouncement, the finding of a court, or maybe the sentence it handed down.

She offered me some weed. I declined and sat down to read. She went on smoking and watching the rain, which made a sound like a simmering pot. It was companionable.

We were the only ones at home that rainy week, and every day we met up here and talked about this and that. She didn't tell me much about her marriage, but enough for me to know it was all but over. I didn't tell her much either, a little about my time in the service, some of the places I'd been—there wasn't much else I was allowed to say. I declined her ongoing offers of weed, but by the end of each day spent in the fog she generated my head was very far north.

Companionable, and then—that day before everyone returned—more than that.

I haven't come up in months, and there's a meat-locker chill in the big room and an air of abandonment and privation—like it's Lent every day here, and always will be. I search for Deirdre, but she's not around. It starts to rain—a hissing drizzle—but even this doesn't coax her. I stretch out on one of the sofas, close my eyes, and measure my breaths in the way I was taught summons sleep, but sleep doesn't come.

PERMANENT LENT

* * *

The morning sky is a hard blue, and I'm up early—battle-tuned, my blood iced coffee. I'm downstairs before the sun comes through the garage windows, gingerly easing the final hookups into place. It's slow work, but I'm rock steady all the way and I'm done before nine. I wipe a sleeve over my brow and have a last look at the Daytona, shiny as an apple, front-and-center under a spotlight. Then I sling a rucksack on my shoulder and step into the cold.

I press the garage door remote and watch the big metal door roll down. I check the monitor I'm running on my phone. Green lights. I get in the Jeep and drive up to the folly.

There's a breeze up there, moaning through the roof tiles like a ghost and turning the blades on the veranda fans. I open the shutters and pull up one of the bamboo chairs.

Everything is sharply etched in the morning light, and the property looks like a game board from here, the buildings like bright plastic pieces. I pull field glasses from the rucksack, sight in on the garage and front gates, then sit back. I pick up my phone to check the monitor and all of a sudden I've got messages from Orla, all from this morning, the first ones sent hours ago.

my stupid father got back last night and he's seriously pissed thanks to her
pissed at YOU
why don't you pick up your fucking phone???
I check it and see it's set to silence. Shit.
are you there???
my father and that bitch are headed up soon
she's got him twisted up over that stupid fucking video
i should've known

I see voice mail messages too and I'm about to listen when there's movement on the game board—his lordship's black Range Rover, passing through the gates. It goes straight to the garage and pulls up in the gravel turnaround. I pick up the field glasses.

The central bay door rolls up and their highnesses stride through like they're staging a raid.

I keep watching and in five minutes the Daytona pulls out, gleaming in the clear light, fishtailing on the gravel because his lordship doesn't drive as well as he thinks. The garage door rolls down and I glimpse her majesty in the passenger seat looking self-satisfied. I smile too as they drive out the front gate. I put down the glasses and look at the monitor app. Yellow lights now.

I look up and Deirdre is on the veranda, peering through the window, and for an instant relief floods through me. And then drains away. Deirdre is frowning and shaking her head. Her lips move, but the only sound is the moaning wind. Then Orla's voice message plays. She's scared and excited.

"I tried talking to him, told him nothing happened, but she's got him crazy. He's going to fire you or worse. Don't be there when they get there. Just leave. Why don't you answer your fucking phone?"

Another message after that.

"Just call me, okay? Tell me you got my messages. Tell me you're getting out of there."

There's a frantic sound in Orla's voice that spikes my heart rate. There's a third message in the queue and I press play as a movement at the front gate catches my eye. An SUV is waiting there while the gate sweeps back. A gray Honda, like Nanny's car. Shit. What's Nanny doing here? The Honda heads up the drive, pauses at the fork, then heads to the garage. The third voice message begins to play—Orla again.

"Okay, you're not answering. Maybe you're dead or something. Whatever. I'm coming up there. Nanny won't mind if I take her car. It's our fucking car anyway, and she's off with her boyfriend. I know the way and the app says there's hardly any traffic this time of day, so if I can just get out of the city in one piece…Anyway, call me when you get this. I really hope you're not dead."

Shit.

I'm out the door before the Honda makes it to the garage. I jam the Jeep through the gears, skidding on the trails. Adrenaline locks my chest, and I'm struggling to breathe. I catch a glimpse of the road that runs along the edge of the property and see a streak of red. The Daytona, returning.

I fumble one-handed with my phone and call Orla. She answers in a landslide of words.

"So, you are alive—that's good. Also good you're gone, 'cause the assholes are around here somewhere. Did you know you left your door unlocked? I mean, I'm glad you did, but—"

"Orla, stop talking and get out of there. Get out now."

"What are—"

"Now, Orla. Out the door, down the stairs, away from the garage as fast as you can. I'm not fucking around—do it now! Run!"

"Okay, okay—I'm going," Orla says. "Jesus Christ, what the hell is your problem?"

I'm approaching the main drive when something flashes past—the Daytona, like a red dagger catching the sun, speeding toward the garage. I pull in behind, standing on the gas, leaning on the horn. The Daytona doesn't slow.

I look up and see Orla stock-still at the top of the stairs that lead from my rooms, a golden statue in the sun.

"Oh fuck, it's the assholes," she says. "Is that you behind them? Why're you driving like that? And what's with the honking?"

Ahead of me the Daytona slows and I see the center garage door begin to roll up. I can't get air in my lungs and my voice is a whisper even as I shout into the phone. "Orla, please—get away from the garage. Run!"

Orla takes the stairs two at a time but it's much too late. I see the flash and feel the pressure wave through my bones, and then comes a storm of jagged metal and shattered glass, crumpled beams, shredded pieces of cars, stair treads and most of the Range Rover. Right at me.

***

The next time I see Orla and her mom it's night and the sky is full of stars, like bits of white confetti. We're at the folly, on the veranda, and they're preoccupied, like there's a taxi waiting and their luggage is in the trunk. Orla's pissed—who can blame her—and won't look at me, but Deirdre lays a hand on my cheek.

"Nothing here for you," she says, by way of goodbye. It's the last I see of them.

I'm hoping for a nap inside, because I'm exhausted, but it's not to be. It's cold when I open the door, like crossing the threshold to a tomb, and their highnesses look up at me. They open their mouths to speak but all I hear is the rush of that bleak draft.

THE BEAT
by Raymond Benson

The damn phone rang and interrupted him.

He *hated* it when he was jarred out of the zone.

But it could be Alan calling. Charlie had waited all day to talk to the guy; but if Alan wasn't on the line, then Charlie might throw the device across the room. He picked up the handset of the old rotary dial phone. It had been in his room since he first came to live with Uncle Dan and Aunt Phyllis in their fourth-floor walkup.

"What?"

"Good evening to you, too," Alan said with a sniff.

"Oh, hey, Alan. Thanks for calling me back," Charlie said.

"You sound out of breath. Did I interrupt something?"

Charlie quickly closed the skin magazine and shoved it under the pillow on his bed. He then picked up the tube of lube and threw it in the open nightstand drawer and closed it. It was almost as if Charlie didn't want Alan to see what he'd been doing, but of course there was no way that was possible.

"I was...exercising."

"Really? You exercise?" Charlie heard Alan chuckle.

"Sometimes. Hey, you got what I need?"

The *need* was strong. It had been a few days since he'd had a taste. The *need* made him anxious and irritable.

"Yeah, I got it. It's going fast, though. I'll be at CBGB at ten."

Charlie glanced at the Big Ben windup clock on the nightstand. Eight twenty-five. It was already pitch-black outside since daylight savings time ended two weeks earlier in New York. Before he knew it, Charlie would be even grumpier. He absolutely detested the holidays and had no desire to join the New Year's Eve crowds that would maddeningly celebrate the changeover to 1979.

"CBGB?"

"That's what I said."

He didn't like scoring at CBGB. Aaron and his friends would be there. Sometimes they acted like they were Charlie's friends. He didn't believe they really were, though. But Darlene would likely be at CBGB, too. Maybe—*just maybe*—he'd be able to tell her what he'd always wanted to say.

"Yeah, okay. I'll be there."

"Cool. I'll let you get back to your…exercising."

Alan hung up. Charlie cursed and dropped the handset on the base.

Charlie pulled up his pants and looked in his wallet. Yeah, he had enough cash, thank the frikkin' Lord. Might as well hit the streets now. He could get a slice of pizza, maybe kill some time in some record shops on St. Marks Place.

He threw a shirt over his skinny pale torso, put on shoes and tied them, and stuck his arms through the brown leather bomber jacket that displayed a Ramones patch on one sleeve and an Iron Cross on the other. He then grabbed the battered backpack on the floor and slipped it in place. It didn't contain much, but he felt naked without it when he zigzagged through the sidewalks of lower Manhattan.

Charlie went out of his bedroom and down the hall to the claustrophobic bathroom. No bathtub, just a shower, sink, and toilet. He had to share it with his uncle and aunt, and too often that was a major hassle. Aunt Phyllis was in there *a lot*. Charlie couldn't *wait* until he could get the hell out of that apartment on East 11th Street. But as he was still in high school, that wasn't

THE BEAT

going to happen until after graduation in May. At least he had turned eighteen recently, so that was one hurdle that was behind him.

He splashed water from the sink onto his face and ran a filthy comb through his greasy dark hair. Charlie felt frustrated that he didn't get to finish what he'd been doing earlier, but he needed to get the Beat. It had become a mantra in his head, something he silently chanted to manufacture a rhythm to his movements. Walking. Running. Combing his damn hair. Nearly everything he did.

Just the beat…yeah, on the Beat…beating…keep the beat…the Beat…beat beat…

Charlie laughed at the irony of his inside joke, peered into the mirror at the ring in his nostril to make sure there was no dried snot on it, and made sure his eyes weren't too bloodshot. He then took a piss, didn't bother washing his hands, and left the bathroom.

Aunt Phyllis was in the kitchen cleaning up the remains of her dinner, which smelled like last year's model.

"You're going out now, Charlie?" she asked. Aunt Phyllis reminded Charlie of Edith Bunker on that dumb TV show they used to watch when he was younger. Very ditzy lady, but at least she and his uncle had taken him in when he was orphaned at the fucking age of six.

"Yeah, I told you I was, and I'll be home late."

"Don't you want some of the dinner I made? I had to put a dish in the fridge for your uncle. He works late tonight."

"Yeah, you said. I told you I'm eating out with friends."

"You have homework?"

"I did it."

"Have to keep up your grades, honey. You've been missing school a lot."

"It's fine, Aunt Phyllis. I gotta go."

"You sure you don't want dinner? Your uncle will be home soon and we can sit—"

"I'm eating out with friends. Don't wait up for me. I—" Then he remembered. The package. "Oh, I forgot something in my room." He turned and hurried back to the bedroom, closed the door, and rummaged through his clothes closet. The drawstring cloth bag was where he'd left it, inside a battered suitcase. The object inside the cloth bag felt comfortably heavy. He put it in his backpack, closed the closet door, and left the room.

He didn't say goodbye to Aunt Phyllis.

Charlie bounded down the stairs and noticed that Darlene's door on the third floor was open. Her mother, Mrs. Wilson, stood on the threshold smoking a cigarette. She was dressed in a nightgown and robe, and it wasn't yet nine o'clock in the evening.

Darlene and her mother lived alone in their apartment. Charlie had no idea where Darlene's father was, and he didn't care. As much as he was obsessed with Darlene—who normally didn't give him the time of day—Mrs. Wilson was *mighty fine.* The woman was likely in her forties and she seemed to enjoy showing off her magnificent body. Word in the neighborhood was that Mrs. Wilson worked at one of those joints in Times Square. She often usurped Darlene as the star of Charlie's fantasies, but he would never tell Darlene that.

"Well, hello, Charlie," Mrs. Wilson purred as she exhaled a puff of smoke.

Charlie halted in his tracks and couldn't help staring. The woman was a disheveled goddess, but he could smell the booze from six feet away.

He couldn't find the voice to respond at first. Then he managed to croak, "Oh, hi, Mrs. Wilson. How are you?"

"*I'm* fine, Charlie. How are you?" She grinned, amused at his awkwardness.

Charlie didn't know if she was flirting with him or laughing at him.

"Uh, I'm okay. I'm, uh, just going out."

Mrs. Wilson raised an eyebrow. "I see. Or would you like to come in for a...glass of milk?"

What the hell? Was she serious? She was inviting him *inside?* In her *nightgown?*

Mrs. Wilson laughed a little. "Oh, my, you look like you're about to swallow your tongue. You know, Charlie, you don't have to be so shy. You're a cute young man."

He tried to speak but all he could do was make a gurgling sound as his throat attempted vocalization.

"I...uh..."

Mrs. Wilson rolled her eyes. "You shouldn't mumble when women talk to you."

He was unable to respond to that.

"Oh, go on, get out of here," she said. "I don't mean to keep you. You probably have things to do. There are all those girls your age out there waiting for you, Charlie."

Yeah, right.

"I, uh...I have to..."

The Beat...get the beat...

"It's okay," she said. "Run along, little man. Oh, if you see Darlene, tell her that she's in big trouble. I know you two frequent the same filthy music clubs. She's supposed to be studying. School tomorrow, and, Lordy, she's never going to graduate the way she's going." The woman shook her head.

"I...If I see her..."

Mrs. Wilson gave him a look that Charlie interpreted as disgust, and then she turned, moved inside the apartment, and shut the door.

What just happened? Had she insulted him?

Charlie took a breath and continued down the stairs all the way to the street.

The night air was cool, crisp, and invigorating. The smells of 1st Avenue were always the same, though, no matter what season of the year it was. The pretzel guy tended to park near Charlie's building, and the odor of roasting pretzels and hickory nuts was simultaneously mouthwatering and revolting, if that was feasible. The trash bags from the Chinese takeout next door were rank. And yet the aroma of exhausts—from buses, taxis, delivery trucks, cars—was somehow refreshing. It reminded Charlie that he was in the BIG CITY. As much as he hated his daily existence, the *need* that dictated his actions *all the fucking time*, and living in the hell hole that was his aunt and uncle's apartment building, Charlie couldn't imagine being anywhere else.

New York City was the rock and roll heartbeat of the world.

Charlie killed some time wandering around Alphabet City and Tompkins Square Park. Avenues A, B, and C had bad reputations. Supposedly a lot of crime took place in the area, especially at night. Muggings and knifings and even shootings occurred all the time. Or so Charlie had heard. *He'd* never seen anything happen. He knew kids who lived on Avenue B and they said nothing ever happened. Charlie paid the rumors no mind. Besides, occasionally he'd been able to score Beat from a street dealer in the park.

No such luck tonight, though.

After browsing in a couple of his favorite record shops on busy St. Marks Place, Charlie made his way down the Bowery to just below Bond Street. Like it or not, the door to the little club beckoned to him. And when Charlie entered the dark, noisy, smoky, crowded, stinky, but often exhilarating CBGB, he felt as if his nerves would split and become electric agony. Just as he had expected.

The *need* was getting to him.

The Beat...yeah, the beat...

Alan was supposed to be there somewhere, but Charlie didn't see him.

Surely the guy wouldn't blow him off?

Nothing to do but wait. Enjoy the club. Just make an attitude adjustment. Get into the cacophony, which could be glorious if he allowed it to be so. Some punk band he'd never heard of was on stage. The music was horrendous, but the volume was perfect. Feeling the bass guitar thumping the rhythm in his chest did the trick.

He didn't see Darlene in the crowd either, but it was hard to spot anyone in the shadows. His eyes couldn't help being drawn to the figures hammering away at their instruments under the lights.

Charlie thought he should maybe get a drink. Before he'd turned eighteen, the bartenders had occasionally and surprisingly served him without question. Usually they hadn't. Now he could order an alcoholic beverage with aplomb and arrogance. "I shall have an alcoholic beverage," he would smugly announce to a server. Charlie experienced perverse pleasure to hear the response, which was invariably something like, "Yeah? Well what fucking alcoholic beverage do you want, piss face?"

He approached the bar, but then he realized that he wasn't thirsty at all. When he had the *need*, he lost his appetite for food and drink.

Charlie spun around, deciding that he'd visit the Bathroom from Hell instead. There was no line at the moment. He didn't have to pee, but he knew that trying to access the place when there was a line when you really *needed* to pee was no fun. Ancient words of wisdom from his aunt reverberated in his childhood memory cells: "Better go now, Charlie, so you don't have to go later when we're on the subway!"

The Bathroom from Hell was a scary place. There was a toilet and a sink, sure, but every surface of the floor, walls, and ceiling was covered with new and old concert flyers, bumper stickers, artwork, and Day-Glo graffiti. The little room *screamed* insanity. Expecting to find it empty, instead Charlie opened the door to—

Aaron and his friends. And, oh my God, Darlene, too.

"Lookee here! Charlie boy!"

Charlie's instinct was to say, "Sorry," and immediately shut the door, but Aaron called to him. "Come in, man! Come here!"

What the hell were they doing in the Bathroom from Hell with

Darlene? Or rather, what was Darlene doing in the Bathroom from Hell with Aaron and his friends?

"Close the door!" someone else spat. Maybe it was the one they called Spike.

Charlie did so.

Aaron lived in Charlie's neighborhood, just a block east on Avenue A. He was a couple of years older and was out of school. In fact, he never finished school. They had been friends when the two boys were younger. Much younger. They had shared some things then. That was a long time ago. Now Aaron was a full-blown punk who worked in a record store on St. Marks Place. Charlie always avoided that particular shop.

Aaron gestured toward the toilet. "You gotta pee? Don't mind us!"

"What are you doing in here?" Charlie asked.

Darlene laughed. Aaron chuckled. Then they all laughed.

"How are you, Charlie? Have you been good?" Aaron asked. "Do you still play with it?"

What?

Aaron, noting Charlie's expression, addressed his friends and Darlene. "Yeah, he does."

Charlie felt his cheeks go hot. He turned to open the door.

"Charlie, wait! I have something for you!"

He turned back warily. Aaron held out his other hand, palm up.

The Beat...

"Want some?"

Charlie stared at it.

"Yeah," Aaron said, "Alan was here earlier. He said you were supposed to meet him but he had to leave. I bought your stuff from him."

What? No!

"Oh, don't look so disappointed. I'll let you have a hit."

Charlie wanted to slug the guy, but Aaron was bigger and had an army of friends behind him. And Darlene was watching, wide-eyed and full of Beat.

"Here, it's yours," Aaron said, thrusting his palm out again.

Charlie swiftly grabbed the Beat, examined it closely to make sure he wasn't being conned, and ingested it like a dog snarfing a biscuit.

"Oh, look, he had the *need*," Darlene said.

"He *really* had the *need*," Spike said.

Charlie coughed and then said, "I have money. You can sell me what Alan was going to sell me."

"The hell I will," Aaron answered. "You're lucky I gave you that. Beggars can't be losers. Oh, wait..."

Darlene laughed.

It was then that Charlie got a good look at his third-floor neighbor, the girl who occupied his dreams. Darlene, who was a year older but still a senior in school. Her mother was right to be concerned. Darlene had been held back a grade at some point in her education. She was dressed in ripped denim shorts, fishnet stockings, a tank top under a distressed black leather jacket, and definitely no bra. A dainty silver nose ring sparkled at him. Her droopy eyelids and bloodshot green eyes betrayed her condition. She was currently on another plane of existence.

Charlie thought she was stunning. He would give anything to be her victim.

"What have you been up to, Charlie?" she asked him. "I don't see you in the building much."

Suddenly everything went silent. The Bathroom from Hell disappeared. Aaron and his friends didn't exist. He was all alone with Darlene. It was as if he and the girl who lived on the floor below him were together in a bubble.

Bliss. Blessedness.

But it also scared the shit out of him.

"Nothing much," he muttered. Then he remembered what her mother had said about mumbling, so he cleared his throat, and then spoke louder and more clearly. "Nothing much."

"Oh yeah? Up there in your room on the fourth floor?

Nothing much?" She raised an eyebrow and gave him an intoxicated, lopsided grin. "I hear you like magazines. They keep you busy, huh."

When Aaron and his friends laughed, they all reappeared in the space. Charlie was abruptly back in the Bathroom from Hell with all of them.

And they were laughing at him.

He glared at them—Aaron and his friends and Darlene—and he felt ridiculous. "I'm going to hear the band," he said. He turned, opened the door, and exited into the club.

The Beat was strong.

Charlie felt it in his head, behind his sternum, in his eardrums…the pulse of the drummer and bass melded with it in his blood and his brain.

Thump…thump…beat…Beat…thump…thump…

He felt a hand on his shoulder.

"Charlie!"

He jumped, startled, and turned. Darlene stood beside him. Or was it her mother?

Mrs. Wilson said to him, "Are you all right?"

"What?" he shouted. The band was loud.

She pulled his arm toward the front door.

What the hell?

Mrs. Wilson was dragging him outside! Did she want *him*? How would he handle that? While it might be nice, it would be really fucking weird. It was Mrs. Wilson's *daughter* that he wanted. He didn't think he could *perform* with Mrs.—

In a flash, he felt the cool night air and they were standing on the Bowery sidewalk in front of CBGB.

Oh my God…!

Mrs. Wilson wasn't Mrs. Wilson after all. She was Darlene all along. She was saying something, but Charlie had to rub his eyes and scrunch his face a couple of times before her words made any sense.

"Charlie, listen to me!" she demanded.

"What, what?" He shook his head and blinked several times. She was so lovely...

"If my mother asks you, don't tell her you saw me here."

"Your mother?"

"Come on, Charlie, *my mother*. Don't tell her, okay?"

Didn't she *know*? Couldn't Darlene see how he felt about her? Come on, Charlie, ask her out. Forget about her quip about the magazines. Ask her for a date. Tell her you want her.

He was frozen.

"I'm waiting for you to answer me," Darlene said.

He blurted, "I've been waiting, too. You're not the only one."

She made a face of confusion. "What?"

The club door burst open and Aaron and his friends poured outside. "Oh ho, here you are!" Aaron bellowed. "What are you guys doing out here, huh? Darlene? What are you two up to?"

"I'm coming back in, Aaron," she answered. She moved away from Charlie and took Aaron's hand.

Charlie saw it now. Darlene was unmistakably with *him*.

She said, "You were right, Aaron. Charlie stays up in his room. No holidays for him. You know what? He keeps thinking about *my mother*."

Aaron snorted. "Your mother? Really? Charlie!"

Darlene started laughing. "You don't wanna be a *lover*, Charlie. Not with me, not with any girl here. Not even with my *mother*!"

More laughter from the group. Once again Charlie felt his cheeks flush. The Beat enhanced the humiliation, but at the same time it encouraged and amplified his anger.

He bolted at Darlene, ready to rip out her nose ring. She screamed and moved away; Aaron simultaneously threw out his huge, bulky arm. Charlie slammed into it and staggered. This caused his backpack to slide off his body onto the sidewalk. Aaron then drew back his other arm, made a fist, and pump-jacked it into Charlie's face.

Charlie stumbled a few feet as the Bowery spun like a top.

Aaron moved in and hit him again. This time Charlie fell to the pavement.

"It takes two, Charlie," Aaron taunted. "You getting up?"

Aaron then kicked the prone figure in the side.

Pain. Blood on the tongue. The taste of hate.

The boot smashed into his body a second time.

Laughter.

Charlie rolled over, coughed, and cried out in torment.

"You dropped this, Charlie," Darlene said. She dumped his backpack in front of his face and then moved back to the gang of boys behind him. They were still there on the pavement, laughing. At him.

Then he remembered the package.

Charlie wrapped an arm around the backpack and clutched it to his stomach. He curled into a fetal position and managed to unzip the main compartment. He forced himself to sit up on the sidewalk. Blood from his busted lip and nose dripped onto his hands and lap. He removed the cloth bag he'd placed inside earlier. It wasn't difficult to undo the drawstring. Charlie reached inside and grasped the heavy metal object.

Charlie swerved around. From his position on the sidewalk in front of CBGB, he aimed the Colt .45 revolver at Aaron and pulled the trigger.

Darlene screamed as the big teen fell back into his friends.

Charlie got to his feet with the gun pointed at the others to keep them at bay.

No one moved…for a *beat*. Maybe two.

Then he bolted into the street.

Charlie ran.

Aaron's friends pursued him, hollering and shouting.

They wanted to collar him, swallow him, tear him to pieces…

But he was faster. He was on the Beat.

Charlie hurried toward the darkness, full of the elation of

what he had done. It was a new path forward. It was a direction he hadn't expected, but it was a mystery he embraced.

He ran…and ran…

He had to keep running or the vigilantes would follow him forever…

Running to the beat…

Into the night…into the shadows…the blackness…

Run…run…never stop…keep going…

The mantra in his head pushed him, drove him, and filled him with the voltage of a new beginning…

The Beat…yeah, on the beat…just the Beat…beat…

OUR LITTLE ANGEL
by Mark Billingham

Easy enough to put it all down to the chicken wings, how great they were, but that would be stupid. Yeah, so they were the only reason he was there at all, that first time anyway, but in the end, everything that happened was because of the girl. That dress, that face, the voice that promised so much. The moment he looked across and saw her sitting in the corner, Jimmy pretty much forgot he was eating anything at all.

Where he was and what he was doing there.

It would probably have taken him a second or two to recall his own name.

It was called Pat's Tiki Shack and Jimmy had seen the place every day on his way to work. He'd glanced down from the bridge at the big battered sign below him as he crossed the Manatee River on his commute from Bradenton to an industrial park on the outskirts of Tampa. To a job that depressed him. To an office filled with people he didn't much care for, with the possible exception of Linda (when she wasn't being super snarky) and Andy, who he chatted to about the Rays now and again and who, as it happened, had been the one to recommend a stop-off at Pat's on the way home in the first place.

"Seriously, man, those wings are better than sex. Trust me..."

She was sitting on her own at a table next to the small stage. To begin with, Jimmy wondered if maybe she was going to get up and sing or something, but after a while he decided that she was just perfectly content where she was and she looked equally happy when she turned and saw him staring. Jimmy quickly looked away because he didn't want her to think he was some leering jerk or anything, but when he looked back again a minute later, she was smiling, like maybe she'd been staring at him the whole time.

Yeah, right, like who was he kidding?

Jimmy felt the blood rising to his cheeks all the same and caught the eye of the bartender who cocked his head and smirked. Jimmy slipped off his barstool and asked where the restroom was.

"Over in the corner." The bartender nodded and picked up Jimmy's empty plate and beer bottle. "You want me to set you up with another while you're in there?"

"Sure."

"Coming up." The bartender leaned toward him; a smile or maybe a grimace. "You'll be walking right by her…"

When Jimmy came out of the restroom, he stopped to stare around the bar for a few seconds. He bent to tie a shoelace that wasn't undone. He took a step past the table where the girl was sitting then turned back and spoke fast before nerves got the better of him.

"Tell me to get lost, I mean it's really not a problem—"

She was already nodding. "I'd love one."

"Right." Jimmy sucked spit up into his mouth. "What can I get you?"

The girl raised her chin toward the bartender who was watching them, like he was ready and waiting. "Anthony knows."

By the time Jimmy was back at the bar, the bartender was ready with his beer and was filling a glass with Coke from the soda gun. "I'll keep a tab open," he said.

"That definitely what she wants?" Jimmy asked.

"She doesn't drink."

"Oh…"

"She doesn't have a problem with booze or anything. She

doesn't like the taste, that's all."

"Sounds like you know her pretty well."

"Alison's in here a lot," Anthony said.

The girl slowly kicked out a chair when Jimmy arrived back at the table. He sat and they touched glasses. "I'm Jimmy." She reached to shake his outstretched hand, but didn't say anything, like it was obvious that he'd already know her name. He burbled something about just dropping in on his way home because his buddy had raved about the chicken wings, I mean not really his buddy, just some guy from work, and he was hungry so he'd thought he'd try the place out, that was all.

"Those wings are pretty special," she said.

"Yeah, right?"

She sipped her drink and sat back, blinking slowly and pulling at a wayward strand of black hair. "I saw you looking."

Jimmy felt himself redden again. "Well, you're pretty hard to miss...that dress, you know? I thought maybe you were like...a bride or whatever."

She laughed.

"Like you'd just got married or something and your husband was...not around—"

"You thought I'd been jilted?"

"No." Jimmy took a drink, laughed right along. "I don't know."

"It's just a dress."

Jimmy did his best not to stare while he talked about his job selling insurance that nobody wanted and she smiled and nodded when he told her about the boring stuff he did all day. She laughed a few times when he let rip about snarky Linda and the rest of them, then looked serious, like she was really listening, when he confessed that what he really wanted to do was write.

It felt to Jimmy like she knew she was the first person he'd ever told.

"What kinds of things do you want to write about?"

"I don't know...just stories."

"That's so cool."

"I mean I'll probably never do it."

"Maybe you could write a story about me."

Jimmy nodded. "Yeah…a story about a mysterious girl in a bar."

She wrapped her hands around her glass and stared down at the table. "I'm not mysterious." She sounded disappointed.

"Okay then, so…"

She told him she was a beauty therapist, that people called her up and she went to their houses to thread eyebrows, fix hair weaves, whatever. She said that she loved it, that helping people look better made her feel great and that it was all she'd ever wanted to do.

"I'm not like you," she said. "I don't have any secret desires." Suddenly she was grinning. "Well, not about work, anyway."

Jimmy's mouth was dry again and all he could do was watch her drain her glass, slurping at the straw like a kid might do. She looked at him like she was ready for another and he felt a little uncomfortable suddenly, like he was being observed. He turned to discover that nobody else in the place seemed very interested—chatting, eating, and minding their own business—but he couldn't shake the feeling.

He said, "I've already had two beers and I'm driving, so I'd better head."

"You could always leave the car and grab an Uber," she said.

"Yeah, I could…but you know, work in the morning and I'd be crazy to give Linda another excuse to be shitty with me."

"So, be crazy."

"I mean, I don't want to go…"

She smiled and nodded, but she was already turning away to stare out at the water; the sun that was just beginning to dip below it, pinking the sky. "Well, maybe next time," she said.

More than anything, Jimmy wanted to see her again. At home

that night and all the next day at work he thought about little else. Yeah, so Alison was drop-dead gorgeous and was probably beating guys off with a stick, but he also sensed that maybe she was lonely, so he didn't want her to think he wasn't interested. He didn't want to come over like a dog with two dicks either, so he decided to leave it a day or two. To play it cool, even if that was the last thing he was. Or had ever been. Obviously, there was no guarantee she'd even be at Pat's next time, but Anthony had said she was in there a lot, so Jimmy reckoned he had nothing to lose by stopping by and ordering those chicken wings one more time.

He'd taken a change of clothes to work and scrambled into them in the parking lot. He pulled on khakis and a polo shirt, then folded up the shiny suit he wore to the office every day and laid it on the back seat. Having had a bit of time to plan ahead, he'd also got the number for a local cab firm tucked into his back pocket. A cab ride home and another to bring him back to collect his own car the next morning wouldn't be cheap, but he decided it was worth it.

She was worth it.

Walking in, that white dress was the first thing he noticed…

Anthony looked up as Jimmy approached the bar. "A beer, right?" He knocked the top off then reached for the soda gun. "And I'm guessing a Coke…"

Jimmy looked across and saw Alison waving. He waved back.

"Word of advice, man."

"Sorry…what?"

"Just go easy." Anthony tucked a straw into the glass and his eyes slid toward the corner. "All I'm saying."

Jimmy took the drinks, waited.

"Alison's been hurt a time or two, so things with her can be…tricky."

"What does that mean?"

"I'm not telling you how to live your life, bro. Just that if you want happy ever after, you're almost certainly looking in the wrong place." Anthony held Jimmy's eyes for a second or two then moved away to serve another customer.

"I didn't think you'd be back," Alison said, once Jimmy had sat down.

Jimmy smiled. "Yeah, you did."

"Okay, you got me..."

She told him she'd been hoping he would come by, that she'd been thinking about him. That the day before he'd been on her mind while she was fixing an old lady's eyebrows, that she'd been so distracted she'd messed them up.

"That's good," Jimmy said.

"I don't think the old lady would agree," Alison said. "She looks a bit...startled."

Jimmy cracked up and she joined in and, when they were both done laughing, Jimmy took a deep breath and said, "So, like...you don't have a boyfriend, right?"

She stared, mock serious. "That's awful forward, Jimmy."

"Yeah, no...I mean—"

"You think I'd be sitting here with you if I did?"

"I was just...checking."

"I've had boyfriends," she said. "One or two. Nothing that lasted very long."

"Okay."

"I think maybe it's me, you know?"

"It's definitely not you," Jimmy said.

Once he'd finished his beer, Jimmy went and got himself another two. He told her he didn't need to worry about drinking too much because he was planning to get a cab, that he was in no rush. She looked pleased and leaned across to squeeze his hand.

"You got far to go?" he asked. "Later, I mean."

She shook her head, curled another wayward strand of hair round a finger. "I live local."

"Why you're in here so much, I guess," Jimmy said.

She shrugged. "I like it. The...atmosphere, whatever. People are friendly."

Jimmy nodded, thinking that Anthony the bartender hadn't

seemed that friendly, however much he'd been smiling.

"It's a family place, you know?"

"Right." Jimmy looked around. "So I guess Pat's in the back somewhere?"

"Pat's long gone," she said. "It's his family, though."

He wanted to ask her why she was on her own, why she didn't come here with friends, but it felt a bit mean, like he was judging her or something. "Tell me about your family," he said.

She sat back and sighed, like it was a long story, or a painful one. But in the end she just said, "My parents are both dead."

"Sorry," Jimmy said. He figured that neither of them could have been very old, considering that Alison was no more than late twenties. "That's tough."

"It's fine," she said. "I still have family around, you know? We're all real close."

"That's nice," Jimmy said. "Family's important. The most important thing, you ask me."

"You?"

He drank his beer and told her about his mom who lived close by in Sarasota and his dad who'd left when he was a kid and was holed up in Ohio somewhere with a new wife. "His third marriage," Jimmy said.

"Holy crap," Alison said. "I sometimes wonder if I'll ever manage one."

He talked about his sister and her kids who he adored, and a younger brother who was still in college. He got more drinks in and before long he was telling her how much he wanted kids of his own. He knew he probably shouldn't be talking about stuff like that, like he was getting way ahead of himself and that he wouldn't be coming out with any of it if he wasn't putting the beers away so fast, but she didn't seem to mind.

"I want kids myself," she said. "I reckon three's a good number."

"Right, three." Jimmy remembered a stupid joke Andy had told him. "One of each."

She was laughing as she stood up to visit the bathroom, but she waited and stared down at him. Like she'd been sizing him up all this time and had finally decided he was a pretty good fit. "You're easy to talk to, Jimmy," she said. "I mean, real easy."

Jimmy just sat there and grinned. "Yeah?"

There were still a couple of stragglers and one guy at the bar who looked like he was asleep, but by the time the shout went out to drink up—from a guy Jimmy decided was probably the manager—he and Alison had more or less closed the place down.

The number of empty bottles on the table made it obvious how long they'd been sitting there, but Jimmy couldn't believe how fast the time had gone. She was real easy to talk to as well. Real easy on the eye, real easy to...

Christ, he couldn't remember the last time he'd been so drunk.

She walked him out to the parking lot when his cab arrived, moved close to him when he opened the car's back door. She smiled as he stood there, hovering, unsteady on his feet.

"I had a lot of fun," she said.

Jimmy was desperate to kiss her and he was fairly sure that she wanted him to. Course that might have been down to the beer, too; thinking stuff that wasn't real, misjudging things, whatever. In the end, he just reached out and rubbed her arm, which was probably stupid.

"Tomorrow night, then?" she said.

When he'd finally fallen into the cab and it had begun to pull away, Jimmy let out a loud whoop, then said sorry when the driver turned to give him a dirty look. He craned his head round to see Alison walking slowly after the car and blowing a kiss; acting silly like she was Marilyn Monroe or something. Jimmy felt like the King of the Fricking World. Of Florida, anyway. He was buzzing, indestructible, even if—drunk as he was and dark as it was—he was pretty sure he could see Anthony, the bartender, talking to some other guy and watching from the doorway.

They ordered food together this time, and had drinks delivered to their table by one of the wait staff. Jimmy was more than fine with that, happy to sit staring at her for as long as possible and not particularly keen on getting any more friendly advice from Anthony.

Waiting for their order to arrive, he said, "I talked about you in the cab last night. I talked about you a lot."

She beamed at him. "You did?"

"All the way home. I talked the driver's ear off. I was pretty wasted, mind you, so I don't know if I made much sense."

Jimmy had been even drunker than he'd realized and the conversation hadn't actually been quite as long or in depth as he remembered.

"I met a girl."

"Oh, yeah?"

"An amazing girl...never met anyone like her before, you know? You've got no idea, man..."

"You throw up in the back of my cab, it's a one hundred and fifty bucks cleaning charge, just so's you know."

Alison looked at him. "You don't have to drink so much, Jimmy. Not tonight."

"Oh, okay. Sorry if I was—"

"You were fine," she said. "You were great, okay? Look, it's not for me to tell you how many beers you can have, it's just that when people get drunk they don't always say what they mean. It's like...you can't always believe it's how they really feel."

"I always thought it was the other way round," Jimmy said. "Like with some people that's the only time they do say what they feel." The truth was, he didn't know if that was how it was for him because he rarely got that drunk. He did know he'd needed a good few drinks the night before, so as to be brave enough, but maybe he didn't have to go down that road with her anymore. He was certainly ready to tell her exactly how he felt, if he hadn't made it plain enough already.

"It's up to you," she said. "I'm just saying it would be nice to spend a few hours with you when you're not drinking too much."

"You got it." Jimmy clapped a hand to his chest. "Tonight, I'm on the ginger ale. I'm not sure I can keep stumping up for a cab anyway."

Certainly not if it was costing him an extra one-fifty a pop.

The food was fantastic: a blackened grouper sandwich for him and a chicken Caesar salad for her, and of course a portion of Pat's famous wings for the two of them to share.

As the server was taking their plates away, Jimmy pointed across. "You've got a…there on your…"

Alison looked down and saw the stain on her dress: the blood-red sauce from the buffalo wings. She groaned, then dipped her napkin in water and began to dab furiously at it. "I'm so clumsy. Jeez, I eat like a child."

"How come you always wear the same dress?" Jimmy asked.

She stopped, looked over at him for a second, then began working at the mark again. "It was my mom's. The dress she got married in."

"That's nice." Now, Jimmy didn't feel like such an idiot for thinking she might be a bride that first time. "Like a what-do-you-call-it…tribute."

She paused again and cocked her head. "Yeah, I guess. She changed it up after she got married so she could wear it as an everyday thing. Not quite so fancy as it was, you know? She didn't wear it very often, just special occasions or whatever, but she could still get into it, you know? Right up until the day she died and she was real proud of that." She stopped worrying at the stain and shrugged. "I do wash it every night, in case you thought I was being a bit…slutty."

"No, I didn't mean…"

"It'll be wore out soon. Bits of it are almost see-through now." She grinned, seeing Jimmy blush. "I know where your mind is right now, mister."

Jimmy just grinned right back because there was no point

denying it.

With no room for dessert—not even Pat's "famous key lime pie," which was by all accounts as spectacular as the wings—they stepped outside, where a series of decks and short piers ran around three quarters of the building.

They leaned against a wooden rail and stared out at the water, at kayakers catching the last of the sun and a pair of large boats passing each other beneath the bridge, their passengers waving. It was still pushing eighty degrees and humid. On the deck below them an egret worked its stiletto beak into a dead fish, then looked up to scream at a blue heron swooping low across the water, before rising up into the trees.

"Is that for real?" Jimmy pointed to a rusting sign that read *Please Don't Feed The Alligators*; a cartoon gator winking and showing its teeth.

"Oh, sure," Alison said. "You don't see them here very often, but there's definitely plenty around."

"That guy looks like the one in Peter Pan," Jimmy said. "The one that swallowed the alarm clock, remember?"

"The kid who never grew up, right?" Alison smiled, though she suddenly seemed a little sad. "I used to love that story."

"Oh wait, that was a crocodile…"

For a minute or so they said nothing, just stood watching as the light began to fade. Jimmy reached for her hand and she let him take it. The egret finished its dinner and hopped up onto a pole to preen its feathers.

"I need to go to the little girls' room." She squeezed his hand before turning away to head back inside.

"Cool," Jimmy said, watching her go. "I'll stay and watch out for gators."

He wasn't one for views, never had been. He'd seen enough big skies and sunsets to last him a lifetime, but he had to admit this place was pretty special. Maybe that was because she was here, though, and he still couldn't get his head around the fact that she was choosing to be here with him.

He watched a squadron of pelicans glide low across the water and saw the heron take off again. A fish jumped just below him and there was a peal of laughter from inside before a group began to sing happy birthday.

What had Alison said? Something about a great atmosphere...

He turned at the sound of footsteps to see a short, thick-set guy step out on to the deck behind him. The guy had a shaved head and wore a grubby apron. He leaned back against the wall, lit a cigarette, and sighed out a plume of blue smoke. He looked wiped out.

Jimmy took a step toward him. "You're the chef, right?"

The guy glanced down at his apron. "What gave it away?"

Jimmy laughed a little too loudly. "Seriously, man, those wings."

The chef grunted.

"I mean, everything else too, though. All of it was so...great, you know?"

The guy just nodded and took another drag, like he wasn't in the mood for a chat. Jimmy was about to step away again when the guy rolled his head around on his neck and said, "Glad you enjoyed your food."

Jimmy just nodded.

The chef stuck out a meaty paw which Jimmy shook. "Sean."

"Jimmy. Good to meet you. Busy night?"

Another grunt. "Always."

They both turned to lean against the railing. The smoke from Sean's cigarette was drifting straight into Jimmy's face, but he didn't really mind. He'd only quit six months before.

"You're the guy who's with Alison, right?"

"Yeah...I guess. I mean, we've only just—"

"Good luck."

Jimmy looked at him, but the chef was staring straight ahead, the cigarette between his lips and his eyes half closed. Not good luck like "all the best, man," like bros sticking together. Not good luck like a wink or a big old pat on the back.

Good luck like "you're going to need it."

Jimmy opened his mouth, but it was suddenly too dry to speak, which was no bad thing, because he hadn't got much idea how to respond anyway. He straightened up and waved away the cigarette smoke. He could do little but stand there and wait for whatever it was his new friend was clearly itching to get off his chest.

"It never ends well, is all."

Jimmy cleared his throat. "What never ends well?"

Groaning with the effort, the chef pushed himself back from the rail and turned to look at Jimmy. He seemed pained. "Look, it's up to you, but I've seen other guys come in here and try and it never works out the way they want. It just…never does. That girl's got baggage, you know what I'm saying?"

"Not really."

"She's got a reputation, okay?"

"For what?"

Sean puffed out his cheeks. "For making bad choices."

"I'm not a bad choice," Jimmy said. "And even if I was, it's her choice, that's the point. The choice is hers."

The chef sighed, like being the bearer of bad news was weighing heavily on him. He lowered his head and shook it. "She's been hurt a lot of times."

"I'm not going to hurt her." Jimmy held his arms out. "Why the hell would I—?"

"Nobody's saying you will."

"So, what's the problem?"

"It don't really matter if you do or you don't, that's not what this is about."

"Listen, she already told me she's had other boyfriends, okay? She told me things hadn't worked out for her in the past. I'm fine with that."

Sean sucked in a breath, took a few seconds. "I'm just telling you that she carries all that hurt around with her. Like a great black sack of it, and it gets…passed on."

"Passed on, how?"

The chef shook his head again, frustrated that whatever message he was trying to send wasn't getting through. "Alison's real easy to fall for, I get that."

"Yeah, because she's sweet and she's beautiful."

"Nobody's arguing, all right?"

"So, what's the big deal? Maybe she just wants to have some fun."

"It won't be fun, trust me."

Jimmy was starting to get more than a little irritated. "Look, I get that you're looking out for her, because she's a regular and you've gotten to know her a bit and you think she's…vulnerable or something. Same as the guy behind the bar and that's nice, okay? But I'm not just some horny teenager and I've had my own fair share of relationships that haven't worked out, so I think her and me are about even on that score. I think she's an amazing girl…that's it. I'm not planning on hurting her or messing her around, so you really don't need to worry."

"I do, though."

"I can't help that," Jimmy said. "You good if we say no more about it?"

The chef shrugged like he didn't really have a lot of choice, then turned to walk away along the dock. He stopped at the corner, flicked his cigarette butt into the water and said, "It's not going to end well, Jimmy…"

Jimmy was all set to shout after him, something about minding his own business, when he saw Alison stepping out of the door. "Hey," he said.

"Hey, yourself." She walked across and leaned close to him. "So, you spot any gators? Dolphins, maybe?"

"Just the chef."

Alison rolled her eyes. "Sean."

"Yeah, Sean." Jimmy could see from her expression that he didn't need to go into details, that he wasn't the first of Alison's suitors the chef had spoken to that way.

"He's…protective."

"Well, he doesn't need to be," Jimmy said.

"I know." She reached for his hand again. "Why the hell would I want to be protected from you, anyway?"

Jimmy leaned in then moved to slide an arm around her waist. The anger he'd felt with the chef was all but gone.

"Even so…"

Jimmy looked at her. "What?"

"I think it wouldn't hurt if we took a couple of days."

"Seriously?'

"Just step back a bit, take things a little slower, maybe."

"Is this because of Sean?"

"No…not really," she said. "I'm just saying we don't need to do this every night. Not yet, anyway. Let's meet back here in a couple of days and we'll see if you still feel the same way. I mean I know how I feel." She pushed her head against his chest. "I mean here I am presuming you feel anything at all."

"You can presume all you want," Jimmy said. "I feel plenty and that's not going to change."

"So, there you are then. A couple of days isn't going to make any difference, right?" She leaned back and smiled up at him. "We're all set."

"Can I at least have your number?" It was weird, Jimmy thought, that here he was thinking he could spend the rest of his life with this girl, that he would chuck in his stupid job if she asked him to, move anywhere in the country she wanted, and he didn't even have her phone number.

"Sure, Jimmy." She waited until Jimmy took his phone out and reeled off a number.

"Got it." Jimmy stared down at the new number in his phone, waiting.

"You think I'm flipping you off?"

"No, just…"

She grinned, shaking her head. "Call it."

Jimmy dialed the number and a few seconds later a phone

started to trill in Alison's bag. He nodded, feeling like an idiot. He felt a flutter in his stomach, a second or two of concern that she had not asked him for his number, but it was no big deal.

She stepped across and placed her hands on either side of his face. "So, I'll see you back here in two nights' time," she said. "Yeah?"

"For sure," Jimmy said.

"You promise?"

"I swear."

She leaned in to kiss him. Her mouth stayed closed more or less, but Jimmy was fine with that because she kissed him plenty long enough. She said, "It's going to be special."

He sent her a message as soon as he got home:
can't stop thinking about you x
And again when he woke the following morning:
not going to pretend I dreamed about you 'cause i actually dreamed I was at a springsteen concert and the boss got me up on stage to play guitar (i can't play guitar) but i swear you were the first thing I thought about when I opened my eyes. J x

He called her at lunchtime from work, but it went straight to voice mail, so he left a message:

"Hey, it's Jimmy…just wanted to talk to you is all. Hate that I won't see you for like another day and a half…work's even shittier than usual. Not like I'm getting much done anyway, thinking about you all the time. Thinking about tomorrow night…can't come quick enough. Have some wings for me, okay?"

He sent another message before he went to bed and lay awake for another hour waiting for her to reply.

He sent a message first thing next day:
you ok? you obviously have my number now so let me know everything's all right xxx

He left another voice mail at lunchtime:

"Me again…obviously. So, I guess you must be busy or your

phone's not working or something...but I'm not going to make out like I'm cool with you not getting back to me, because I'm not. Anyway, I'm sitting here at work and Linda's being a bitch and I'm going crazy thinking about you...CRAZY!! Just a few hours until I see you for our special night...so I'll just have to get by until then with imagining. I'm sure you can guess I'm imagining lots of things. See you real soon. Did I tell you I can't wait...?"

As soon as Jimmy had walked into Pat's, he made a beeline for the corner table where Alison was waiting. He'd seen that white dress straight away. Something jumped in his guts when he saw her stand up and wave like she was thrilled to see him, but he was still ticked off that she'd ignored all his messages and the truth was he'd gotten himself a little worked up in the car.

She walked around the table, arms ready for him. "Hey, you..."

"You said you weren't flipping me off, but you didn't get back to me even one time. You said—"

She shut him up with a kiss. "I was busy, okay? I had clients back to back."

"You couldn't even find...like a minute?"

She kissed him again, longer this time and when she'd finished, he didn't have much else to say for himself. "That stuff doesn't matter," she said. "I'm just so happy you came."

"I told you I'd come." Now, Jimmy couldn't stop smiling.

"I wasn't sure."

"Why the hell wouldn't I come?"

"I think that's why I was a bit nervous about getting back to you." She was smiling and her fingers were in his hair. "Like I wasn't busy all the time, I guess. I was just scared in case you'd changed your mind about me."

"Not a chance," Jimmy said.

"So..." She stood back and folded her arms. "You going to

sing with me?"

"Sing?" Jimmy saw her nod and turned to see the equipment being set up on the small stage. "Whoa..."

"You gotta love karaoke, right?"

Jimmy had done it once, a year or two before on a night out with folks from the office. He and Andy had stumbled through some old Bowie number and he hadn't come away feeling it was something he wanted to do again.

Alison clasped her hands together, simpered in a little girl voice. "Please. It's only one night a week, baby."

"I'd better go and get a drink," Jimmy said.

He ordered Coke for her as usual and a beer for himself, with a shot of Jim Beam on the side. He was happy enough that Anthony did no more than nod while he was serving him.

When she saw the drinks he'd brought back to the table, Alison nodded and said, "Easy there, big boy."

"Well, if you want me to sing."

"Oh, I do," she said.

They sat and listened as the first few customers took to the stage and, if "Livin' on a Prayer" and "Summer of '69" weren't quite murdered, they were certainly the victims of serious assault. Jimmy and Alison clapped and cheered along with everyone else, though and while a middle-aged woman belted out a pretty decent version of "Hopelessly Devoted to You," Jimmy went back to the bar for another round.

"Same," he said.

Once again, Anthony said nothing while he fetched the beer and poured the bourbon and, when Jimmy turned round, he saw Alison talking to the guy in charge of the karaoke machine. A few minutes after he'd sat down again, the guy was calling out his and Alison's names.

Jimmy said, "Shit," and downed his bourbon as he got to his feet.

The crowd cheered and shouted Alison's name as they clambered on to the stage. Jimmy enjoyed seeing her grin and give the crowd a little bow. He wasn't exactly surprised that most of the people in the place knew her, and he wondered if any of them knew her quite as well as Anthony and Sean seemed to. He wondered how widespread that reputation really was.

She had an amazing voice.

Jimmy thought so, anyway.

The crowd shouted their approval when the two of them sang "I Got You Babe," and again when they came back a few songs later and giggled their way through "You're the One That I Want." It was their version of "Islands in the Stream" that brought everyone to their feet though, even if Jimmy was largely oblivious. He was just looking at her; stunned that she was really singing the song to him and at the way her eyes went wide and bright when she was singing about the two of them "making love with each other."

A couple of hours later, when things were winding up and there were only a few die-hard drinkers or karaoke enthusiasts left in the place, Alison said, "Let's go outside."

Jimmy had put four beers and as many bourbons away when he half-stumbled onto the deck and, as soon as the warm air hit him, he could feel the sweat pricking at the back of his neck.

"You okay?" she asked.

"Yeah, I'm good." Jimmy leaned against the rail, gulped in a lungful of air which tasted a little of fish and motor oil. "I'm great."

She stood behind him and slid her arms around his waist. "That was so sexy."

Jimmy wasn't sure what she meant, not exactly. Was it the two of them singing together that had turned her on, or was she just buzzing from the reaction of the crowd? Maybe a bit of both. He just hummed his agreement, wondering why the hell he'd been drinking bourbon and wishing that the water would keep still for one damn minute.

"You're so sexy, Jimmy."

He turned into her arms. "Am I?"

This time she opened her mouth to him and Jimmy kissed her like he'd been wanting to all along. She moaned into his mouth like she was enjoying it and, when they broke away briefly from the kiss, she nuzzled his neck and pulled at his hair. When their mouths met again, Jimmy moved his hands a little further down her back. She tensed, just a little, when they slid down to her ass, but seemed to relax quickly enough.

She said his name.

Jimmy's head was swimming, but the rest of him was working just fine and before he could stop himself, his hands were clawing at the material of her dress, lifting it up towards her back.

She pulled away, breathless. "No..."

"I'm sorry. I was just—"

"Not yet."

He stepped across and pulled her gently back towards him because he believed that she wanted him to. They started to kiss again, hungrier still and, as she stroked his neck, Jimmy's hands moved down one more time, then further still to the hem of her white dress.

She pushed him away. "I said not yet, Jimmy."

"I don't understand. I thought...special, you said?"

"It was special, but then you spoiled it."

"I thought you wanted to—"

Jimmy turned at the sound of footsteps behind him and found himself being grabbed by a guy in a dark jacket and open-necked shirt.

"That's enough..."

The guy was strong and, even if he hadn't been, Jimmy wasn't in any state to put up much resistance as the guy frog-marched him back inside and across the room toward the door.

"Hey...who the hell are you?" Jimmy struggled, but the guy had one hand on the back of his polo shirt and the other on his belt. He was dimly aware that the few customers left in the place were staring at him, that whoever was still on stage had stopped singing, and that Alison was calling his name somewhere behind him. "You can't just—"

"My name's Liam and I'm the manager of this place, so I can do what I want, you got me?"

"I didn't do anything."

"The young lady was clearly not happy back there, okay?"

"She was kissing me."

Jimmy grabbed hold of a table and planted his feet, but the manager prized his fingers away and shoved him towards the exit. "Right, until you took advantage."

"But that's not me," Jimmy shouted. "I'm not...like that."

"I've heard it all before, so don't waste your breath." He pushed Jimmy hard through the door and out into the parking lot. "I will not have young women being pawed at in my bar. That's just the way it is. So you need to leave..."

Jimmy turned and stared at him, breathless and tearful. He leaned down to put his hands on his knees. After a few seconds, he stood up straight and took a couple of unsteady paces back toward the door, but the manager moved to block his way. "How the hell do you expect me to get home? I can't drive, for God's sake..."

The manager was already punching in a number into his phone.

"There's a cab on the way," he said.

"Jesus..."

"So you really need to do the sensible thing, which is to get in it and go home. While we're talking about being sensible, Jimmy, I really don't think it would be a good idea for you to come back here, because you will not be welcome. Not at all. The food and drink you had tonight are on the house, but that's the end of it. Oh, and if you've got Alison's phone number, I strongly suggest that you delete it. It's no use to you, you understand?"

Jimmy nodded, but he didn't understand any of it.

The cab was quick and Jimmy did as he was told. He watched the manager walk back into his bar as the car pulled out of the parking lot. He took out his phone, crying harder now and belching Beam as he stared down at Alison's number.

Ten minutes later, when they were halfway across the bridge, he leaned forward and dropped a hand on the cab driver's shoulder.

"Turn around when we get to the other side and take me back…"

When Jimmy barged through the door into Pat's, he saw that Alison was still sitting at the corner table. Her head was lowered and she might have been crying, but he couldn't be sure. Jimmy started to move, a little unsteadily toward her, but he'd been spotted straight away by Liam, the manager, who was sitting at the bar talking to Anthony and moved fast to intercept him.

Alison raised her head and, even though he couldn't hear it, Jimmy was almost certain she mouthed his name.

They were the only four people in the place.

Liam stood between Jimmy and Alison. He raised his hands. "We've been through this already, pal, so let's not do anything stupid."

Jimmy wanted to smash the place up, he wanted to grab the girl and run, he wanted to lie down and curl up into a ball. Truth was, he had no idea what he was going to do, but there was a fair chance that, whichever way he decided to jump, it would turn out to be stupid. He said, "I just want to talk to her."

"Not going to happen," Liam said, hands still raised and ready.

Jimmy nodded, like he'd got the message, then made his move, but he was far too drunk and Liam was too quick. Once again the manager was holding him fast, easing him away from Alison's table and across to the bar.

He held Jimmy fast against the counter and looked at him hard. When he was convinced that Jimmy wasn't about to try anything else, Liam lifted him up on to one of the stools. Said, "We good?"

Jimmy nodded, panting. "I feel like crap…"

"Sure you do." Liam nodded to the barman. "Tony, get the guy a coffee, would you?" He climbed on to the stool next to Jimmy and wrapped an arm around his shoulder. "Why the hell you back here, man? Did I not spell things out for you?"

Jimmy grunted, felt like he wanted to laugh but didn't know why. "I had to come back." Anthony laid a mug of coffee down next to him on the bar and Jimmy took a welcome slug. "What else was I going to do?"

"Go home," Liam said. "Like I told you to."

"Why would I want to be home when she's here?"

Jimmy tried to turn his head to look at her, but Liam reached across, took Jimmy's face in his hands and dragged it right back. "That's exactly why you should be at home."

Jimmy drank more coffee and shook his head. "We were getting on so great, you know?"

"Oh, I know." Liam looked at Anthony.

"Same old story," Anthony said.

Jimmy stared down into the mug of coffee, tried to figure out how long it had been since he'd been staring down at the Manatee River. The brown water swirling, right before he'd turned round and Alison had kissed him. Really kissed him. "She said it was going to be special." He was feeling woozy and his chin was on his chest. "She said all kinds of things…"

"I know she did," Liam said. "She always does."

Liam said plenty of other stuff after that, and Anthony chipped in once or twice, but Jimmy only caught fragments. Something about quitting while you're ahead and walking away. Something else about how stupid it was to ignore good advice.

Their voices seemed to be coming from far away, like the bottom of a hole Jimmy could feel himself tumbling into.

Christ, he needed to sleep…

"Come on, Jimmy, get up."

Jimmy groaned as he was lifted from the rough concrete floor onto his knees. He opened his eyes and immediately tried to cry out but couldn't. There was something across his mouth—duct tape, he guessed. He couldn't even force his tongue between his lips. He instinctively tried to stand, but his wrists and ankles were bound with cable ties.

"What are we going to do with you, Jimmy?" Liam asked.

"Don't worry," Sean said. "It's a what-d'you-call-it...rhetorical question."

They were in some kind of storage room, Jimmy reckoned. There were crates piled up against one wall, barrels and pipework. It couldn't be under Pat's, there wasn't any kind of basement, but he guessed it was somewhere nearby. He could smell the water.

"This isn't what we wanted, you get that, right?" The voice came from behind him, then he saw Anthony step around and squat down in front of him. The bartender leaned in close. "It's never what we want, but guys just don't listen. I mean, yeah, a few have listened...the smart ones, but most are just pig-headed, same as you." He shook his head, like this was all a matter of some regret, and got to his feet.

Jimmy grunted behind the tape and struggled against the ties. His head was thumping and he tried in vain to piece everything together from the moment he'd marched back into the bar. He swallowed and all at once he figured out just how they'd managed to get him out of the bar and truss him up in this place.

He could still taste the coffee.

Blinking back the tears, he stared up at the three of them: the bartender, the chef and the manager. It was easy enough now to see the resemblance between them.

And to Alison.

It's a family place, you know?

"It's not like you weren't warned," Liam said.

"More than once," Anthony said.

Sean stepped close and jabbed a finger into Jimmy's face,

clearly the most agitated of the three. "You were fucking told."

Liam waved a hand and Sean stepped back. When Liam nodded at him, he moved purposefully away to the far corner of the room.

"Just so we're clear," Liam said. "Nothing was ever going to happen between you two. There was never a chance in hell. None of those things you imagined doing to her and none of the things you dreamed about her doing to you. Not with Alison."

"Not with our little angel," Anthony said.

"Those things are saved for us."

Sean stepped back to join his brothers, something held behind him.

"You understand me?"

Jimmy was already screaming against the tape as Sean raised the bat.

She would be up there singing alone tonight, but that was okay. She'd done it often enough because people almost always asked her to and it wasn't like the perfect partner came along every day. Besides which, she liked it when the cheering and the applause was just for her. Who in hell didn't like to be appreciated?

She sat sipping Coke and watched while the equipment was set up.

She didn't love it that Jimmy had left her and she'd cried plenty of tears for him, but it wasn't a big surprise because they always went away. Some stuck around a bit longer than others, but she always ended up on her own.

What was it she'd said to Jimmy that first night?

I think maybe it's me.

Which was the truth of it, more or less.

She turned to look out at the water and it warmed her heart a little to think that Jimmy would have company, at least. Down there drifting around and yakking about her with Pete and Marcus and Brad. All her loves together, right underneath that stupid old sign about not feeding the alligators.

Which was real ironic, considering that's what they all did, eventually.

Alison's soft red lips twisted into a sad kind of smile, thinking about it and she was still smiling when she turned back to look over at the man standing by the bar.

He'd been staring at her ever since he walked in.

ABOUT THE CONTRIBUTORS

JIM FUSILLI is the author of nine novels including *The Mayor of Polk Street* and its predecessor *Narrows Gate*. His story "Chellini's Solution" was included in an edition of the Best American Mystery Stories and "Digby, Attorney at Law" was nominated for the Edgar and Macavity awards. He edited the anthologies *The Chopin Manuscript*, *The Copper Bracelet*, and *Crime Plus Music: Twenty Stories of Music-Themed Noir*. The former Rock & Pop Critic of *The Wall Street Journal*, Jim is the author of *Pet Sounds*, his tribute to Brian Wilson and the Beach Boys' classic album.

RAYMOND BENSON is the *New York Times* bestselling author of over forty books, most known for being the third—and first American—author of James Bond continuation novels between 1997 and 2002. Raymond's recent work, *The Mad, Mad Murders of Marigold Way*, won the IPPY Gold (first place) Award for Mystery from the Independent Publisher Book Awards. His critically acclaimed and popular five-book serial, The Black Stiletto, is in development as a possible feature or television series. Website: RaymondBenson.com.

MARK BILLINGHAM is one of the UK's most acclaimed and popular crime writers. His series of novels featuring DI Tom Thorne has twice won him the Crime Novel of the Year Award

ABOUT THE CONTRIBUTORS

and, in 2021, he received the award for Outstanding Contribution to Crime Fiction at the Harrogate Crime Writing Festival. His latest novel is *The Last Dance*—the first in a new series featuring DS Declan Miller. When not living out rock-star fantasies as a member of the Fun Lovin' Crime Writers, Mark is hard at what is laughably called 'work', writing his next novel.
Website: MarkBillingham.com.
Twitter: @MarkBillingham

PETER BLAUNER is the Edgar winning, *New York Times* bestselling author of nine novels, including *Slow Motion Riot* and *The Intruder*. His work has been translated into twenty-five languages and been anthologized on *Selected Shorts from Symphony Space* on NPR. A lifelong New Yorker, he has also been a journalist and a TV writer for shows like *Law & Order* and *Blue Bloods*. His most recent novel *Picture in the Sand* was published by St. Martin's/Minotaur in 2023.

MARY ANNA EVANS is the author of *The Traitor Beside Her*, the second WWII-era suspense novel featuring physicist Justine Byrne, the Faye Longchamp archaeological mysteries and is co-editor of the Edgar-nominated *Bloomsbury Handbook to Agatha Christie*. Her books received the Benjamin Franklin Award, two Oklahoma Book Awards, and a Will Rogers Medallion Award. Her short works appeared in publications including *The Atlantic*'s Technology Channel, *The Louisville Revie*, and *The Faking of the President*. Evans holds an MFA in creative writing from Rutgers-Camden and is a licensed professional engineer. She works as a professor at the University of Oklahoma, where she teaches fiction and nonfiction writing.

MEG GARDINER is the #1 *New York Times* bestselling author of sixteen novels. Her thrillers have won the Edgar Award and been summer reading picks by *The Today Show* and O, the Oprah magazine. In August 2022 *Heat 2*, co-authored with Michael Mann,

ABOUT THE CONTRIBUTORS

debuted at #1 on the *New York Times* best seller list. A former lawyer, two-time president of Mystery Writers of America, and three-time *Jeopardy!* champion, Gardiner lives in Austin, Texas.

GAR ANTHONY HAYWOOD is the Shamus and Anthony award-winning author of fourteen novels and dozens of short stories. His crime fiction includes the Aaron Gunner private eye series and Joe and Dottie Loudermilk mysteries. His short fiction has been included in the Best American Mystery Stories anthologies and *Booklist* has called him "a writer who has always belonged in the upper echelon of American crime fiction." His most recent novel, *In Things Unseen*, was published by Slant Books in December 2021 and would be best described as a thriller for fans of nontraditional Christian fiction.

REECE HIRSCH is the author of six thrillers that draw upon his background as a privacy attorney. His first book, *The Insider*, was a finalist for an International Thriller Writers Award. His most recent books, *Black Nowhere* and *Dark Tomorrow*, feature FBI cybercrime investigator Lisa Tanchik. Reece is a partner in the San Francisco office of an international law firm and co-head of its privacy and cybersecurity practice. Website: ReeceHirsch.com.

ED LIN is a native New Yorker of Taiwanese and Chinese descent. He's the first author to win three Asian American Literary Awards. His latest books are the YA title *David Tung Can't Have a Girlfriend Until He Gets Into an Ivy League College*, and *Death Doesn't Forget*, the fourth book in the Taipei Night Market series published by Soho Crime. He lives in Brooklyn with his wife, actress Cindy Cheung, and son.

CATRIONA MCPHERSON (she/her) writes historical mysteries, contemporary comedies, and psychological suspense. Her books have won multiple Anthony, Agatha, Lefty, and Macavity awards and been finalists for the Mary Higgins Clark Award, the Edgar and the UK Crime Writers' Association Dagger. She was born in Scotland, where most of her books are set, but immigrated to northern California in 2010. Catriona is a proud lifetime member and former national president of Sisters in Crime.

ROB OSLER's debut novel *Devil's Chew Toy* was a 2023 best first novel finalist for the Anthony, Agatha, and Lefty Awards. His first publication, "Analogue" (*Ellery Queen Mystery Magazine*), won the 2022 Mystery Writers of America Robert L Fish Award for best short story by a debut author at the Edgar Awards. On good days, he writes, plays tennis, and eats pie in California, where he lives with his partner and Andy Action Cat. Website: RobOsler.com.

GEORGE PELECANOS is a novelist, screenwriter, and film and television producer. "New Amsterdam," from Get Happy, was spun at his wedding reception.

GARY PHILLIPS has published various novels, comics, short stories and edited several anthologies including the Anthony-winning *The Obama Inheritance: Fifteen Stories of Conspiracy Noir* and *Get Up Offa That Thing: Crime Fiction Inspired by the Songs of James Brown*. The *Washington Post* named his novel *One-Shot Harry* as one of the best mysteries of 2022. He was also a writer and co-producer on FX's *Snowfall* about crack and the CIA in 1980s South Central where he grew up.

NAOMI RAND is the author of *Surviving Amelia* (Bink Books, 2018), a literary novel, and three mysteries featuring divorced criminal investigator Emma Price—*The One That Got Away*, *Stealing for a Living*, and *It's Raining Men* (all from HarperCollins). She has stories in *Crime Plus Music* (Three Rooms Press) and *Hardboiled Brooklyn* (Bleak House Books). Her fiction, nonfiction, personal essays, and literary criticism have appeared in

ABOUT THE CONTRIBUTORS

many national publications including *Redbook*, *Parents*, *Ladies Home Journal*, *Huffington Post*, *The Boston Globe*, and *The New York Times*. She is at work on a new mystery, *My Little Town*.

RAQUEL V. REYES writes Latina protagonists. Her work has won a Lefty award, an International Latino Book Award, been nominated for Anthony and Agatha Awards, and optioned for film. Raquel's short stories appear in various anthologies, including *The Best American Mystery and Suspense 2022*.

ALEX SEGURA is the bestselling and award-winning author of the *L.A. Times* Book Prize Award-winning *Secret Identity*, which *The New York Times* called "wittily original" and named an Editor's Choice. NPR described the novel as "masterful," and it received starred reviews from *Publishers Weekly*, *Kirkus*, and *Booklist*. *Secret Identity* was also listed as one of the Best Mysteries of the Year by NPR, *Kirkus*, *Booklist*, the *South Florida Sun Sentinel* and more, and was nominated for the Lefty and Barry Awards for Best Novel, and won the *L.A. Times* Book Prize in the Mystery/Thriller category. His next novel, the YA Spider-Verse adventure *Araña/Spider-Man 2099: Dark Tomorrow*, is out now from Disney Books/Marvel Press.

PETER SPIEGELMAN is the Shamus Award-winning author of six novels, including *A Secret About a Secret*, *Dr. Knox*, *Thick as Thieves*, and three books—*Black Maps*, *Death's Little Helpers*, and *Red Cat*—that feature private investigator and Wall Street refugee John March. Peter's short fiction has appeared in many collections, including *Dublin Noir*, *Hardboiled Brooklyn*, *The Darker Mask*, and *Wall Street Noir*, a crime fiction anthology that he also edited. Peter lives in New York City.

MARTYN WAITES was born on the North East of England. Before becoming a writer he was an actor. He has written over twenty novels including the award-winning *Born Under Punches*

ABOUT THE CONTRIBUTORS

and been nominated for every major British crime writing award. He has also written eight internationally bestselling thrillers under the name Tania Carver. He has also written *Doctor Who* for Big Finish and along with Mark Billingham, Stav Sherez and David Quantick he wrote *Great Lost Albums*, the funniest music book ever written. Apparently. He is currently working on a new novel.

On the following pages are a few
more great titles from the
Down & Out Books publishing family.

For a complete list of books and to
sign up for our newsletter,
go to DownAndOutBooks.com.

Roulette
Thomas Locke and Jyoti Guptara

Down & Out Books
October 2023
978-1-64396-342-6

Don't trip. It could cost your life.

Experimental science meets heart-pounding suspense in this thriller about a dangerous new drug.

When a former special agent tracks rumors to a remote clinic in Florida, he allies two local women to stop a powerful pharmaceutical company. The race is on to expose a terrifying truth—before it rewrites the human genome.

Ruins of Midnight
An Ecclesfield Division Novel
Colin Campbell

Down & Out Books
November 2023
978-1-64396-343-3

Mick Habergham enjoys the nightshift. Sunday night should be quiet, but it will prove to be anything but.

From the mad knifeman of Hill Top Hostel to the suicide attempt at the House of Pain, Mick will face all manner of obstacles to a peaceful night.

If Mick wants a happy retirement he will first have to walk through fields of heartache and survive the ruins of midnight.

The Moonlight Falcon
A Dick Moonlight PI Thriller
Vincent Zandri

Down & Out Books
November 2023
978-1-64396-344-0

Headcase Dick Moonlight PI finds himself in a world of hurt and deception when he agrees to take on a job for the Blaze Construction Company. It seems its portly, "midget" owner, Greg Blaze, believes his workers are stealing tools from him and he needs Moonlight to gather the proof.

But the more Moonlight digs into the case, the more insidious things become, including a mysterious ancient, Egyptian falcon statuette made of pure obsidian believed to be priceless that the crooked construction owner has allegedly stolen.

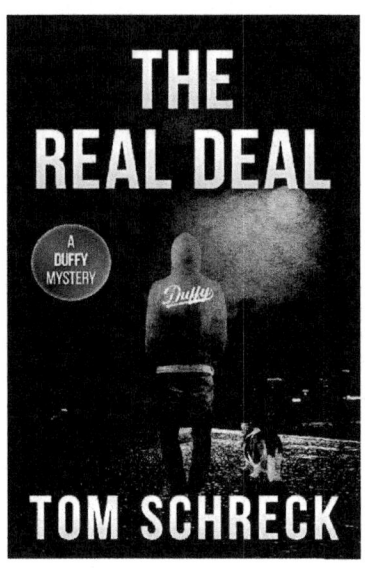

The Real Deal
A Duffy Mystery, 7th in Series
Tom Schreck

Down & Out Books
November 2023
978-1-64396-361-7

When Mushie, the popular street hustler of counterfeit watches, sneakers, and kitchen gadgets, comes into Duffy's bar bleeding from a gunshot wound to the stomach, Duffy and the gang are baffled. Everyone loved Mush who didn't have a mean bone in his body, Sure, he operated on the edges of what's considered proper society but, hey, so did a lot of Duffy's friends.

For Duffy, it's different. Mush was Hymie's, Duff's father-like mentor, grandson, and Duff had promised to keep an eye out for him. Now, it meant righting Mushie's wrong after his death.

Printed in Great Britain
by Amazon

38562208R00158